H̶a̶r̶m̶ans Water Library

C000037303

Robert Woods was born in the UK in 1996. He studied Aerospace Engineering at the University of Southampton for four years, a course which was partly taken due to his deep-rooted interest in science fiction, and has been a season ticket holder at Reading Football Club for the majority of his life.

Throughout his childhood, Robert has harboured a passion for books and for writing fiction. This passion eventually culminated itself in the form of Hunted, which he wrote as his first novel during his third year at university.

44139001543648

Robert Woods

HUNTED

AUSTIN MACAULEY PUBLISHERS™

LONDON · CAMBRIDGE · NEW YORK · SHARJAH

Copyright © Robert Woods (2018)

The right of Robert Woods to be identified as author of this work has been asserted by him in accordance with section 77 and 78 of the Copyright, Designs and Patents Act 1988.

All rights reserved. No part of this publication may be reproduced, stored in a retrieval system, or transmitted in any form or by any means, electronic, mechanical, photocopying, recording, or otherwise, without the prior permission of the publishers.

Any person who commits any unauthorised act in relation to this publication may be liable to criminal prosecution and civil claims for damages.

A CIP catalogue record for this title is available from the British Library.

ISBN 9781788233583 (Paperback)
ISBN 9781788233576 (Hardback)
ISBN 9781788233569 (E-Book)

www.austinmacauley.com

First Published (2018)
Austin Macauley Publishers Ltd.
25 Canada Square
Canary Wharf
London
E14 5LQ

Acknowledgements

Hunted is my first major literary work. I have learnt a huge amount from the experience, but the book would not be in the form it is today without the advice and support of a lot of people.

In particular, I would like to thank my housemates, Greg McAusland and Marcus Taylor, for their help with brainstorming ideas, discussing the plot and read-throughs. My family, for their endless support and encouragement, particularly to my dad for suggesting so many great books to me that have inspired my writing, and my mum who has always encouraged me to begin writing. Helen Keelty, for making English such a fun and interesting subject for me, and for proof-reading and supporting this book. James Essinger, who has given me so much professional advice when no one else would and for helping hone my skill as a writer. James Entract, for the long discussions and feedback to make the final draft. And Callum, Richard, Jamie and David for their support and advice. Finally, and most importantly, my special thanks to Sydney, for putting up with me when I was stressed, for reading through every chapter, and for giving me her love and support when I most needed it.

Prologue

It was one of the first settlements to be officially declared as "deserted", and survivors had labelled the place as abandoned, dead – a ghost town. But now the dilapidated buildings stood covered by shoots and leaves that sprouted from every crack; the flora all desperately competing to catch the first rays of the summer morning. It was clear to see that what had once been devoid of life was now another place to have been reclaimed by the force of nature.

It was quiet.

Every time he made his journey into the town for a supply run or to do his usual patrols, the same thought always struck him. It was so damn quiet. He still remembered when the streets had teemed with the life that it was built to accommodate, when the roads hummed with the sounds of commuters in their cars heading to work or school, the pavements reverberating with footsteps and hurried conversations of people on their phones or in groups, and the occasional shunting of trains leaving the station carrying workers and trade across the country.

It seemed so long ago – it was so long ago – but he still remembered, and so it still made him shiver to hear the silence that now encompassed the place he had once called home.

That was why he had left. Or at least, it was one of the reasons. He simply couldn't handle the silence any longer; not in a place that reminded him of how life used to be. He had moved out of the decaying city and headed for the relative safety of the surrounding forest when he could no longer bear the constant silence that surrounded him; that accompanied him to sleep every night and was there waiting for him when he woke up every morning. That, and because Hunters never ventured far from the town.

He had woken early, just before the sun had started to rise, and had set off within minutes from his little camp in the trees. His backpack, which went everywhere with him, was secured tightly to his shoulders. Its simple contents consisted of an old cereal bar that went out of date, months ago and a bottle full of water that he had gathered straight from the stream. His knife was strapped tightly around his waist, as was his small revolver. Accompanying them was a thick cord of rope that hung loosely from his belt.

He reached the bottom of the hill that surrounded the settlement, his view of the town reduced to the buildings in front of him and the taller towers at its centre. Here the coniferous forest ceased, giving way to the sprawling concrete jungle, the division between the wilderness and what used to be civilisation still apparent.

He knew the route. He had walked it more times than he could remember, both before and after it had been abandoned, and over the years he had seen it change from a walk through a small, bustling industrial town, to a walk through everything that had been left behind. Carefully, he traversed his way through the warehouses and storage containers – stripped of all useful contents long ago – and headed into the town's suburban area.

He always liked going through the suburbs, he reflected silently, even now. The houses here were the least dilapidated, and the front gardens that used to be carefully tended by their affluent owners, now resembled small meadows of long grass and scattered flowers. Bird song could still be heard from the deciduous trees that grew in the streets and gardens, and he occasionally stumbled across foxes or rabbits on his journeys through. The silence here, though it still made him slightly uncomfortable, seemed more peaceful than unnerving, and at one point he had even considered staying in the suburbs rather than retreating as far as the forest.

But despite the apparent calm he still forced himself to remain alert, the sense of unease that was more prevalent near the centre of town not yet gripping him. It was rare to see a Hunter venture this far out, and even if one did, there was less opportunity of it sneaking up on him in the wide open spaces. The more central estates, where houses became terraced and space a rarer commodity, was where they were a greater threat, and he never ventured too close to the centre unless he absolutely had to.

Today was different, however, and his destination was the tower that stood directly in the town's centre. It was the tallest on the horizon, rising a good ten storeys higher than its shorter counterparts, all of which were huddled together in a neat little cluster – what was once a successful financial district that housed businesses both small and large, and now housed at least three Hunter dens that he knew of.

8

He stood staring at the tower for a few minutes, lost in his thoughts once again of how much had changed, how much simpler life seemed now compared with then, and found himself longing to go back to the way things were, longing for the company of people and the joy of simple conversation.

He shook himself from his thoughts, scolding himself for his sloppiness whilst quickly scanning the street around him. The suburbs were still dangerous, even if it was further from the town's centre, and he had found himself losing focus more frequently of late when he ventured in. It wouldn't be too long before something caught him out.

He began to move off again, his pace quicker and his gaze more alert than before. Soon he found himself passing houses that were more run-down, the spaces between them getting smaller and the streets narrower, and knew he would soon be passing into the inner city. The silence grew stronger still as the foliage grew denser, and the birdsong that had calmed his nerves only moments before had faded into the distance.

Suddenly the silence was shattered by a high-pitched scream. At first, it seemed distant and the sound hung in the air for an eternity, making his hand shoot instinctively to the gun at his hip. He stood frozen to the spot for a full minute as his eyes darted nervously between the houses, searching inside the windows and through the flora for any sign of movement.

That was a scream. That was definitely a scream. Not a Hunter's call, a fox's bark or an owl hooting, but a person's scream. He was sure of it. Yet he couldn't quite believe it.

He hadn't seen another living person in months – maybe longer. And even then it had been from the safety of a pair of binoculars. Often it was just a group of travellers going around the town's outskirts, not daring to venture in for fear of what was inside. He hadn't seen anyone in the town itself for years, not since the early days when the sight of another person wasn't so rare.

The second scream brought him tearing back from his thoughts, the unnatural sound making him jump just as much as the first. This time it sounded slightly deeper and more pained than before.

A tremor ran through his body that made his spine shiver. Could it be a trap? He had heard of travellers on the road falling prey to such tricks. A person feigning injury, begging for help from a rare passer-by, only for the unfortunate victim to be pounced upon when they got close enough to help. But that didn't make sense, not this far into town. Noise drew the Hunters, like it drew any predator to its prey, and it would be insanity to try to trap a Hunter.

No, it couldn't be a trap, which meant someone must be in serious trouble. So much so that they were prepared to attract a far greater danger.

His conscience and curiosity battled with his logic. The man who had survived years in a post-apocalyptic ghost town told him to keep moving, use the distraction to his advantage and press on through the inner city. But the human in him…

He headed in the direction of the scream, moving swiftly and silently and keeping out of sight where he could. The sound had come from his left, which led no closer to the centre of town but no further away from it either. As he moved, he kept his ears pricked for any further screams, but the town seemed quieter than ever after the sudden disturbance.

Five minutes later he found himself standing in the shadow of a house covered in creepers, looking out over an empty cul-de-sac he vaguely remembered visiting before.

Could he have gone the wrong way? He could have sworn the scream came from this direction. But then sound travelled strangely between the buildings, and he could easily have wandered in the opposite direction by mistake. Had he even heard the scream at all? Or just imagined it, his mind finally giving in to years of loneliness and desperation. His shoulders slumped as he let out a long breath, unsure if he was relieved or saddened at not finding the screaming's source.

He was about to head back the way he had come when a low moan cut across the cul-de-sac, the sound filled with pain and anguish. The blood turned cold in his veins.

He stared directly across the cul-de-sac at a house that he now saw was less run-down than the rest. The windows were mostly intact, with curtains drawn across them to conceal the inside. The house was still covered in plant life, no surface able to escape the natural barrage, but the front door had been repaired and cleared of all foliage and the path between the low wall surrounding the front garden and the doorway looked trampled and used.

He hadn't been in this part of town for a long time, but he would have remembered if such obvious signs of life had existed the last time he was here.

Slowly, he started to creep round the edge of the cul-de-sac, his eyes scanning the rooftops and houses for any movement. He saw none; and couldn't stop his gaze from continually returning to the overgrown house with the well-kept doorway.

He was only two houses down when he heard the screaming start again. This time it did not stop, and he was now certain that it was coming from the house with the well-kept doorway. He darted across the front gardens, the long grass whipping at his trousers and making his legs feel heavy. He vaulted the low wall and sprinted to the door.

He tried the handle, but it was locked and he didn't have time to pick it. Instead he retreated down the trampled path a few metres, before running straight back up to it and slamming into the doorway with speed. His shoulder buckled, but the door held strong, and he fell backwards onto the floor, clutching his arm in pain. As he sat on the pathway, he heard a second scream join the first, this one deeper and recognisable as a man's.

Jumping up to his feet he ran to the downstairs window that faced out over the cul-de-sac and brushed aside the leaves frantically. He swore when he saw wooden planks nailed across the inside and sprinted around the side of the house in the hope that the back would be less fortified.

As he rounded the corner, he saw shattered glass covering the floor and looked up to see the window where the glass had been. His eyes were instantly drawn to something that had been caught in the jagged window frame and his heart skipped a beat when he looked at it more closely. Grey fur. At that moment, he heard a deep, low growl shudder ominously from the window. This time his blood froze.

It was inside the house.

Quickly, and without thinking, he cleared the jagged glass shards from the window frame and hurled himself through the narrow gap. He landed with a crunch as his feet fell on more glass that was scattered around what must have once been a living room; its leather sofas now faded with mould and the wallpaper yellowed and peeling.

He scanned the room quickly and saw a staircase out in the hallway. Suddenly he realised the man's screaming had stopped; the sound replaced instead with a deep, painful sobbing. He was almost certain that this crying came from a woman.

Inside the house it was dark, the sunlight dulled by the curtains that covered the rest of the windows. Those without curtains were mostly barred by planks of wood, allowing only cracks of light to illuminate the room, but it was just enough for him to see by.

He pulled his gun out from the holster at his hip and started moving slowly towards the stairs, stopping at the doorway to check the hall was clear. The woman screamed once more from up the stairs, a high, shrill shriek that split his ears and rooted him to the spot. The scream was followed by a low gurgle, and then the house was silent.

He put his foot on the first step, aimed the gun up the staircase and slowly ascended, hardly daring to breathe. To his right the floor continued into a landing, and he turned to cover it as he reached the top of the stairs. Three rooms faced out towards him, the two to his right each hidden behind its own wooden door. He could see straight into the room that lay directly in front of him; the door having been smashed clean off its hinges from the now splintered and cracked doorframe. Inside lay the motionless body of a man; his midriff torn to pieces. The knife that lay next to him was clean and unstained.

From inside the room he could hear a wet smacking sound and he braced himself for what he knew he was about to see as he stepped up to the threshold. The first thing he saw when he peered around the doorway was the long, thick tail sitting contentedly on the floor. Two huge, muscular back legs were resting either side, supporting a back that was thick with fur and muscle. He couldn't see its face; only the legs of a woman that were sticking out from underneath the beast.

He approached it slowly, knowing the Hunter would be too engorged in its meal to notice him creeping up on it. Besides, it was a Hunter. It didn't need to keep its guard up. Once he stood behind the creature he held out the gun in front of him, training the sights on the soft spot at the back of its head. The Hunter stopped eating, slowly lifting its head to sniff the air as it started growling quietly.

The man emptied the clip into the back of the monstrous creature's head.

The house was still, the heavy breathing of the man with the gun the only noise breaking the silence. His hand was shaking, arm still outstretched and pointing the gun at the Hunter. Slowly he let his arm fall to his side and wiped the sweat from his forehead as he glanced around the room. He couldn't see a gun anywhere, just the knife lying by the man's body, and realised that the couple hadn't stood a chance.

He pulled the Hunter's body off the woman and immediately regretted it. There was a large, bloody hole where her chest should have been and her face was badly scratched. Her eyes were red and blotchy, her cheeks wet with tears from where she had been crying. The man winced and looked away from the body, trying to work out why two travellers had thought they could shelter safely when they were this close to the centre of town.

He thought about burying them, but quickly discarded the notion. It would take too long and more Hunters were bound to be on their way. He reloaded his gun, a grim determination settling over him and cast one last look at the gruesome scene that lay before him. He was just about to turn to leave when he saw something move.

The man froze, eyes fixed to the spot where he could have sworn he had seen movement. But the room was still and silent. Then he saw the movement again, over by the woman's legs. He started to creep over slowly, afraid of scaring away whatever it might be. Could be a rat, he thought, ready to finish the Hunter's meal for him or maybe the first of the flies that would soon be swarming the place. He reached the woman and stood over her, looking down at the floor between her legs.

He dropped the gun.

He didn't believe in miracles, had never decided if some divine power existed or if there was such a thing as fate. He had seen a lot of things since the world had gone to hell, been surprised more times than he could remember, but as he stood there, surrounded by death and carnage, he experienced pure and utter shock as he had never felt before.

Between the woman's legs, still attached by the umbilical cord, lay a baby. It was still covered in blood, the bright pink of its head broken up by soft tufts of hair. The child looked tiny lying on its back, the miniature arms and legs moving in gentle circles through the air. Its eyes were barely open and it wriggled its head softly from side to side on a soft blanket of towels.

The man choked, unable to tear his eyes away. Thoughts raced through his head faster than he could register them as he desperately tried to explain what his eyes could see but his mind couldn't comprehend. It now made sense. The couple, the house, the screams. But he still couldn't believe it.

Standing there, his mouth agape and body numb with shock, he realised in that moment what he had to do.

Slowly he drew the knife from his belt, bending down so that he could cut the umbilical cord and pick the child up in his arms; gently cradling the new born as the silence was pierced by its first cries of life.

Chapter 1

Mark awoke as the first signs of day began to drive away the night, the dim light from the wintry sun not yet bright enough to dispel the darkness that filled the log cabin.

He lay on his back for a while and held his breath while he listened for the usual sounds that accompanied the coming of dawn. The pine needles bristled as the chill wind blew through them, making the branches creak and the trees moan. The birds were yet to break into their morning chorus, most still huddled beneath their wings in a futile attempt to escape the cold. In the distance, the sound of gently running water could be heard.

His breath came out in a long puff of steam as he relaxed. Everything sounded as it should.

He rolled over and looked to his right; saw the gentle rise and fall of the small bundle tucked warmly under the heap of blankets. The child's breathing was barely audible in the dark of the cabin, but Mark could just make out the little puffs of vapour that came from his nose as his warm breath met the crisp morning air.

He rubbed his face and quickly drew the blankets back, wanting to leave the comfort of his bed as quickly as possible before he was tempted to stay in the warmth. Standing by the two worn out mattresses in the corner of the hut, he waited for his eyes to adjust to the slowly fading gloom.

The cabin which he called home was a simple wooden hut that had taken him a few months to build when he first moved into the forest. It was small, but large enough for him to comfortably move around without having to bend down, and had more than enough space for all that he needed.

In one corner, lay an assortment of cooking equipment and cutlery; some reams of rope, an array of knives and his backpack hanging from hooks nailed into the wall above. In the corner across from this, several shelves had been neatly placed which supported a host of books.

From where he stood he couldn't read the titles but he knew what they all were: a mix of survival guides and wildlife books adorned the top shelf and the middle shelf hosted some first aid and medicine guides. The bottom shelf, by contrast, supported much lighter reading; a few fictional classics that at one time were his favourite reads, and some child-friendly picture and colour books that looked strangely out of place.

A small window was placed in the wall opposite him, through which he could see grey sky peeking through the gaps in the dense canopy. A gust of cold air blew into the cabin, making Mark shiver and reach for his coat. He placed another blanket over the child before walking to his equipment corner and taking two metal flasks that were dented and scratched. The metal was cold and burnt the palms of his hands, so he quickly stuffed them into the pockets of his coat as he headed over to the wooden hatch in the floor that was to the right of the window. The rusty bolt that secured the hatch in place groaned as he pulled it back, and he tried to keep the squeaking of the hinges as quiet as possible as he slowly lifted the hatch from the floor.

He threw a rope ladder out of the hole that had appeared in the floor, the rungs unfurling delicately as it fell, but stopped short of climbing down into the dark of the forest. Quietly, he crept back over to the mattresses and carefully pulled a small, black gun from under his pillow. He then crept back across to the ladder and slowly descended into the morning gloom, closing the hatch silently behind him.

He reached the ground and looked back up at his home. The cabin was built about twenty feet up, nestling in the branches of a tall coniferous pine tree. In this light, it would go unnoticed by any passer-by, which was exactly why he had built it so high up in the first place.

Not that he had many passers-by if any at all.

The lower branches of the tree had all been cut away, making access to the little tree-house virtually impossible without the use of the rope ladder, which he made sure was pulled back up into the cabin every night. Even during the day it was difficult to spot unless you were looking directly at it; the dense mass of pine needles adorning the branches acted as a living screen throughout the entire year.

Naturally, he had painted the little cabin a dark green in order for it to blend in.

Mark turned his attention back to the ground and started to head for the little stream than ran nearby. On his way he passed the circle of stones they used as a fire pit; the embers from the previous evening having long since died away, leaving behind a patch of ground that was blackened and scorched. The stream itself lay a few strides beyond, the gentle sound of the water trickling over the rocky bed guiding him in the half-light.

He cupped the ice-cold water in his hands as he stooped down on the bank of the stream and gasped as he splashed it over his face and felt it trickle down the back of his neck. The water was refreshing and instantly dispelled the tiredness from his face; the icy cold instead making him feel fresh and alert.

He was starting to fill the flasks he had brought from the hut when he heard something move behind him. He turned round quickly, his hand moving instinctively for the gun in his pocket, but relaxed when he saw the child walking sleepily towards him.

"Did I wake you?" Mark asked softly, quickly scanning the trees around them. "You may as well go back to sleep, Jake. We're not going into town until it gets a bit warmer."

Jake rubbed his eyes and let out a loud yawn. He looked small wrapped up in his thick winter coat, and his hair was wild from where he had slept. In his arms was clutched a ragged teddy bear, its black, beady eyes staring emptily into the distance.

"No, I just woke up," Jake replied, his voice quiet and gentle. "I was having that dream again, the one with the monsters."

Mark sighed, and gave Jake a sympathetic look. Jake often had nightmares. Frequently Mark was woken up by him tossing and turning in his sleep, moaning softly to himself, or even waking up screaming in the night with tears filling his eyes.

"Come and have a drink," Mark replied, turning to continue filling the flasks, "then we can go to watch the sunrise and we can talk about it."

Jake nodded and wandered over to Mark, taking the flask that was held out for him. He sipped at it slowly as they walked downstream to where the brook disappeared over a sharp drop.

Here the ground fell away into a steep slope, providing the perfect vantage point that looked over the trees covering the bottom of the hill and out onto the town beyond. On the other side of the valley the sun was just beginning to appear over the treetops. It looked pale and watery in the grey sky, and was doing little to drive away the cold of the winter morning.

Below them the town glistened as the dull light reflected off the armour of frost that covered the buildings, the blandness of the concrete jungle more apparent now that the vines and creepers had shed their leaves. In the town's centre, the tall skyscrapers stood silhouetted against the sky, looking as if they were huddled together in a futile attempt to escape the cold.

Mark and Jake sat down on a rock by the stream that was just on the edge of the treeline and listened to the water as it trickled over the cliff. Mark had often used to sit here, gazing over the town and trying to imagine the pavements bustling with people and the roads jammed with cars. In fact, before he had found Jake, this is where he had spent most of his free time, just sitting on this rock and contemplating all that had happened. It was also here where he had taught Jake how to use a rope, reload a gun, and, most importantly, to read.

"Was it the same dream you usually have?" Mark asked, his voice breaking the silence as he turned to look at Jake huddled on the rock.

Jake nodded, his eyes not leaving the buildings spread out below them. His voice was meek and fragile when he spoke.

"Yes. The monsters came and took you away again. They took you away and left me on my own. I tried to stop them, I did! But there were so many, and I…I couldn't. And then I was on my…my…my own, and it was dark and…and…"

Tears filled Jake's eyes and he started to cry softly while squeezing his teddy bear tight to his chest. Mark put his arm around him and brought Jake closer, gently stroking his hair to calm him down.

"Shh, it's all right, it was just a dream." Mark's voice was soft and caring, and gradually Jake's breathing began to slow. "Nothing is going to take you away from me, OK? You know that the Hunters don't come out this far. And you know we are extra careful in town so that they can't get us."

Jake looked up at him, his eyes glistening.

"But what if they did? What if they sneaked up on us and managed to take you. I don't want to be on my own." His voice started to crack again.

"Stop it," Mark's voice was still gentle, but reassuringly firm. "Nothing is taking me away from you. Be it Hunters or people or anything! I would never let them. So stop crying."

"Promise?" Jake asked uncertainly.

"Promise."

Jake nodded gently, wiped the tears from his eyes, and then slowly nestled his head back into Mark's chest. "Thanks, Dad," he said softly.

Mark winced. Jake had only recently started calling him "Dad", and he still wasn't used to it. Jake had read in one of his books about a family, and had noticed what the children called their father. Soon after, he had started referring to Mark as Dad. Jake still didn't know that he wasn't his true father.

Mark hadn't yet told Jake the truth about how he had found him. About how Jake's real mother and father had been ripped apart by the same monsters he had nightmares about almost every night. About how Mark, when standing over his dead mother's body and looking down at the new born baby, which he couldn't believe was real, had made the irreversible decision that he would take it and raise it as his own, despite living in a world full of danger and death.

How were you meant to explain that to a five-year-old?

"It's OK, Jake," Mark said, still softly stroking his hair. They sat in silence for a while as they watched the sun climb higher into the sky and begin to thaw out the frosty town below. After a while Mark continued.

"We need to head into town later today, search for some food and get some more blankets before we end up freezing to death. I swear these winters are getting colder."

"Are we going to stay in the suburbs?" Jake asked tentatively, doing his best to look unafraid by the mention of heading into town.

"Yes. Just the suburbs," came the reply.

Mark had started taking him on supply runs when he had turned three. Before that it was far too risky to take Jake into town, when he was too young to sense the danger that surrounded him. Not only would he move too slowly, but he would also make noise, and Mark wasn't prepared to risk attracting the Hunters when he was travelling with Jake.

Mark used to head into town when Jake had his nap in the middle of the day. It gave him a few hours to gather supplies and he knew that Jake would be safe locked in the treehouse – a few small toys left out for him in case he woke up before Mark got back. It had been tougher when he was only a few months old and his sleeping pattern was more erratic. Back then he had hated leaving Jake behind, but had needed to in order to gather everything a new born needed to survive. Whenever he returned Jake would always be OK, sleeping peacefully in the cot that Mark had scavenged from a nursery, or at worst bawling loudly for food and attention. But although he had always been safe, Mark could never help feeling guilty, and he never stopped worrying whenever he had to leave Jake on his own.

He decided that he much preferred having Jake with him on supply runs, although it seemed more dangerous. Mark felt calmer knowing he could keep an eye on him, and that he would be there in case anything went wrong.

It hadn't been an easy decision. Three was a very young age, and at the time Mark had spent countless hours worrying if it was too young. But he had to teach Jake how to fend for himself, how to survive in case anything went wrong – and besides, he never ventured too close to the centre of town when Jake was with him.

Mark remembered teaching Jake how to move quietly before they went on their first supply run, and what signs of danger he needed to watch for whilst they were in the town. Later he had given Jake a knife and shown him how to use it properly. Mark had felt uncomfortable giving him a weapon when he was so young, but felt safer knowing that he had it on the off chance that he would need to use it. Luckily, so far, he hadn't.

Now Mark worried about when he should give Jake a gun. He had taught him how to aim and fire properly and how to reload a pistol, but had stopped short of giving Jake one of his own. It didn't seem right for a five-year-old to be walking around with a gun in his pocket.

Soon enough he knew that he would need to put aside his worries and do what was safest. Like the knife, Mark doubted he would need to use it for a long time, but at the moment the thought of Jake carrying a gun made him feel deeply uneasy. Jake was smart enough to use one, and careful enough – Mark had made sure of that. But if some accident did occur and Jake ended up hurt, then Mark knew he would never forgive himself.

When he's six, he decided, as he watched the light begin to fill the desolate streets below. I'll give him a gun when he's six.

Chapter 2

It was mid-afternoon when they set out into town. Mark's knife was strapped tightly around his waist, sitting comfortably next to the dull metal of his gun. He carried some water and a torch in a backpack that was pulled tightly against his shoulders; along with a few snacks which would have to make do for lunch.

A cold breeze rustled through the trees and Mark zipped up his thick winter coat to protect him against the chill. The sun had already started to go down, the warmest part of the day having gone and the temperature beginning to plummet once more.

Beside him Jake was also wrapped up warm, his cheeks a rosy red above the woollen scarf around his neck. On his head sat a snug, woolly hat and thick gloves covered his hands that made them look comically big. He also had a backpack for collecting anything of use they might find.

They set off silently down the slope leading to the storage yard that marked the edge of the forest. When they set out into town, Mark didn't allow any unnecessary talking.

The plan was to go through the old storage yard and head west around the edge of the houses. Their destination was a home-ware shop that used to sell all types of goods, and Mark hoped he would find some blankets, winter clothes and firelighters still lying around. They were the kind of things that were now essential.

All seemed peaceful as they started to walk through the storage yard. A thrush sang lazily from a thorn bush nearby and the chains hanging from the warehouse doors clinked together softly like giant wind chimes in the afternoon breeze. But despite the calm Mark could feel the pit of anxiety growing deeper in his stomach, seemingly at a faster rate than usual.

It was probably Jake's nervousness affecting his mood, he thought to himself, as he scanned the rusting containers that surrounded them warily. Everything seemed perfectly normal. He tried to ignore the feeling and pressed on through the yard, never letting Jake out of his sight.

They travelled for some time around the edge of the suburbs with little event, not bothering to search the houses they passed, which had long since been picked clean of all their worth.

At one point, Mark felt Jake tug at his hand insistently and a surge of panic ran through him as he quickly scanned the surrounding buildings to see what had alerted him. He sighed with relief when he saw what had caught Jake's attention.

In a front garden across from them sat a rabbit, grazing leisurely on the grass. Jake stared at the creature in awe, squeezing Mark's hand tightly with excitement. Mark stared too, letting Jake enjoy the moment.

It was too risky to shoot it, he thought, watching the rabbit nibbling on a withered patch of lawn. They had enough food back at camp for tonight and the noise of the gunshot was likely to send the Hunters their way.

Suddenly the rabbit sat back on its hind legs and turned to look at the two strangers, twitching its whiskers feverishly as it tried to measure the danger. Jake gasped and Mark felt his hand being squeezed more tightly as he met the creature's gaze. After a few seconds, the rabbit returned to all fours and hopped out of sight through a hole in the garden wall.

Jake looked up at Mark, his eyes wide with wonder and a huge smile across his face.

"A rabbit!" he mouthed silently. Mark smiled.

"I know!" he mouthed back, sharing in Jake's excitement. "Come on, we're nearly there."

They carried on for another block around the outskirts of the suburbs before starting to head further into town. The houses around them began to get closer together and Mark tried to remember the last time he had ventured into this area.

It must have been well before he had found Jake. He noticed how wild it had become. The dormant husks of the creeper plants and bushes that had long since shed their leaves for winter could be seen on every surface and the ground was covered by a carpet of rotting leaves. In some places, the plants had forced themselves through narrow cracks in the walls, making the brickwork crumble and collapse.

As they ventured deeper, Mark realised that he could no longer hear the occasional chirping of the birds that had accompanied them only moments before, and nothing stirred in the undergrowth around them.

Things didn't seem quite so peaceful anymore.

Mark felt his feeling of unease grow. His eyes scanned around them for any signs of danger and he briefly considered turning back, but decided against it. He was being over sensitive, and the store was only a few minutes away. Jake must have sensed the change in his mood, as he started to shiver and huddled closer to Mark's side.

At the end of the street, they rounded a corner and Mark let out a quiet sigh of relief. The shops lay ahead of them; five small outlets in a row with a storey of flats above. The roof had collapsed in at the far right of the buildings and all of the shop windows had been smashed long ago.

Mark and Jake darted quickly across the street, heading for the small home-ware store that was second in from the left.

They reached the shattered window at the front of the store and stopped, holding their breath as they listened for any sound coming from within.

Nothing. It was as quiet as a grave. Mark drew his gun and entered. Jake followed closely behind.

They walked through the aisles silently, eyes scanning over the shelves for anything they could use. It was oddly tidy, most of the clothes hanging on rails and goods still neatly in place. Everything was covered in a thick layer of dust and in places the clothes lay in heavy piles where they had fallen from their displays.

The children's section was at the back of the store and seemed completely untouched. Around them stood an array of miniature outdoor gear and winter clothes, all guarded dutifully by a small army of toys.

Jake walked up to a thick woollen jumper that was hanging from a rail and felt the material between his fingers. Beneath the grey outer shell of dust he saw a faded dark blue. Quietly, he took it from its hanger and stuffed it into his backpack, then grabbed a pair of gloves and a hat that looked as if they would fit him. Close by, Mark walked over to a still-full shoe rack and found his eyes being drawn to a pair of sturdy walking boots with thick soles and low ankle support. He picked them up and turned them over in his hands, wiping away the dust to reveal the little number he was looking for.

Size four. Too big. He would need to find a smaller pair in the stockroom.

He saw the entrance to the stockroom nearby, the small window in the front of the door revealing only the darkness that lay beyond. Mark tapped Jake on the shoulder and pointed to a pile of blankets that sat on a table a few metres away. Obediently Jake walked over and started filling his backpack with as many blankets as he could.

Meanwhile, Mark crept up to the stockroom door, his hand reaching for his gun as he pushed down on the handle and slowly opened it. The rusty hinges moaned in protest at being used after so long and Mark winced at the sudden noise. Nothing stirred in the room ahead of him and all he could see was a black, foreboding darkness that threatened to engulf him.

He quickly slid his backpack off of his shoulders and got out his torch, clicking it on as he aimed it into the black. The beam cut through the darkness like a scythe and illuminated row upon row of shelves full of boxes. Mark scanned the beam around the rest of the room, revealing more rows of shelves and a tower of boxes against the far wall that were stacked to the ceiling.

It looked deserted.

Mark beckoned for Jake to hold the door while he grabbed the nearest box and jammed it in the doorway so they wouldn't get trapped. The shelves were labelled and he began searching for the footwear stock while Jake waited in the doorway. He found it and quickly located the pair of size threes he was looking for before stuffing them into his backpack.

As Mark stood to leave, he noticed the beam reflect off of something metallic at the back of the stockroom. A door was set into the far wall and he realised it must lead out into the courtyard that stood at the back of the shops. He headed for it, gesturing for Jake to follow as he navigated his way through the dark, and pushed open the door to the outside.

The daylight, though dim, was enough to make them both squint after the darkness of the storeroom. As their eyes adjusted to the brightness, they found that they were standing in a small service yard that backed out onto a street. A metal staircase stood to their right that led up to a walkway from which they could access the flats above the shops.

They headed for the stairs and ascended quickly, taking a moment to look at the street behind them when they reached the top.

It too lay in ruin. The walls of the houses were covered in vines and branches, most of them crumbling, and bricks were strewn over the floor. The ominous silence still surrounded them and Mark noticed with a start how low the sun had fallen in the sky. It wouldn't be long before they needed to head home.

They went through the flats quickly and methodically, Mark picking the locks of the first four doors with relative ease. They didn't find much: some tins of food that had gone out of date years ago but should still be safe to eat, some painkillers, and a box of matches.

Mark knelt in front of the fifth and final door as he prepared to pick the lock. He put his gun down on the floor beside him as he tested the door handle and, to his surprise, found it was already unlocked. That was strange, he thought, as he pushed the door gently open. Ahead of him lay a short hallway, the carpet filthy and the wallpaper peeling off the walls in reams. Cold air blew gently down the corridor and out of the doorway, carrying with it the smell of rotting, damp and decay. Mark felt himself shudder involuntarily, and picked up his gun from the floor before getting to his feet. The feeling of unease had returned in the pit of his stomach and he found himself no longer wanting to go inside.

He needed to search the flat, he told himself sternly, trying to shake off his anxiety. Search the place and then head home. Slowly, Mark forced himself into the hall.

It was cold in the flat. A lot colder than it had been in the others. Jake must have felt it too, as he wrapped his scarf tighter around him and hugged himself to try and keep warm.

Together they walked down the hallway, the carpet muffling their footsteps to maintain the eerie silence; gently pushing open each door they passed to check that the rooms were safe. At the end of the hall, they came to a final door and stopped.

The smell had gotten worse as they had crept deeper into the flat and now Mark found his unease was making him feel sick. Something didn't feel right. Something was out of place.

Mark motioned for Jake to retreat down the hallway and aimed his gun at the door. He took a deep breath, bracing himself for what might be in the room. In his head he counted to three, then quickly pushed the door open and stood back abruptly.

The chill wind rushed in at him and stung his face with cold. Ahead of him he could see house after house underneath a grey sky and it took a moment for him to realise he was looking outside.

This must be where the roof had collapsed, he thought, the exterior wall collapsing with it. At the far side of the room, the floor had fallen away into the grocery store below.

Mark stepped into the room, testing the floor cautiously with each step. As he rounded the doorway, he saw a large bundle lying on the floor. He froze.

It was a person.

They weren't moving.

Mark aimed his gun at the bundle and tried to control the torrent of thoughts that had begun gushing through his head. What the hell was a person doing here? Should he turn around and leave before he was noticed, or should he shoot them? No, he couldn't shoot them. The gunshot would draw the Hunters, but he couldn't just leave either. It was the first person other than Jake he had seen in years.

"Hey," he hissed at the body, his voice barely more than a whisper. "Hey!"

The bundle didn't stir.

Carefully Mark crept over to the bundle and gave it a sharp kick in the back.

Still no reaction.

Slowly, with one hand gripped firmly on his gun, Mark knelt down and held out a trembling hand. He grabbed hold of a shoulder and quickly pulled the body over, at the same time jumping backwards to aim his gun towards it.

Mark gasped. Then sighed. Then lowered his gun.

The body was that of a man's, and the man was dead. A small red hole sat in-between glazed-over eyes that stared emptily up into the grey sky. His face was a ghostly white, streaked with dark red where blood from the hole had trickled over it. The streak continued down his neck before soaking into his clothes, making what was once a faded jumper look dark and wet. Mark looked at the floor around the body, but the gun that had caused the bullet hole was nowhere to be seen.

Confusion replaced his relief, but before Mark could make sense of the scene in front of him he heard the door creaking behind him and turned to see Jake peering into the room, his mouth open in disbelief.

"Is that a person?" Jake whispered excitedly, his eyes growing wider by the second.

"Look away!" Mark whispered sharply. "Go back into the hallway!"

"It is, isn't it? It's a person!"

"I said, look away!"

Jake looked down at the floor with a huff of annoyance. He waited for Mark to turn back to the body and start examining the corpse before stealing another look.

It was definitely a gunshot wound, Mark was sure of that. Right between the eyes. He picked up the lifeless head and looked for an exit wound, but couldn't find one. That was strange. The corpse itself looked fresh, maybe only a few days old. It had started to decay but only slightly, the smell not yet strong enough to attract the usual scavengers that accompanied dead bodies.

He turned to look back at Jake and noticed him staring again.

"Jake! I've already told you. Don't look at it!"

Jake huffed again, clearly disappointed, and pretended to turn his attention towards the street outside. For a second, Mark felt guilty for being so stern.

The dead body was the first person other than Mark that Jake had ever seen and Mark understood that he was bound to be curious. But Jake already had enough nightmares and Mark didn't want him to get too close for fear of making them any worse. It didn't seem right for a child to look at dead bodies.

Mark returned his attention to the corpse and began rifling through its pockets for anything of value, or for any clue as to why it was here. As his hands fumbled around in the coarse fabric, his mind continued to race with questions.

Someone had shot this man, by the looks of it executed him, and that someone could still be around. Someone who was prepared to kill in cold blood. But where? Who? And were they alone?

He found nothing in the pockets.

Mark sat back and looked nervously at the dead man, suddenly feeling the need to get back home as soon as possible. He needed to think about what this meant; to work out if Jake was in any danger. More importantly, he needed to decide what he was going to do about it. He turned to the doorway to see that it was empty. His brow furrowed.

"Jake?" he whispered quietly. His gaze shifted to the edge of the room, where the floor had given way, and he saw Jake standing there, silhouetted against the sky. Mark's blood froze.

Jake turned around, a confused expression plastered across his face, and opened his mouth to say something when he heard the crack. Below Jake's feet the floorboards splintered and the wood groaned as it gave way.

"Jake!" Mark shouted, leaping forward to try and catch him, but he was too far away, and he could only watch helplessly as Jake disappeared through the floor.

Chapter 3

The floor boards and beams crashed loudly into the shop below, kicking up a cloud of dust that filled the small, abandoned grocery store. A second later Jake started screaming; a loud, high pitched squeal that travelled out into the street, bounced noisily around the deserted houses, and filled Mark with complete and utter panic.

Mark leapt down the hole that had appeared where Jake had just stood, landing heavily on his front and inhaling a mouthful of dust. He scrambled to his feet and turned quickly around, his eyes stinging from the dusty air, and felt a spike of terror jar through him at what he saw.

Jake was lying on his back in the middle of the store, still screaming loudly and writhing in pain. His right hand was pinned to the ground under a heavy wooden beam and his legs were scrabbling uselessly against the floor as he tried to free himself. The sound of Jake screaming was almost deafening after being in silence for so long.

Mark knew he had to act quickly. He dashed over to the fallen beam and grabbed it by one of its splintered ends, grunting in his effort to try to lift it from the floor.

As soon as the beam was high enough, Jake withdrew his wrist, clutching his forearm with his left hand as he continued to scream. Tears were pouring down his face and his screams turned into splutters as he choked on the dust that caught at the back of his throat.

Without thinking Mark pulled Jake to his feet and started dragging him to the shattered window at the front of the shop. Jake was sobbing heavily; his splutters now turning to whimpers as the shock set in. Mark stole a quick glance down at his hand and winced when he saw the extent of the injury.

Jake's wrist was twisted at an awkward angle, the skin bulging where the bone beneath was threatening to emerge and his right hand hung limply from his forearm. Blood dripped in a steady stream from his fingers where the nails were cracked and bleeding.

Mark swallowed hard, trying to drive away the panic rising in his chest. They needed to get out of the town. Get out and get home. He tightened his already firm grip on Jake's coat. He would sort his wrist out later.

Mark pulled Jake to the smashed window at the front of the shop and was about to drag him out onto the street when he suddenly froze. Jake stopped too, still sobbing loudly to himself as he stared at his ruined hand. In his despair, he hadn't noticed what had caught Mark's attention, which was now fixed on the houses across the street.

The Hunter was perched on one of the rooftops. Its eyes gleamed menacingly as it stared down at its prey, its mouth pulled back to reveal a sharp set of fangs. Above the grey fur on its back its tail was quivering; a thick cord of muscle that ended in a razor sharp point. Mark held his breath, not daring to move in case he tempted it to attack.

Tension hung thick in the air as they stared each other down, the yellow eyes of the Hunter surveying Mark before settling on Jake, who was still crying. Mark heard Jake's sobbing begin to slow and turned in time to see his eyes glaze over. Suddenly Jake's eyes shut and his head lolled forward helplessly.

Mark caught him before he fell, but knew it was already too late.

The Hunter leaned back on its hind legs and held its head high in the air. A long, low howl cut through the silence, sending a shudder down the back of Mark's neck and making his spine tingle. From somewhere close by came another howl…and another.

Mark couldn't wait any longer.

He threw Jake over his shoulder and as he turned, he saw the Hunter leap from the rooftop out of the corner of his eye. He sprinted back through the shop, Jake's weight pressing down on him as he dodged the debris from the collapsed roof, and smashed through the back door that led out into the service yard.

As he barrelled through the door, he half expected to see one of the Hunters waiting for him, but for now the yard was clear.

He sprinted towards the street that lay at the back of the courtyard and rounded the corner at speed. The Hunter was running down the street towards him, its powerful legs dancing over the concrete.

The house across the street had a low gate at its front and Mark sprinted through it, barrelling into the alley that ran down its side. Dead, thorny branches whipped at his face, but fear urged him on and numbed his cheeks from the pain. At the end of the alley, he found himself in a backyard, his path blocked off by an impenetrable line of bushes at the end of the garden.

Mark knew they couldn't stop, so instead he turned and ran full pelt at the fence to his left. His shoulder smashed into the rotting wood, the panel giving way easily under the force of the impact, and he found himself staggering through to the garden on the other side.

For a second, he felt himself falling under the weight of Jake on his shoulder, but managed to catch himself before it was too late. He carried on running, vaulting over a low wall and heading for the next fence.

Out of the corner of his eye Mark caught a glimpse of the Hunter as it raced through the hole he had left behind him. Panic filled his chest and his legs screamed in protest as he forced them to move faster and carry him towards the fence ahead. Maybe there was something he could use on the other side, he told himself. Maybe he could find a way out.

He was halfway across the garden when he saw another flash of grey dart out from the bushes to his right.

The realisation hit him like a brick.

There were two of them.

Mark swerved left, knowing that he would never reach the fence in time. Instead he sprinted towards the house, drawing his gun from his pocket and firing it at the large glass doors ahead of him as he ran. The glass cracked, but only shattered when he hit it with his side. It took him four steps to cross the conservatory and slam the door that led to the main house shut behind him.

He didn't stop to see where he was, just headed straight for what he took to be the next exit. Behind him he heard a loud crack as the Hunter threw itself into the door and from somewhere else in the house he heard a window smash as the other one leapt through it.

Mark sprinted down a hallway and out through the front door, not wanting to get trapped in the house. He jumped down the steps in one go, his shoulder sagging under Jake's weight when he landed, before barrelling down the front path and back onto the street.

When he reached the road, he found himself turning right before he knew why. He was heading diagonally across the street for a house whose doorway was hanging off its hinges; the rest of the building in a similar state of decay. Mark knew he couldn't outrun the Hunters over open ground, especially not with Jake on his shoulder, and that

31

his best bet was to keep moving through the maze of houses until he found somewhere safe.

He sprinted through the doorway of the ruined house, stealing a glance backwards at the two Hunters that were already halfway across the street. Mark was down the hall and out of the back door in seconds, eyes searching for any means of escape. He saw a fence lying on the floor at the end of the garden and he made straight for it, the long grass whipping at his legs and threatening to trip him up.

Leaping over the toppled fence, he landed in a small back alley where he immediately turned right and started to sprint down. Old air conditioning units that were brown with rust blocked out the sky above him and the floor beneath was slippery and wet.

Mark ran to the end of the alley, slowing down to turn the corner at the end when he was suddenly forced to stop. It was a dead end.

He looked up, but there was no way he could climb out, even if he wasn't carrying Jake. He looked back down the alley and saw the two Hunters sprinting towards him, their powerful legs propelling them forward. Their teeth were bared menacingly as they hounded towards them, each tooth as big as the barrel of his gun and sharp as if filed to a point.

Mark took a deep breath and shifted the heavy weight pressing down on his shoulder. Jake was still unconscious: he hadn't moved since he had passed out in the shop. Mark found himself hoping he would stay that way for just a little bit longer.

He ran at them – the distance between them getting smaller and smaller as he hurtled down the alley. Ahead of him the Hunters quickened their pace, growling menacingly when they got to within striking distance. Mark tensed, bracing himself for the impact – and at the last second smashed through the door to his right, throwing Jake into the room as he fell through the doorway.

Back in the alley the Hunters had been moving too fast and their sharp claws slipped uselessly on the floor when they tried to turn. Mark kicked the door shut, a thick metal fire exit that still looked like it would hold. The Hunters crashed into the other side of door and clawed angrily at the surface as they tried to get through, but Mark had already picked Jake up and started to run through the building.

He found himself in a white tiled room that was filled with metal work surfaces and large ovens, all dimly illuminated by large windows in the roof. At the end of the room, there were two doors that led out onto a dining area. They must be in a restaurant.

It was quiet in here, the only sound coming from the Hunters as they continued to slam into the door. The quiet was strangely unsettling and Mark headed straight for the exit at the front of the restaurant that led back out to the street. But when he started to move, he heard glass smashing behind him and loud clattering as metal pots fell to the floor.

They couldn't have got through the door that quickly, and there was no way they had already reached the roof. Dread began to creep over him as he realised what it meant. There must be a third Hunter.

Quickly Mark placed Jake on the table next to him and turned to face the door to the kitchen. He pulled out his gun from his pocket and aimed it at the doorway, holding his breath in an attempt to steady his hands. A second later, a Hunter darted into the room and headed straight for them, its tail thrashing viciously at the tables behind it.

Mark opened fire, flinching at the sound of the gunshots which were deafening in the quiet room. The first bullet struck the doorframe to the Hunter's left, sending a shower of splinters exploding into the air. The second hit it in the shoulder, but did nothing to slow it down.

It cleared the space between them in three great leaps and launched itself at Mark, its front claws digging into his shoulders as it forced him backwards onto the ground. As Mark fell under its heavy weight, he felt the gun fly out of his hand.

In the time it had taken for the Hunter to reach him, he had only managed to fire two more shots, and although he was sure they had hit their mark they had not had the effect he had hoped for. Now the Hunter was on top of him, its jaws bearing down on his face and claws digging deep into his shoulders.

Mark jabbed his thumb into the Hunter's right eye, making it flinch involuntarily. It gave him a second, just enough time to grab its jaws and push its fangs as far away from him as he could.

Warm, stale breath hit his face and he nearly gagged as the stench of rotting flesh filled his nostrils and mouth. The Hunter tried to force its head back down onto him, its claws still digging into his shoulders, but Mark pushed back with strength he didn't know he had.

Somehow he managed to keep the gnashing teeth at bay. The gunshots must have weakened it.

Saliva dripped off glistening fangs and onto Mark's face, making him flinch and turn his head to the side. When he turned, he saw a dark object lying on the floor next to him; a glass bottle that was just within his reach.

His arms ached under the strain of the attack, his shoulders burning from the claws that were stuck in them, and he could feel his strength beginning to fade quickly. He would be dead before his hand reached the bottle, the Hunter was too quick, but he knew now that it was the only chance he had left.

With one last effort he pushed the Hunter's head away from him with every ounce of strength he had left and shot his right hand out for the glass bottle. Immediately he felt his left arm give way and Mark gritted his teeth as he prepared for sharp fangs to pierce his face.

But they never did.

Instead the Hunter's body spasmed violently and the creature let out a yelp of pain. Mark's hand reached the bottle, his fingers gripping tightly around the neck, and he swung his arm at the Hunter's head. The glass smashed across the side of its face and Mark flinched as a shower of broken shards fell over him.

Above him the Hunter growled with fury and launched its head back at Mark's face with its teeth bared – but it was too late. Mark brought the broken neck of the bottle quickly up towards its throat and the Hunter found itself impaled on the glass, the jagged edge slicing through the fur and piercing its gullet.

Warm blood spurted out from the Hunter's neck and sprayed across Mark's face. He felt the pressure release on his shoulders and he rolled quickly away as the beast fell heavily onto its side. A strange hissing sound was coming from the creature's neck as blood and air poured out of its throat, and its legs and tail flailed helplessly on the ground. Mark watched on in a mix of shock and disbelief as its struggles got gradually weaker, until eventually the beast was still.

Mark sat up, breathing heavily as his mind tried to process what had just happened. He stared at the dead Hunter that now lay in a growing pool of blood, unsure of how he was still alive. That was when he saw the handle of a knife protruding from the creature's back.

He looked to his left and saw Jake standing there, his eyes wide with terror and right hand held loosely in his left. Jake was staring aimlessly at the floor, mouth slowly opening and closing. The blood that was dripping from his fingers had slowed to a gentle drip.

Mark jumped up and grabbed his gun from where he had dropped it on the floor before throwing Jake over his shoulder again. The other two Hunters were still chasing them and they needed to keep moving if they were to get somewhere safe.

He made straight for the front door and out onto the street, heading again for the edge of town and the safety of the forest. The pain in his shoulders made him feel sick, but he tried to ignore it and forced himself to start running again and get away from the restaurant.

It was darker now, the daylight fading away as the sun set over the hills. They were still some distance from the forest, and it wouldn't be long before the sun disappeared altogether. He tried to shake off the thought of being chased through the town in darkness.

When they reached the end of the street, Jake started whimpering and Mark turned to see the other two Hunters sprinting headlong towards them. He felt a sinking feeling form in the pit of his stomach. He couldn't keep up this chase for much longer.

Mark sprinted to the end of the street. When he rounded the corner, he saw their final hope.

At the end of the road, stood a large building, the walls still intact and a large metal security door hanging invitingly open in the wall that faced them. It was a straight sprint to the opening. A hundred yards at most.

Mark ran. Fast. Faster than he had ever run before. Focusing all his attention on driving his legs forward and using his free arm to pump faster and faster while he clung onto Jake with the other.

Eighty yards.

The roar of the wind rushing past him filled his ears, the cold air making the tips of his ears burn and his eyes water. His breathing was ragged and he tried to control it, barely stopping himself from choking as the cold air caught at the back of his throat.

Sixty yards.

He felt Jake slipping, but managed to catch him before he fell and hauled him back onto his shoulder. The joint screamed in protest as pain lanced down his arm and up his neck, making him gasp and almost lose his balance.

Forty yards.

He heard Jake whimper again and knew that the Hunters had rounded the corner. Mark didn't bother to look back. Instead he just kept on running, desperately trying to fight the slowly rising panic that was filling his body. He was so close… Twenty yards.

Behind him he could hear the thud of their paws striking the ground as they gained on him. He knew their strides were larger than his, their legs stronger and more powerful. His legs burned, his shoulders screamed and his head pounded, each stride more painful than the last. The thudding sounded closer than ever, and he could hear their low growls as the Hunters closed in for the kill.

Mark threw Jake ahead of him as they reached the entrance to the building. As soon as he was through the doorway, he turned and slammed the door shut. Just as he heard the sound of the lock clunking into place, he felt the whole frame judder as one of the Hunters hit the outside at speed, and the loud thud it produced reverberated round the entire room.

The first impact was followed quickly by a second...and a third.

Mark ran over to a tall, metal cabinet that stood by the door, knowing he could use it as a barricade. The cabinet didn't budge when he first tried to push it. It was heavy. Really heavy. But he summoned what little strength he had left and pushed harder. This time the cabinet moved – but only slightly.

Slowly, and with great effort, Mark managed to push the cabinet across the door, the sound of the metal scraping along the concrete floor making him grit his teeth. When the entrance was finally blocked, he stopped and turned to look at Jake.

Jake was standing rock still, his eyes wide with terror and fixed on the entrance. Tears were streaming down his face, which was covered in a mass of cuts and scratches, and he was clutching his right wrist loosely in his left hand as his body shook uncontrollably.

The thudding continued.

Mark scanned what he now took to be an old car workshop for anywhere that could provide an escape. The shutters on the far side of the room were down to the floor and the only windows were high up; lying just under the ceiling and well out of their reach. None of them were open, but he knew that wouldn't stop a Hunter if it could get up to them. It would be through in an instant, and with their only way out blocked off...

The sound of scratching joined the thuds.

He would just have to hope that they couldn't reach the windows.

Mark grabbed Jake by the hand and ran to a smaller room that stood at the side of the room. At one time, it must have been an office, for inside he saw an old chair sitting in front of a wooden desk that was covered in sheets of paper and a window on the inside wall that looked out over the workshop.

He grabbed the desk and pulled it across the tiny room, slamming the door shut before blocking it off. Jake was still shaking, his eyes staring out of the window and fixed on the barricaded entrance.

Mark grabbed him and sat opposite the office door, his back against the wall and Jake pulled tightly against his chest. Outside the building the Hunters had started howling; a hollow, chilling sound that filled Mark with terror and made Jake tremble and whimper in his arms.

The thudding was getting more intense.

Mark knew the office door was a lot weaker than the external security one, knew the desk would do nothing to stop the Hunters from breaking it down, knew that even if it did hold then they would come through the window anyway – but he had run out of options. They were trapped.

He pointed the gun at the doorway and waited.

Chapter 4

Mark pulled up the handbrake as the car came to a gentle stop, the low drone of the engine cutting out at the same time. He looked through the murky windscreen at the red light that glared down at him, listening to the pitter-patter of the rain as it bounced gently off the glass.

It was a Friday afternoon and Mark was heading home to his family for the weekend. It had been a relatively straightforward week; business always seemed to be quieter at this time of year and most of the office seemed to have either taken holiday or were off sick. He glanced into the rear-view mirror and saw the tall skyscrapers from which he had just come. Most of the floors were dark, the staff having all left for the weekend, but some were still blazing brightly against the dark clouds, tiny silhouettes milling about behind the windows as they raced to get their work done.

A sharp toot of a horn from somewhere behind brought Mark's attention back to the road ahead and he noticed that the traffic light had now turned to a pasty green. He quickly put down the handbrake and pushed down on the accelerator. The engine immediately kicked back into life and the car pulled smoothly away.

The traffic on the roads was unusually light today, Mark reflected, as he passed through another set of lights.

Usually he would sit impatiently in queue after queue as he fought his way back from work, desperate to get through the door and kick off his shoes so he could relax for the weekend. It wasn't that he didn't enjoy his work, quite the opposite in fact, but the weekends spent with his young family were always what he looked most forward to in his week.

He indicated right and turned into a quiet street. Terraced houses ran along either side of the road, some more modernised than others, and Mark smiled when he saw his wife's small hatchback parked in their drive. He pulled in alongside it, slipping his car into neutral before pulling up the handbrake. Again, the engine cut out and for a while he just sat there, resting his eyes as he listened to the rain continue.

Claire would be sitting on the sofa, her feet tucked up under her while she read one of her fashion magazines. Abby would be sitting next to her, sucking on her thumb whilst she watched her cartoons. Leah, the older of their two daughters, would be upstairs somewhere, her head lost in a book or doing some drawing.

Mark felt a smile spread across his face. He had been looking forward to seeing them all day.

He opened his eyes and got out of the car, bristling as the chill autumn wind struck him across his face. His front door was only a few steps away, but by the time he reached it he could feel his trousers sticking to his legs where the rain had soaked them. His wet fingers fumbled with his keys as he tried to unlock the door and, after a few frustrating seconds, he pushed it open and stepped inside. The moment he was inside he was pounced upon by a giant mass of white fur and he almost fell backwards under the sudden weight on his chest.

"Down Bear!" Mark laughed softly. Bear dropped his front paws to the floor, his tail wagging feverishly behind him. His eyes stared imploringly up at Mark, begging for his owner to pay attention to him. Mark obliged quickly and ruffled the thick fur under his chin, which was met with a satisfied whine.

At an age of four years old, Bear was the youngest of the family. He was a large, white Samoyed that Mark and Claire had rescued from a dog home nearby when he was just a puppy. Mark had promised the girls that they could get a dog, and the two of them had instantly fallen in love with the little ball of fluff asleep in the corner of his cage. It seemed almost comical to Mark that Bear had now grown to almost twice their size.

He kicked off his shoes into the little shoe cupboard by the front door and hung up his coat to dry. It was warm in the house, and grew warmer still as Mark stepped into the lounge with Bear following closely behind.

The scene had been exactly as he'd expected. Abby was curled up at the edge of the sofa, sucking on her thumb and watching some cartoon birds flying around on the TV. She turned to look at him and her face broke into a smile, then she hopped down from the sofa and ran into his arms.

"Daddy!" She squealed excitedly, throwing her arms around Mark's shoulders when he picked her up.

"Hey darling," Mark said gently. He looked over her shoulder at Claire, who was sitting with her legs tucked underneath her. She had turned to look at him and was smiling softly, an open magazine placed face up on the coffee table next to her. Her blonde hair shimmered either side of her face, falling neatly over a smart black top he had seen her put on this morning.

Mark felt a warm feeling settle in his stomach. He knew she'd had a long week, but somehow she still managed to look amazing.

"Hey, honey," her voice was soft and calming, but Mark could tell that she was tired. It was the little signs you picked up on after being together for twelve years that gave it away.

He put down Abby, who ran back to the sofa, before embracing Claire in his arms. She let herself rest on him and Mark breathed in the smell of her shampoo that still lingered in her hair from this morning.

"How was work?" he asked, taking a step back and heading into the kitchen to make them both tea.

"Tiring", she answered, following him into the kitchen. "We're still understaffed. And I had to collect Leah from school just after lunch."

Mark frowned, taking the kettle off its stand so he could fill it under the tap.

"Really? Is she OK?"

"She'll be fine. She's just started coming down with the flu. Half the class has already caught it and Miss Claret doesn't want it spreading any further."

Mark nodded, putting the now full kettle back on its stand and turning it on. The moment the temperature had dropped people had started catching the flu and as autumn had dragged on the number of cases had grown. It had been part of the reason why his week had been so quiet; most people were working from home to stop it passing on. Inside the kettle the water had started to bubble and Mark had to strain to hear what Claire was saying.

"In fact, I think I am starting to come down with it. I can feel something at the back of my throat."

Mark walked over to her and put his arms round her before kissing her gently on the lips.

"Let's take it easy this weekend then. We can get a takeaway for tonight and just relax tomorrow."

Claire smiled warmly and nestled her head into his chest. Behind them Mark heard the click that told him the kettle had boiled and slowly he unravelled himself from her embrace and fetched two mugs from the cupboard. He heard her mumble behind him and move back into the lounge. He finished making their tea, his white with one sugar and hers black and without, then took them through and placed Claire's on the coffee table.

"Thanks, hun," Claire mumbled. She had picked up her magazine and was browsing through it again. Beside her Abby was still watching cartoons, one hand on Bear's head who was sitting dutifully on the floor in front of her.

Mark looked at them enviously, wanting nothing more than to sit down and join them. But he knew he wouldn't be able to relax until he was out of his work clothes, so with his tea in hand he left them on the sofa and headed quietly up the stairs.

When he reached the upstairs landing, he stopped by the door to Leah's room. He listened to see if he could hear her, then gently pushed down on the handle and opened the door. Inside the room was dark and he saw Leah tucked up in a ball under her duvet. She turned as the light from the doorway fell across the carpet and when she spoke Mark was taken aback by how dry her voice sounded.

"Hey dad," she said, followed by a low groan.

Mark walked over to the bed and sat down beside her, running his fingers through her mousy brown hair.

"Hey Leah. How are you feeling?"

"My throat hurts", she moaned softly. "And I have a bad headache." She was turned away from him and Mark listened to the gentle rasping of her breath. She didn't sound healthy at all and he found himself wishing he could make her suddenly better. He hated seeing his kids sick. It made him feel irrationally scared and helpless.

"It will be OK, darling," he whispered softly. "Why don't I get you some hot squash?"

She nodded gently and hugged herself more tightly. Mark let out another sigh and slowly got up from the bed, already feeling slightly anxious as he headed towards the door. He was about to step onto the landing when Leah started coughing violently. He turned and went back towards her, placing his hand on her back and patting it gently as she brought up her hands to her mouth.

41

"It's all right," he said comfortingly. "It's all right."

Leah continued coughing, a horrible hacking sound that reverberated around the room, and for a horrible moment Mark thought that she was never going to stop. But eventually she did, and the violent coughs were replaced by ragged gasps as she tried to catch her breath.

"Are you OK, Leah?" Mark asked, failing to keep his concern out of his voice. He had already decided that tomorrow he would take her to the doctors.

For a few seconds, Leah didn't answer and Mark was going to ask her again when suddenly she turned to him.

Her face was a deathly pale, as white as the duvet she was wrapped in, and she looked up at her father with a horrified expression.

Mark felt his stomach turn and for a moment he was lost for words. He knew that he should act like it was OK, that there was nothing to worry about, but his anxiousness from before had intensified and for the first time he felt like his fear might not be so irrational. His eyes darted quickly between the two things that had caused his panic; from the pool of dark blood that had appeared in her hands, to the terrifying red in her bloodshot eyes.

Chapter 5

The first rays of light filtered through the dirty windows of the old workshop, slowly filling the darkness and driving away the long shadows that reached out across the floor.

Ice covered the insides of the windows where the condensation had frozen hard against the surface, and was now slowly thawing in the gentle warmth of the sun. Across the floor was a thick layer of dust that lay unbroken apart from a small scattering of weeds, and two sets of footprints that led to the little office at the workshops side.

It had been a long, cold night, and Mark and Jake had spent it huddled together meekly against the office wall under a thin layer of blankets. The workshop was like a freezer; the cracks in the roof letting through an icy draft and the brick walls doing nothing to protect them against the bitter chill.

But although it had failed at keeping out the cold, it had somehow managed to keep out the Hunters.

The scratching and thudding had stopped in the middle of the night. How long after he had barricaded the door Mark couldn't say, but the painful silence that had dragged on until the morning was enough for him to be sure that they were gone.

Jake had slept sparingly; the exhaustion from the chase and the pain in his wrist had eventually overpowered his fear and taken him into an uneasy, disturbed sleep. Mark hadn't slept a wink.

"We need to get back," Mark said softly. Gently he removed Jake from his embrace; he was now stirring quietly and looking around the small office space with bleary eyes. Mark got up from the floor, shaking the stiffness from his legs and looking out through the office window at the workshop's calm interior.

"It should be clear by now."

Jake nodded in reply, whimpering softly as he got to his feet. His right hand was still hanging limply to the floor and his fingers were a mess. Dried blood encrusted the edge of his nails, which were cracked and black from the bruising underneath. His wrist was twisted at an awkward angle, the bone bulging beneath the skin where it had snapped.

Quietly they shifted the desk away from the door, creeping back out into the workshop and the slowly brightening light. The exit was still barricaded and Mark grunted as he pushed the heavy cabinet back where he had found it against the wall. They stood holding their breath for a moment, straining to hear what was outside, before opening the door.

Sunlight streamed in, stinging their eyes and making them squint after spending so long in the dark. Mark took a quick step back from the doorway, his gun drawn, and allowed his eyes to adjust to the daylight as he scanned the street in front of him for any sign of movement.

Nothing. It was clear.

Despite Jake's injury the couple moved quickly and headed straight back to the forest, not wanting to linger for any longer than they needed to. When they finally reached the forest's edge, they stuck to the treeline, skirting around the town's outskirts and keeping away from the buildings.

Neither of them spoke until they had made it back to the bottom of the tree which housed their home. Once there Jake collapsed heavily onto the floor, whimpering quietly as he clutched his hand to his chest, then pulled himself up to rest his back against the tree trunk.

"Pass me your flask," Mark said, his voice dry and hoarse. Jake removed the backpack from his shoulders, passing the strap gently over his broken wrist, and dropped the bag on the floor. Mark opened it and pulled out the metal container. After a quick scan of the surrounding forest he left Jake by the tree and headed for the nearby stream.

Mark knelt down by the gently running water and started filling the flasks. He watched as the water trickled into the bottles and felt something rise in his throat as air bubbled to the surface. His eyes began to water and he felt himself starting to choke. The back of his throat was clogged with something thick and heavy.

He put the bottles to the side and started to cry; letting the emotion pour out in deep, painful sobs that racked his body and robbed him of his breath. Curling up into a ball, Mark rocked back and forth as the fear and helplessness began to swallow him whole. Memories from the previous night flashed before him with sharp, new clarity, the possibilities of what could have been torturing him now that the initial shock had worn off.

What if the Hunters had caught him? What if they hadn't found the warehouse? What if Jake hadn't stabbed the Hunter when he had tried to grab the bottle? What if they had got Jake?

For a while, Mark lay by the river, sobbing into the ground as he let the fear and uncertainty take him over. It seemed like forever before he mustered up the strength to calm himself, steadying his breathing with a few deep breaths and bringing his thoughts back to the present.

The Hunters hadn't caught him, he reassured himself firmly. They had found the warehouse when they needed to. Jake had stabbed the Hunter as he went to grab the bottle. And, most importantly, Jake was safe.

Slowly Mark got back to his knees and finished filling the flasks, before splashing some water over himself to hide the tear marks that streaked his face. As he walked back to the camp, he drank from his bottle greedily, the ice cold water soothing the soreness at the back of his throat.

When he got back to the hut, he found Jake fast asleep against the bottom of the tree, holding his wrist carefully against the rise and fall of his chest. A sad smile crossed Mark's face as he watched him sleep, and for a second he thought that he might start crying again.

He hated what he would have to do next.

Quietly he crept up to Jake and examined his wrist. The break was nasty: the skin was already turning a deep violet as the bruising set in. He would need to splint it, that was for sure, but luckily it was a closed fracture, the bone bulging under the skin rather than tearing it where it had snapped.

Gently Mark pulled Jake's right arm away from his body, causing him to stir slightly in his sleep at the movement. In his head he began to count slowly, breathing softly with each second. When he reached three, he pushed down hard.

The bone moved suddenly under Jake's skin, clicking loudly as it shunted back into place. Jake sat up sharply with his eyes open wide and started shrieking in pain, holding his arm out uselessly and clenching his left hand. He screamed for five more seconds before suddenly falling silent, his body slumping unconsciously against the tree.

"I don't want to go into the suburbs again," Jake protested loudly. "Not ever! Ow!"

"We won't go back for a while," Mark replied gently. "But eventually we'll have to. You know that, Jake."

They were sitting at the edge of the slope that looked over the town, the stream trickling softly out from the forest beside them. The sun was at its highest point, its light shining down to warm them as they sat on the ground. A pot full of water lay next to them, along with a small bag full of medical equipment that Mark had salvaged over the years. Jake's hand was resting on a small stack of cushions, his wrist now in a more natural position after being reset.

When Jake had regained consciousness, Mark had given him painkillers to try and calm him down. They had taken away the worst of the pain, but Jake's wrist still throbbed with every heartbeat and now he was wincing, occasionally yelping with pain, as Mark delicately tried to clean the wounds on his hand.

The skin around the break was now a palette of purples and blacks. The nails too had turned a dark purple where the blood underneath had dried and the skin was swollen. The nails themselves would fall off soon, but for now Mark was more concerned about the cuts getting infected.

"Was that…ow…was that a person? A real one?" Jake asked, the excitement in his eyes still evident despite the pain.

"Yes," Mark replied bluntly. "It was a person. Hold still! I need to splint your wrist."

He grabbed a stick he had found which was reasonably straight and about the right size for what was needed. Carefully Mark began to bandage Jake's hand and wrist, the stick working crudely to hold it straight and in place. Once he was finished Mark examined his handiwork with a grimace. It would have to do until he could find a proper cast.

"He was dead, wasn't he?" Jake asked, examining the make-shift cast for himself before looking back up. "Like most of the people? But why haven't we seen more dead people? Why just him?"

Mark turned away to look over the town and let out a deep sigh. He had been waiting for the question ever since they had got home, but now it had been asked he found himself unprepared. For a second, he considered pretending he hadn't heard, but knew that would be unfair.

Jake was curious. Who wouldn't be? The only person he had ever seen in his life was the one that had found him at his birth and it was only natural that he wondered who else was out there. Now that he had seen someone else, even if it was just a body, that curiosity would only intensify.

Of course he was aware that at one time more people had existed. The books Jake had read talked about how life used to be, when it was rare to go through the day without seeing anyone else and families and friends still existed. But to him they were fantasy, not history, and the thought of meeting another person was a distant dream that filled him with awe and excitement. However, the world was no longer what it used to be, and if they were to bump into a stranger Mark would be thankful if it still consisted of just a passing acknowledgement.

He needed Jake to be prepared for when that happened.

"He was dead," Mark confirmed, turning back to Jake to make sure he was listening. "He was dead because someone killed him. You understand that, don't you?" He waited for Jake to nod before continuing.

"People aren't friendly anymore, Jake. They're dangerous now. They're nothing like the people in your books. Out here people will do anything, and I mean anything, to survive, Jake. You need to understand that. If a stranger was to see something that we have, and they needed it for themselves…then they wouldn't think twice about shooting you for it. Do you understand?"

Jake frowned with disappointment, but didn't appear surprised by what he had been told. It wasn't the first time he had heard it.

"Is that why the man was dead?" Jake asked. "Because he had something somebody else wanted?"

"Probably. Or maybe some other reason. In fact, there may not have even been a reason."

Jake had turned to look off into the trees, his brow furrowed with concentration. He was clearly thinking hard about what Mark had said.

"Jake."

Jake turned his attention back to him.

"If we ever see someone, you don't go to them. OK? You don't talk to them or even let them know you're there. Be silent, keep out of sight, and tell me. All right? Just like if we see a Hunter."

Jake nodded, flinching at the mention of the Hunters, but the expression on his face said he was still confused.

Mark was confused too. Ever since they had found the body he had been trying to work out why it was there.

He wanted it to be suicide –was desperately hoping that it was – but deep down Mark knew that that couldn't be the case. If it was suicide, then the bullet hole wouldn't be between the eyes – the hand position to put the gun there was too unnatural – and the weapon itself would have still been by the body. That meant that somebody else was responsible – that it was murder. And if that was true then the murderer must still be out there.

Gently Mark picked up Jake's arm and placed it in a sling he had made from an old sheet, his mind tying itself in knots while he worked.

Whoever it was that had left the body surely wouldn't find them here. It was more than likely just a traveller passing through the town. They would have been searching through the flats when they bumped into the stranger. The two of them had an argument, maybe over some supplies or something similar. Things got a bit intense so the traveller shot him, either out of protection or out of need.

Whatever the case, the killer would have moved on after realising how little there was left to find and be heading for the next city. Mark didn't need to concern himself with it anymore.

The sound of Jake talking suddenly roused him from his thoughts.

"So if we met another person," Jake was saying, "and they tried to steal from…OW! They tried to steal from us.

Would we kill them?"

"Yes," Mark answered, without hesitation.

"What if they didn't try to steal from us? Would we, would we steal from them?" Jake asked curiously, seemingly uncomfortable with the idea.

"No," Mark answered, slower this time. Then with more clarity, "No, we wouldn't. What's theirs is theirs and what's ours is ours. We wouldn't try to steal from them and if they left us alone we would leave it at that."

"Couldn't we talk to them, though? Maybe we could invite them back for tea, like they do in my book. The kids alw…"

"No Jake," Mark cut him short. "It would be far too dangerous. If they knew where we lived, where all our food and supplies are, they could come back at any time and take it. Couldn't they?"

Jake lowered his head with a sigh of frustration. He knew it would be useless to argue. For a while, they sat in silence as Mark finished off the sling and Jake sulked. Mark felt bad for crushing Jake's hopes so brutally, but knew that it had to be done. Jake needed to know how dangerous people had become, needed to understand that he couldn't trust anyone.

"There," Mark said, tying off the final knot to finish the sling. "That should work for now. We'll need to change the bandage every few days and it's important that you rest your arm until it heals. So you have to keep it straight, like a stick." He held out his arm to demonstrate what he meant. "Does it still hurt?"

"A bit," Jake mumbled, still upset.

"OK," Mark checked his watch. "You can have some more painkillers in an hour. That should help."

Jake stood up and began swaying from side to side. His eyes were fixed on the ground where he had been sitting. Mark sighed.

"What is it, Jake?"

"Nothing," Jake mumbled.

"Are you sure? We can talk about it if you want?"

"I'm sure." Underneath the scratches his face was full of defiance.

Mark shrugged. "OK. Well, if you change your mind we can talk about it. I'm going to get some beans from the hut so we can eat."

He turned and started heading off for the treehouse, feeling suddenly very tired. He would need to sleep after they ate. He must have been awake for nearly forty hours.

"I thought he could be our friend! I was going to invite him to tea!" Jake suddenly shouted angrily.

Mark froze mid-step, all thoughts of sleep instantly dispelled. Slowly he turned back to face Jake, feeling almost as confused as when they had found the body.

"Invite who to tea?" Mark asked quietly.

"The man in the other house! Who I saw across the street, when I fell!"

Chapter 6

The camp had appeared at the east side of town, a stone's throw away from the road that travelled several miles to the next settlement.

Hammocks hung from the trees around a large circle of tents, creating a mismatch of fading colours that cast an ugly stain against the natural green of the forest. A large pit surrounded by rocks stood in the middle of the camp, the floor within blackened with soot from the previous night's fire.

Just outside the perimeter of the tents, lay a tree that had been cut at the base. Its trunk had been stripped of all its branches and large gouges pitted the surface where chunks of wood had been hacked away. On the road just outside of the forest stood three large pick-up trucks that were each adorned with a paintwork of jagged scratches and dirt.

Next to the fire pit in the centre of the camp a deer hung loosely from a wooden stand, a large hollow pit replacing the space where its insides used to be. Its head hung limply from its neck, from which small black eyes stared emptily at the small group of men that were sat around the fire pit, all of whom were staring into the blackened ground as if the flames were still roaring away.

"Not a lot lying about," drawled one of the men, the dense mass of scraggly hair that covered his mouth muffling his words. "This place cleared out long ago and no one bothered to come back."

"Better than the last town," replied a smaller man, whose nervous, shifty eyes darted around the trees at the Camp's edge. "We've already found one traveller, and he was carrying enough food to keep him fed for a week."

"Yeah but there's a lot of us and one of him," shot back a tall, skinny man with deep bags under his eyes. "Last us one or two days if we ration it right."

"Quit your bitchin', Joseph," another man joined in the conversation, this one adorned in camouflaged clothing and sitting with a rifle between his legs. "That's what the deer's for! Town may be pretty dry, but the game in this forest is good! That deer will be the first of many."

"That's great," Joseph shot back. "You find any fuel for the trucks while you were out there, Dave? Or some ammo, maybe? Or new shoes?"

Dave shrugged and turned his attention back to the fire pit.

"Exactly," Joseph continued, turning to face the rest of the group. "Pickings are getting slimmer with every town we go to. We need to start thinking about heading back north. Places there were never this empty, and I could swear there weren't as many Hunters either."

"That's a load of crap!" a different man with a gruff voice joined the argument. "Name one place we have been to that didn't have Hunters. Granted some had more than others, but there were just as many up north as there are down here." He pointed off somewhere in the distance. "We had some close calls up north. Right, Mike?"

Mike, who was also sat around the pit, grunted quietly under his breath and began rubbing the stump where his left arm abruptly ended.

"I'm just saying," Joseph carried on, shaking his head and folding his arms defensively. "We should never have ventured this far south. It's only going to get worse from here."

"Are you finished?"

The men around the pit suddenly fell silent at the sound of the calm, quiet voice, whose owner they had not noticed approaching. The voices owner took up a vacant seat that stood at the edge of the circle and took out a large, silver revolver which he began to polish delicately. His hair was crudely cut in order to keep it short and tidy and only a thin layer of stubble covered his face. Cold, blue eyes looked up from the gleaming revolver and fixed Joseph with a hard stare. Four large scars ran menacingly across his right cheek, the skin marked and angry where the claws had struck.

Joseph looked away quickly.

"I said, are you finished?" his voice demanded an answer.

"I...I didn't mean nothing by it, Gabe. I'm, I'm just hungry, that's all. Ignore me, you know I like to whine, right, guys?" He laughed nervously as he looked around at the other men. No one joined him.

"No, it's OK," Gabe said, his voice still level and calm. "You're not happy, I get it. We're finding less and less with every town we go to. Maybe we should start thinking about heading back north."

Joseph's eyes widened in surprise. "I mean, if you think it's a good idea…"

"Why not?" Gabe continued with an unmoving stare, "It can't be any worse than here, can it?"

"I, I guess so," Joseph shrugged. He was starting to feel unsure of himself.

"Don't guess so," Gabe replied, his voice suddenly firm. "You seemed so sure of yourself a minute ago."

"I was just talking, Gabe. I di–"

"Maybe you should start making decisions." Joseph's face dropped like a stone.

"Maybe we should be going where you think is best. In fact, maybe you should be in charge." Gabe's stare had grown more intense as he spoke, and his voice was now as hard as ice.

"I didn't say that, Gabe!" Joseph protested, shaking his head furiously.

"But that's what you meant. Isn't it?"

"No Gabe, I would never say that!"

"Why don't, if you are so smart, why don't you go off and fend for yourself?" Gabe said, his voice getting slowly louder. "Why don't you go out there, on your own, without us, and see how long you last back up north?"

Joseph's face turned a bright red and he quickly turned back to the fire pit. He didn't dare to respond.

"No? You don't want to? Then shut up and stop bitching!"

An uncomfortable silence settled over the campsite. Everyone's eyes were fixed on the blackened ground, none of them daring to speak in case they made themselves a target. Gabe's stare moved slowly around them all, his eyes only returning to his gun when he was sure that he had got his message across. He started speaking as he polished.

"Daniel, why don't you get a fire going and start cooking up that deer for us? The others will be back soon."

Daniel, the youngest of the group at around his mid-twenties, nodded in compliance and walked off to gather some firewood. He returned with an armful of kindling and began to build up a fire in the middle of the rocks. Once it was built he put a match to the tinder and watched as the flames caught. The orange glow and the warmth that accompanied it helped relieved some of the tension and gradually the mood started to lift in the camp. Daniel started cutting strips of meat from the deer carcass and placed them in a cooking pot over the fire.

Gabe continued talking once the meat was cooking.

"We've already found one traveller here, so there are bound to be more. And we aren't going anywhere until we find them and we're stocked up again. If anyone has a problem with that, the road's over there and the next town is fifteen miles east."

No one replied. They were all watching Daniel while he cooked the deer.

"Now, Jack says there's a lot of Hunters in and around the town centre, so it's a safe bet that not many travellers have had the chance to pick it clean. That means if there's fuel anywhere, it will be right in the middle. So that's where we need to look."

The men around the camp nodded in agreement.

"Joseph, for that little outburst earlier, you can start scouting it out tomorrow for us."

Joseph flinched at the command, but nodded slowly. He still didn't dare to make eye contact. Gabe, satisfied, returned his attention to his revolver, polishing off an invisible speck on the barrel.

Truth be told, things were getting desperate and had been for a while. Each town that the group travelled to seemed more barren than the last and travellers were becoming few and far between. They had been heading south, or in that general direction, because that's where there were more cities and towns and so a better chance of finding supplies. At least, that's the reason Gabe had cited when he had declared where they were headed.

In all honesty, Gabe had no idea what lay further south; if it would be better or worse than where they had come from, or if there was anything of value there. But he couldn't let his men know that; that he had no idea what lay ahead and he was leading them blindly. They might see through the mask he had put on to control them, the mask they all feared so much and that he had done terrible, terrible things to keep wearing.

Things that he would do again in an instant if he had to.

The sound of a stick cracking nearby made the men in the circle turn their heads sharply, but they relaxed when they saw it was just one of the scouts returning from town, a bag slung loosely over their shoulder.

"Not got much unfortunately," the scout said, as he approached. "Just some medicine, and some boots that should fit you, Cal."

The small man with shady eyes nodded in way of thanks.

"Other than that, just a few cans."

No one responded. The report didn't require one. They had heard it before and would hear it again. Their attention was better focused on the deer meat that was cooking nicely on the fire.

Gabe continued polishing his gun, also not surprised at the bleakness of the news, and felt a sense of unease at the group's discontent. He needed something. Something to boost morale and keep them all going. The one traveller they had found with some ammunition and ration bars was nothing, and when they had found him they had shot him the moment he drew his gun. Maybe they should try to capture the next one, bring him back to the camp and play with him for a bit. Or even better, a woman. That would keep them happy for a while.

The smell of cooking deer stirred Gabe from his thoughts and he turned to look at the meat that was now evenly browned and sizzling with fat. Daniel retrieved some metal plates from one of the tents and put the largest strips onto one of them before handing it to Gabe.

Gabe ate in silence while the rest of the meat was handed out and devoured by the men. The venison was warm and flavoursome and it wasn't long before the meagre scraps had gone.

"Jack," Gabe said, when he had finished eating and had put his plate on the floor. "How far in did you go?"

"Not too far," the scout replied, whilst chewing on a particularly tough piece of meat. "I was still about a mile out from the centre, maybe. Wasn't much there. Some of the cars look like they could have had fuel but…" He shrugged and returned to his meal.

Gabe nodded and stared deep into the fire, acting as if he was unaffected by the news.

In reality, his mind was racing.

They would need to raid the centre. Eight of them. Leave two back to guard the camp and trucks. Daniel and Dave were the obvious choice, he didn't want to lose them. The rest he would take with him to see what they could find. With any luck he might lose one or two to the Hunters. A few less mouths to feed would do some good.

"Boys!" A voice from outside the circle made them suddenly all jump. "Got some ammo for you."

Another scout stepped into the circle and dropped a bag on the floor with a thud. The sound was met by impressed nods from the rest of the camp. The new scout grabbed a plate and served up the last of the deer meat, sitting down in a chair to complete the group. He started chewing ravenously on the venison, talking casually between mouthfuls.

"Found all that in one house. Some freak with a gun obsession probably. Couldn't find any of the guns, but that was lying under the bed. Bloody goldmine!"

"Good work, Paul," Gabe said. The good news helped to slow the pace of his thoughts. "That means we can head into the centre in a few days and try and drain some of the cars out. Get enough to run the trucks for a few weeks."

Paul nodded, licking the fat from his fingers. "Saw something else though. Could hardly believe it. Still don't actually." He finished licking his fingers. "Was going past the place where we shot that guy the other day, last night this was, and I saw two people across the street, in the same room that we left the body."

Gabe suddenly sat up straight; the other men turned to listen with interest.

"So I'm looking at them, a middle aged guy, right, bending over the body, and the other one standing by the door. And then I think, wait! That's a kid!"

"What?" said Joseph, the disbelief plain in his voice. Gabe winced at the interruption and waited for Paul to continue.

"Seriously!" replied Paul. "He was tiny. Can't have been older than six. Or seven maybe, I don't know. I couldn't believe it! Then suddenly this kid looks at me, and I mean right at me, and starts walking to the edge of the room."

"Cut the crap," said Dave, quickly losing interest in the story. "Haven't seen a kid for years! They aren't about anymore."

"Why would I make this up?" protested Paul, holding out his hands in front of him. "Anyway, so this kid is walking towards me, looking straight at me because he's obviously seen me, and I am looking straight back. Then he turns around to the older guy, who must be his dad or something, and I'm thinking, I better get out of here before the dad sees me. When suddenly...bang! The kid falls right through the floor!"

Some of the men around the fire laughed, others just shook their heads and turned back to their meals, not believing the story for a second. Gabe was the only one to not have moved. He was staring at Paul with his sharp, blue eyes, searching for any signs of lying on his face. He found none.

"What happened then?" The sharpness in his voice stopped the laughter immediately.

"Kid starts screaming the place down," Paul continued, happy that his story was being believed. "The dad jumps down the hole after him. I stayed to watch. You know, see what happened and go in after to see what I could find, but then I saw about three Hunters approaching so I turned and ran." "You see them escape?" Gabe asked.

Paul shook his head.

"Didn't stay for long. Hunters got them, though. No way that they got out of that."

Paul turned his attention back to his food now that he had finished his story. The rest of the group put their plates down and sat staring into the flames, still chuckling or shaking their heads at what they'd heard. Gabe felt himself smiling coldly.

A kid. He hadn't seen a kid for years, not since before he had formed this group. Most children hadn't been strong enough to survive, and now it was far too dangerous, especially during a winter as cold as this, to travel with one.

That meant that there had to be a camp somewhere. A camp that was warm, safe and full of provisions.

Suddenly Gabe found himself feeling a lot better about the town him and his men had stumbled across. He needed to know if the dad and child had survived, and if they had, then where they were now.

He sat back in his chair and returned his attention to the flames. He had a goal. An objective. Something to keep the men busy and the group's morale high. He sensed a hunt was coming, and the thought of catching his prey was already making his blood rush. Who knows, maybe there was a mum around as well.

Either way, Gabe was certain of one thing. He had found his distraction.

Chapter 7

A thick blanket of cloud lay low across the sky, making the sunlight a dull and gloomy grey. Beneath the towering pines that formed the forest canopy it was gloomier still; the light barely managing to filter through the thick mass of branches.

A thick layer of frost covered the carpet of leaves and shrubs, ready to crunch loudly when stepped on to reveal the presence of anything passing by. But Mark and Jake had hunted these woods before and knew how to walk amongst the forest in silence, even in the poor visibility cast by the eerie half-light.

They picked their way through the leaf litter; Jake following exactly in Mark's footsteps. It had been almost an hour since they had left their camp and in that time they had not seen or heard a thing. The forest was well and truly within winter's grasp.

Jake had a brand new knife strapped to his waist, a suitable replacement for his old one which he had stuck in the back of a Hunter. Mark had found the knife in town earlier that week, along with a cast he'd found in a doctor's surgery which Jake now wore on his wrist. They'd taken his arm out of its sling in an attempt to restore some movement.

They had replaced Jake's bandages that morning and Mark was pleased to see that the wounds on his hands were healing well. One of the shattered nails had already fallen off, the new nail beneath filling the space it had left.

Ahead of Jake Mark was moving silently, his eyes and ears peeled for any signs of life within the forest. In addition to the gun and knife that he always carried, was an archer's bow slung tightly across his shoulder.

The bow was finely made, from the time when things still were made, and would once have been considered a high-end product which enthusiasts would not have hesitated to pay the top price for. But Mark knew little of such things and to him it was something that allowed him to kill quickly and quietly, in times when stealth was of a greater importance.

Now was one of those times.

It had been over two weeks since they had been chased through town, when Jake had broken his wrist and the world had almost claimed its next two victims. Two weeks since they had stumbled across the dead traveller with the hole between his eyes, the discovery filling Mark with confusion and Jake with awe. Two weeks since Jake had seen the person who had undoubtedly killed him.

Fortunately in that time very little had changed. They had stayed in the safety of the hut, giving Jake's wrist time to heal and using their supplies to get through the cold winter days. Mark had only gone into town once, in order to find the cast and knife, and the trip had led to no more unpleasant discoveries. He had left Jake, who was far too scared to head back into town just yet, back in the forest.

They also hadn't had a fire in those two weeks. Mark wouldn't allow it for fear of the smoke being spotted and this meant that Jake had moaned incessantly about the cold. To keep warm they had instead huddled under heaps of blankets, whispering quietly to each other about the books they had read and Mark answering the hundreds of questions that were heaped upon him.

But soon their supplies had started to get low and now they needed to be replenished. They hadn't eaten anything fresh for a while, so Mark had grabbed the bow which he had kept for years and set out into the forest to hunt their next meal.

They weren't fussy about what they caught, not that they had much choice. In fact, any game would do, but so far they had been unable to pick up a single trail; the only sounds of life they had heard had been quiet birdsong trickling down from the high branches. Mark could sense Jake's impatience behind him and knew that soon they would need to turn around and head back. He would just give it a little longer.

"Dad," whispered Jake from behind him. "Nothing's here!"

Mark kept his eyes forward, his focus still on moving silently and looking for movement amongst the trees. "I know, Jake. Just a few more minutes and we'll head back."

"But I'm tired!" Jake persisted.

"A few more minutes," he repeated,

Jake sighed behind him, but continued to follow. His eyes wandered to the tops of the trees and the grey sky beyond.

Jake hadn't slept well last night; for the last two weeks in fact. Ever since the chase the nightmares had gotten worse, the monsters in his dreams now more real than ever. Mark would always be there when the nightmares came, awoken by Jake's unconscious mutterings, and was ready to stroke his hair and whisper reassuringly to him as he tried to ease him back to sleep.

Mark pitied him and felt somewhat guilty for Jake's nightmares. He himself barely ever dreamed.

They carried on for another five minutes, Jake's footsteps beginning to drag amongst the leaves. Still nothing moved in the forest around them. Eventually Mark stopped, ears pricked in the hope of hearing anything in the quiet, before sighing disappointedly.

He turned to Jake, about to admit defeat and whisper to him that they would head back, when suddenly they heard the sound of a stick cracking under the weight of something heavy. They ducked instinctively, their knees bent as they scanned the treeline for the source of the noise, but could see nothing. The forest was as quiet and still as a graveyard.

The movement was subtle and came from their left and Mark felt his heart skip a beat as the largest stag he had ever seen emerged from the trees. Despite its size it moved silently, its hooves effortlessly navigating the frozen forest floor beneath a head held high with pride and majesty. Two great antlers protruded from its skull, the bleached white bone sparkling in the gloom.

Mark tensed imperceptibly, not wanting to scare the magnificent creature off. Behind him he heard Jake gasp.

The stag stopped, stooping to graze on something it had seen in the leaf litter. Mark turned slowly back to Jake, putting a finger to his mouth to show him that he should be quiet.

Jake didn't notice. His attention was fixed on the creature ahead, his eyes wide with wonder and mouth agape. Mark tapped on his shoulder gently, momentarily breaking his trance, and motioned for him to follow.

Slowly they began to stalk through the trees, keeping the stag within their sight. It was grazing casually on a small bunch of snowdrops it had found amidst the leaves, completely unaware of the pair that were approaching. They reached the base of a tall conifer tree, small juniper bushes scattered around its roots, and knelt down once more.

Carefully Mark slipped the bow from his shoulder and pulled a long, slender arrow from the quiver on his back. Silently he nocked the arrow onto the bowstring.

Meanwhile Jake was silent, his gaze still fixed on the stag. As Mark drew back the bow, he realised that this was the closest Jake had ever been to a deer.

He aimed down the bow's sight and felt the feathers on the arrow's flight gently tickling his cheek. He sighted up the stages midriff and began to question whether the arrow would do enough damage to disable the animal. He would have to hope it did. Beside him he heard Jake's excited breaths and Mark hesitated, deciding he would let him enjoy the moment for a little longer.

A small smile tugged at the corners of his lips. He was glad that they could experience this.

Animals fascinated Jake. He had spent many an afternoon staring at pictures of them in his books and dreaming of one day being able to see them all in person. In light of what had happened in the past few weeks, this was exactly what he needed to lift his spirits, and Mark could feel the same effect working on him.

Who knows, Mark thought, as he watched the stag grazing casually in the clearing ahead, maybe he had overreacted to finding the body. Maybe they should have a fire tonight; cook up the deer and have a small feast to celebrate how well Jake's wrist was healing. After all, it was important to enjoy the little things.

"Jake," Mark whispered almost imperceptibly. The moment was coming to its end and out of the corner of his eye he saw Jake nod.

He refocused his aim. The deer's midriff seemed suddenly smaller in the crosshairs.

Mark's breathing slowed and his fingers tightened their grip on the taut bowstring as a gentle calm descended over him. The rise and fall of the deer's body as it chewed on the flowers was almost hypnotic. He held his breath. The deer started to raise its head slowly, sensing something amiss in the forest's stillness. It turned its head and froze when it saw him, its small beady eyes looking straight into his.

For a second, Mark hesitated.

The sound of the gunshot shattered the silence, deafeningly loud. It echoed off the tall pines, making the birds screech as they flew from their branches, slowly fading as it bounced around the trees.

Mark jumped at the sudden noise and felt his fingers let go of the bowstring. The arrow shot forward, but fell short and wide of its mark, missing the deer completely and landing in the undergrowth. The deer itself was now lying on its side, completely motionless and with a hole in the side of its head.

Mark grabbed Jake, bundling him to the floor and under a juniper bush that stood next to them. He covered Jake's mouth, muffling the screams of pain from where he had knocked his broken wrist before turning him towards him. With his hand still clamped firmly over his mouth, Mark stared seriously into Jake's eyes for him to be quiet.

Jake understood and Mark felt the pressure release from under his hand as the screaming stopped. It was only then that he let go of Jake's mouth; Jake began to cry silently to himself as he clutched at his wrist.

Looking back out to where the deer had stood Mark could see the animal still lying on the ground. He scanned the treeline around the carcass, his mind racing as he searched for the source of the gunshot. This time the movement came from his right.

Two men emerged from the trees, both wearing camouflaged outfits that blended in with the backdrop of the forest, and with rifles slung over their shoulders. Together they strolled casually up to the carcass and the older of the two kicked the animal hard in the side. The stages body remained still.

"Nice shot, Paul," congratulated the older man.

Paul, the younger-looking of the two by more than a few years, nodded his agreement.

"Didn't stand a chance," Paul commented, as he stooped down to examine the deer's head. "Look at the size of those antlers, Dave! They're huge!"

Dave nodded as he eyed the creature, clearly impressed with the deer's size.

"That will keep us all fed for a few days. Hide looks thick, too. Could use that for an extra cover. The nights here are freezing."

Paul looked up from the stag and scanned the forest floor around them.

"Yeah well, hopefully Gabe gives up this wild goose chase soon enough so we can move on from this ghost town."

Mark watched them from the cover of the bush, his arm held tightly over Jake's back to hold him to the ground. Paul was still gazing over the floor and his eyes suddenly stopped when they looked in their direction.

Mark's heart froze in his chest.

Paul stepped over the deer and started walking towards the small juniper bush, the crunch of the leaf litter under his boots getting louder as he approached. Carefully, Mark moved his hand towards the gun in his pocket, holding his breath as his fingers closed around the grip.

Paul got to within ten feet of the withering juniper bush before he stopped and bent down to pick up a large stick from the floor. He hefted the wood in his hands to test its weight, then turned around and moved back to the deer as he uncoiled a rope from his belt. Mark let out a deep, low breath.

"Gabe won't give up," Dave was saying, bending down to tie the stag's front legs together. "He won't leave until we've found that camp. You know what he's like when he picks up a trail."

Paul grunted, pulling the rope around the stag's rear legs into a tight knot.

"If we haven't found it yet, then we're not going to find it. There probably isn't even a camp. It was another pair of travellers just like the rest of them. And I don't care if there were no bodies. There's no way that they could have got away from the Hunters. I'm telling you, Dave, the kid went right through the floor! Screamed the place down. Those two are dead, bodies or not!"

Mark strained to hear them talking and felt his stomach tying itself in knots. There was a group of them; a group of bandits that robbed and killed whoever they came across. One of them must have seen them in town, when Jake had fallen through the floor, and now they were searching for them.

Something began tugging insistently at his elbow and Mark turned to see Jake looking expectantly up at him. His eyes were still wet from where he had been crying, but now that the pain in his wrist had subsided they were wide with wonder.

"That's him!" Jake mouthed, his lips quivering with excitement.

Mark glared at him fiercely, demanding him to be quiet. Jake's face dropped with disappointment, but he could sense Mark's unease and so remained silent.

"Well, try telling Gabe that," Dave was replying to Paul. "Anyway what does it matter? Every place we go to is just the same. Empty. If you think the next town is going to be any different to this one, you're wrong. Hunting. Hunting, Paul. That's our best bet. And these woods have the best game I've seen in years. I say let Gabe keep trying to find his camp. It's not doing us any harm."

Paul shrugged as he tied the stag's legs to the stick he had retrieved.

"True. The last few towns have all been dry. I just don't like risking my neck scouting out places only to come back empty handed."

"Well, if you hate it so much then find out where the father and son are. Then we'll move on and maybe the next town won't have so many Hunters in it."

By now, the stag was bound to the makeshift pole and Dave and Paul hoisted the load onto their shoulders. Between them the stag hung limp and lifeless, staring helplessly back towards the clump of juniper bushes. They began heading off through the trees, moving more slowly than when they had arrived under the carcass' heavy weight. Within seconds, they had disappeared into the gloom, the heavy crunching of the leaf litter under their boots fading away with them.

Ten minutes later Mark emerged from under the bush, checking around him carefully before summoning Jake to follow. High up in the canopy, birds had returned to their branches, flitting from tree to tree in search of food and chirping quietly to each other. They walked back to the hut quickly, as swift and silent as ghosts drifting through the undergrowth.

Neither of them spoke.

Jake sensed that his dad was not in the mood for conversation, and knew that the hundreds of questions that buzzed around his head would have to wait until they were back in their hut. But he couldn't help but feel excited! So excited that he could no longer feel the pain in his wrist and the cold in his fingers.

He could scarcely believe what had just happened! First the deer, which he had been so unbelievably close to, had been amazing. Of course he had seen deer before, but only ever from far away. The stag had looked exactly like it did in the pictures from his books, only much, much bigger and so much more…alive! And then the people! Real people!

He had recognised one of them instantly as the person he had seen in town, when they had found the dead body and he had fallen through the floor. Dad had said that there weren't many people around anymore, but now, in only a few weeks, he had seen two!

He couldn't understand why Dad was so scared of them. Whenever they talked about meeting people Dad would say how people were dangerous and would try to hurt them, and could even be more dangerous than the Hunters. But Jake had never understood why anyone would want to hurt them. While they had been hiding under the bush Jake had heard the two men talking about them, about how they were looking for a boy that had fallen through the floor. They must want to know if he was all right, that he was OK after the fall. That didn't sound like someone who wanted to hurt people.

Jake looked at his dad's back and frowned. It was tense, and he could tell that he was nervous by how quickly he was walking and how he looked hastily from side to side. Jake shivered. It made him feel nervous too.

Maybe Dad's right, he thought to himself, maybe they should wait to see if these people were dangerous. Dad hadn't been wrong before and he used to know lots of people, so he would have a better idea of what they were like than him.

He bit his lip as he tried to concentrate, racking his brain to figure out what had made his dad so uneasy. The problem bugged him for the rest of the journey home and he eventually gave up as they reached the base of the tree that housed their home in its branches. Mark still hadn't spoken, but as he turned to beckon Jake to climb up the ladder, the look on his face sent a shiver down his spine that left him feeling bitterly cold.

What Jake saw in his dad's face he knew wasn't fear, or nervousness, or anxiety. Nor was it unease, worry, or panic.

Instead his dad's face was set as hard as stone, his mouth set in a thick line that was neither a frown nor a smile. Dark eyes blazed brightly with an intensity he had never seen before and Jake stood bewildered for a moment, confused as to how he should react to this new emotion.

The dark eyes were blazing with fury. Fury and determination.

Chapter 8

Gabe stared angrily at Joseph, who was standing sheepishly in front of him, and looked him up and down for any sign that he was lying.

His coat was open, revealing a threadbare jumper underneath that was stained with dirt. A faded leather holster hung from his shoulder, the cold metal grip of a gun protruding from it, and around his belt was tied a long knife. Large tears cut through his jeans at the knees and the laces on his boots were full of knots from where they had been repeatedly tied together.

His face was nervous; covered in a messy beard that needed trimming and holding eyes that were tired and weary. But in spite of all of his anxiety Gabe was certain he was telling the truth.

"You're sure?" Gabe's voice was curt and sharp.

Joseph nodded, swallowing back his nerves and rubbing his arms. "Not a trace."

Gabe turned away, paying Joseph no further attention, and walked purposefully back to his tent, ignoring the furtive glances from the rest of his men scattered around the campsite. As he walked, he felt his hands curling slowly into fists and his breathing getting heavier.

He unzipped the nylon flap that led into his tent and threw it back angrily, diving inside before pulling it shut again. The moment it was closed he began to punch the ground viciously, his vision becoming blurred at the edges with rage.

The sound of wet smacks filled the tent as his fists pummelled into the soft ground, permeated by short, angry grunts of aggression. Gabe's knuckles screamed at him to stop, but the pain only enraged him further and he struck the ground harder and harder.

Finally, when his knuckles could take the pain no more, he sat back heavily onto his mattress. He looked down at the hole he had made, which was shallower than he had expected, as he caught his breath.

Nothing. Two weeks and still nothing.

Gabe had sent men out every day to search the town's suburbs since Paul had seen the mysterious boy and his father. So far they had found a few ammo stashes, some cars that still held a trickle of fuel in their tanks, and a few rations that were just about edible – but not a sign nor trace of the father and son.

With each passing day their chances of picking up their trail got slimmer and already Gabe could sense the doubt starting to creep into the camp. None of the men had said anything, but it was obvious that they were getting more and more reluctant to go back out to search, and each wasted trip only strengthened their position.

It didn't matter, Gabe reassured himself with a shake of his head. They would still go. And they would keep going until they found something or he told them to stop.

The day after Paul had returned with his tale of the boy falling through the floor Gabe himself had gone to investigate. Paul had led him to the little outlet of shops and they had stood in the wreckage of the collapsed roof from the previous day.

There were no bodies, nor were there any bits of meat or bone left from a feast. Apart from the roof, the only sign they found that somebody had been there was a small patch of fresh blood by a snapped wooden beam, the congealed liquid covering the thick layer of dust on the ground with a sheen of black.

Paul had shaken his head in disbelief, recounting again the screams of pain coming from the shop and the speed at which the Hunters came, but Gabe wasn't listening. He had already moved back out onto the street, scanning the houses around him as he searched for any signs of fighting or a trail of blood.

It took him half an hour before he noticed the gate to a front garden of one of the houses at the back of the shops hanging loosely from a hinge. He walked up to it, kneeling down to inspect the damage and feeling his heart rate spike as he saw the fresh scrapes that marked where the gate had been forced open. He was about to look in the house behind it when he heard his name being called from somewhere to his left.

Paul was standing in the street, pointing at a front door that was still hanging open. The wood around the frame had only recently splintered and Gabe looked confusedly around him as he tried to make sense of the clues.

They must have gone back on themselves, he realised as he ran his fingers over the splinters sticking out from the doorframe.

Carefully they went through the house and out into the back garden, instantly spotting the trail of flattened grass running through. Again, Paul shook his head in disbelief. Gabe let out a cold smile.

The trail had led into an alley that ran along the back of the garden, and it wasn't long before they spotted the heavy security door at the alley's end. The doorframe was blemished by large dents, and the metal surface of the door itself was gouged with deep scratches. Paul prised the lock open with a crowbar and on the other side they found themselves in a kitchen, their boots crunching on shattered glass that covered the floor.

A Hunter was on its side in the dining area, the carpet around it dark and wet where its blood had soaked in. Once again, Paul had shaken his head, muttering inaudibly to himself as he tried to make sense of the scene. Gabe knelt down to inspect the dead Hunter closer and saw immediately where its throat had been gouged out.

Another smile broke across his face, this time leading to a fit of laughter as he pulled the knife from the Hunter's back.

It was the proof he needed to show that they were alive – but since then they had found nothing.

Gabe held out his hand in front of him and flexed his fingers, grunting as he felt the pain dart up his arm. Little streams of blood ran freely from his cracked knuckles and down the back of his hand.

They couldn't be in the suburbs, he decided suddenly. It had seemed the most likely place for the camp to be – most of the travellers Gabe found were on the road or in city outskirts; the houses were good shelter during the winter months – but his men would have found something by now if that was where the father and boy were hiding.

The trickles of blood reached his wrist and started to skirt between the dark hairs of his forearm. If they weren't in the suburbs, that left three options.

They could be in the town's centre, which he now realised may not be as unlikely as it seemed. There were Hunters, yes, and lots of them, but that meant their chances of being found by anyone were small. It also meant there would be more supplies. It was unlikely, but it wouldn't be the strangest thing that Gabe had seen.

They could have just been travellers; another pair wandering the wilderness in the endless struggle to survive. It was the least likely

67

option if Paul had been right about the child's age. Gabe would be very surprised if they hadn't set up camp for a winter as cold as this, especially now that the boy was likely to be injured from his fall. Which left the third option.

The forest.

His lips curled into a smile as the blood reached his elbow and began slowly dripping onto the floor. If their camp wasn't in the town, it had to be in the forest; far enough from the suburbs to be hidden but close enough to head in for supplies when they needed to.

He stood up suddenly and grabbed a coat from the corner of his tent. As he slid his arms into the sleeves, he felt the fabric sticking to the sweat and blood on his skin. From out of his pockets he grabbed a pair of thick, leather gloves which he pulled tight over his cracked hands, his fingers still throbbing with pain. He took a deep breath, then unzipped the tent door and stepped out into the fading daylight that hung low over the trees.

Around him the men were busy tending to the daily tasks that needed to be done to keep the camp running. Beside the felled tree stood two men with an axe, taking turns at hewing logs for the fire from the deadwood. Another stood on the tree itself, chipping off bark and branches and throwing the pieces onto a growing pile of kindling.

Beside the fire pit sat Mike, the stump of his left arm hanging lifelessly by his side as his right hand worked hard at keeping the fire stoked and alive. Daniel sat in the chair next to him, tending to a large pot that hung over the flames; the liquid inside bubbling angrily as it dispelled the faint scent of rabbit. Joseph was also sitting by the fire, fiddling with his beard and staring into the flames with a glum expression. In the distance, he heard someone tinkering with the trucks.

Gabe strode purposefully over to the fire, glad to see that his men were keeping themselves occupied, and let out a shrill, high-pitched whistle. Around the camp everyone stopped what they were doing and began to slowly make their way over.

He sat down in one of the camp chairs, staring into the boiling broth and enjoying the warmth of the burning sensation in his hand when he opened and closed his fists. He stayed with his eyes fixed on the pot until all the men were either sat or stood around the fire, some of them shuffling nervously as they waited for him to speak.

Above the fire the broth began bubbling over the lip of the pot and Daniel jumped up to remove it from the flames. Gabe continued to let the silence stretch.

"Joseph just got back from town," he began, once Daniel had placed the pot on the ground. Some of the men shot curious glances at Joseph, who was now looking at Gabe uncertainly with his head cocked to the side.

"And, unsurprisingly, he found nothing." A few more nervous shuffles; no one was surprised at the news. "Which leaves us with two options."

A stillness settled over the group. The men were watching Gabe with guarded faces as he continued to stare into the fire. Daniel was the first to break the silence.

"What are they, boss?"

Gabe stirred, his eyes flicking to Daniel.

"Two options," Gabe repeated. "We give up and go.

Or we search elsewhere."

Joseph's shoulders slumped and he turned to look at the fire. Jack, one of the men who had been cutting logs, hawked and spat to the side. Gabe turned and fixed him with a cold stare and quickly Jack looked away. Daniel spoke up again.

"Elsewhere?"

"Isn't it obvious?" Gabe said, shifting his gaze back to Daniel. "If they aren't in the suburbs, they must be in the forest." He spread his arms wide to indicate the trees around them. "So tomorrow we begin searching the woods, starting here and moving around to the far side of town."

His attention was suddenly caught by someone spluttering. He scanned the men around him for the perpetrator and his eyes locked on to Jack, who was shaking his head in disbelief. The cold stare returned.

"That's a lot of ground, even for ten men," Jack protested. "It will take us weeks to cover! And we won't find anything else of use in the forest while we're searching."

"Then it takes weeks," Gabe replied firmly. His voice cut the air like ice. "Either way, we don't leave until we've searched it and we've found that boy, his dad and their camp."

"Damn it, Gabe, have you completely lost it?"

The protest came from his right and Gabe turned to see a frustrated Joseph looking up from the fire.

"Just leave it and move on. Those two are long gone by now! Either upped and left or dead in a ditch. If we haven't found them by now, we're not going to find them!"

Gabe stared at him, every last trace of surprise gradually disappearing from his face. By the time he rose from his chair, his face was emotionless.

Joseph twitched, cursing himself for his own outburst but also confused. He clearly hadn't been expecting this reaction.

"Let's just...just call it a day and get going," he stammered.

Gabe walked around the fire until he was in front of Joseph's face. Suddenly, and without warning, Gabe's right hand shot up, his gloved fingers curled into a fist, and struck Joseph across the nose with a satisfying crunch as the bone cracked under the force of the blow.

Joseph staggered back and he let out a cry of pain as he fell over the chair behind him. He flailed on the floor, trying desperately to get to his feet, but Gabe had already walked calmly over and kicked him hard in the stomach.

He curled into a ball as air wheezed out of his mouth, before another hard kick landed square in his face. A spray of blood flew into the air as his head jerked backwards and slammed into the frozen ground with a thud. His hands shot up to his face, desperately trying to protect himself from more blows while he moaned in pain.

The attack only lasted for a few seconds and as soon as it was finished Gabe walked calmly back to his chair and sat down again, gently stroking the leather of the glove on his right hand. He returned his attention to the fire before speaking.

"Jack. Tomorrow you take Dave, Joseph and Greg around the south side of town. Spread out and make sure you cover a few miles of forest each. I'll take Paul, Daniel and Cal round the north side and do the same. Everyone clear?"

He scanned the faces around him. Everyone nodded, trying to keep their attention on the flames and away from Joseph's awful moaning.

"Good."

Gabe stood up, making to leave the circle and head back to his tent. He stopped when he saw the final two of the group returning from the quickly darkening forest, something heavy being carried on a pole between them. He fought back his rising sense of anticipation.

70

One by one the men around the fire turned, watching as Paul and Dave emerged from the woods. As they got closer, the group could make out that the something being carried between them was a stag, its legs crudely bound to a wooden pole. Gabe sighed. Not what he was hoping for, but the meat would be good.

"We are in for a feast tonight, boys!" Paul said, when they were within earshot. They hefted the pole onto the stand by the fire before Dave collapsed into his chair, puffing heavily. Paul rubbed his hands together as he admired the stag, then stuck his finger in the bullet hole in the creature's head, turning to look at the group to show off his achievement. His face dropped when he saw Joseph curled up on the floor.

"What the hell happened to Joseph!" he exclaimed, making to head over to his aid. He was stopped suddenly by the hazardous looks from the rest of the group and he quickly understood what had happened. Instead he seated himself by the fire and accepted a bowl of the rabbit broth which Daniel had started handing out.

"Good work," Gabe commented with a nod to the stag. "You just missed a group meeting. Paul, tomorrow you are coming with Daniel, Cal and me to search the forest north of the town for the boy and his dad. Dave, you are going with Jack to do the same."

Paul looked up from his broth and nodded obediently. Gabe stifled a smile, glad that his message had gotten across. He took one last look over the group, all of whom were now tucking into their bowls of soup before it went cold. As he turned to go, he noticed Dave had not joined in with the meal, but instead was examining a long, thin object that he held in his hands. Gabe squinted to try and make out what it was, but he was too far away so, curiosity getting the better of him, he made his way over.

"What have you got there, Dave?" he asked casually. There were certain rules within the group and stealing was one which even Gabe couldn't break. What's yours was yours, and no one else's. It was as simple as that. And if any one man took from another then the victim was within their rights to punish the thief however they saw fit.

Dave held up the object for him to inspect, the smooth surface twinkling softly in the light from the flames.

"Found it by the stag after we shot it. I almost walked right by it. Was just lying amongst the leaves and thought it might be useful."

Gabe's heart rate quickened as his eyes identified the object, his earlier rage completely forgotten and replaced instead by a sudden surge of adrenalin. For in Dave's hands, was held a long, slender arrow.

Chapter 9

Jake concentrated hard; his tongue sticking out from between cracked lips while his brain whirred. The board in front of him was almost empty, most of the white chips stacked messily in a pile by his side. His eyes scanned the rest of the chips determinedly as he searched for some way to take the last two white pieces.

Suddenly his eyes lit up and a broad grin broke across his face. He picked up his final piece and moved it hurriedly over the two white pieces left, slamming the chip on the board excitedly with each move. He held up his hands in triumph and grinned at Mark, who was sat across from him.

"I win!" he exclaimed happily.

"Yes, you do," Mark admitted, looking up at Jake and grinning softly. "How about best of three?"

Jake nodded enthusiastically, picking up his pieces and lining them up again on the chequered board.

Jake loved playing draughts. It was his favourite board game and Dad said he was starting to get really good at it. He sat back to study the neatly arranged lines of chips before making his first move. Carefully, he picked up one of the draughts to his right and moved it forward.

A ray of sunlight shone through the treehouse's only window, landing on the playing board and reflecting gently off the polished chips. It was warm today, warmer than it had been for a while, and the birds outside acknowledged this by singing merrily to each other as they basked in the sunlight.

Jake smiled. He liked listening to the birds singing to each other. Sometimes he would sit by the window and look for them in the trees as they flitted amongst the branches. One day Dad had brought him home a bird guide, and Jake had whittled away hours with the book in his lap as he tried to identify them all. The inside of the book's cover was full of scribbles where he jotted down what he had seen so far.

"Jake," Mark said softly.

Jake shook his head, tearing his eyes away from the window and back to the game at hand. He took his time before making his next move.

"How does your wrist feel today?" Mark asked, as he took one of Jake's pieces.

"It still hurts to move it," Jake replied, not looking up from the game. "But not as much as yesterday."

His wrist lay on top of a stack of pillows next to him. They had taken it out of the cast that morning, because Dad said it would heal quicker if they let the air get to it. His wrist looked pale and wrinkled atop the dark stains on the pillows and large purple bruising covered the skin around the break.

Mark nodded and started to stroke his beard as he surveyed the playing board.

"It will still be a while until you can move it properly. And even then you'll need to be careful. It won't be back to normal for at least a month."

Jake huffed, the disappointment showing clearly on his face. He hated not being able to use his hand. Climbing up and down the ladder to their house had become extremely difficult, and the pain that shot through his arm in waves kept him awake at night. He started to yawn. The thought had reminded him of how tired he was.

The pain was always worse at night. No matter how still he kept, or how many pillows they used to prop up his arm, his wrist would always throb with agony. Dad gave him painkillers before he went to bed, along with something to help him sleep, but they never seemed to work and he would always lie awake until the early hours of the morning.

Jake shuddered suddenly at the still painful memory. It wasn't just the pain that kept him up. Whenever he closed his eyes he could feel himself falling. Falling and screaming as he fell into the dark.

"Are you OK?" Mark said softly, sensing Jake's unease.

Jake looked down at the board again, nodding quickly. He didn't want to talk about his nightmares again. About how over the past few weeks they had gotten worse.

The monsters came, as they always did, only now when they came he was stuck and couldn't get away. His hand was trapped beneath a wooden beam and he couldn't move his arm. The harder he tried to escape, the more trapped his hand became, and the terrible pain in his wrist would get worse. While he struggled the Hunters would come and Jake could do nothing to stop them as they pounced on his dad, biting and clawing at his face.

Jake would scream. Scream until his lungs burst. Scream at them to stop, to leave him and his dad alone and to go away. But the monsters didn't stop. They just kept clawing and biting and snarling, their tails smacking onto the floor behind them. Dad would shout at him while the Hunters attacked, telling him to go, to run away and leave him.

But Jake couldn't. And even if he could, he didn't want to. He didn't want to leave his dad and be left alone. Lost in the dark with the monsters hunting him. Then suddenly Dad would stop yelling, and the monsters would turn to him...

Last night he had been so scared that he had wet himself.

He knew what he had done the moment he was awake. The warm damp between his legs made him feel ashamed. He had stopped wetting himself years ago; that was what little boys did and he was a big boy now.

He had turned red with embarrassment when Dad had seen the stain in his shorts and thought that he would be angry with him for ruining the sheets. But Dad had just smiled sadly, reassuring him that it was OK and that they could wash them in the river.

Jake hugged himself tightly and tried to refocus his attention on the game. He realised he hadn't played his turn yet and quickly moved a piece forward on the board.

Dad said that he was in shock; that the trauma from falling through the floor, hurting his wrist, and then being chased by the Hunters was making the nightmares worse. He had also said that in time it would get better and that although the nightmares were scary, they were only dreams, and that the two of them were too clever to let the Hunters catch them.

Dad was probably right. Jake still couldn't remember much about that day once he had fallen, only small flashes of being carried and one of the Hunters lying dead on its side.

"Hey," Mark's voice made him look up. "Don't think about it."

Somehow Dad always knew when he was sad. Jake shook his head, taking his dad's advice and trying to think of something else.

His thoughts locked onto the deer they had seen in the woods. He remembered how big and real it was, how it moved almost silently through the trees and how its black, beady eyes had looked straight at them! It was a shame that Dad had needed to kill it, but Jake knew that sometimes they needed to eat animals to survive.

But in the end Dad hadn't killed the deer. Those men had.

Jake felt the corners of his lips tug into a smile. No matter what his dad said, he couldn't help but feel excited at the thought of meeting new people.

He didn't understand why Dad didn't want to talk to them, why he didn't try and make friends so that they had other people to play draughts with. Dad said that they were dangerous, but they looked normal to him. They wore clothes and talked to each other and they killed the deer just like they were going to.

He hesitated, his mouth held open. Then curiosity got the better of him.

"Dad," Jake asked slowly. "Why didn't we try to talk to those people yesterday?"

On the other side of the board Mark bristled. Now it was Jake who could sense the uneasiness.

"Why do you think we didn't talk to them?" came the reply. Mark looked up from the game to focus on him.

"Because you think they want to hurt us."

"I don't think they want to hurt us, Jake, I know they do." Mark's words were certain and he had fixed Jake with an intense stare. "Didn't you hear them talking to each other?"

"Yes," Jake nodded. "They said they were looking for us. They wanted to see if I was OK!"

Mark winced, and Jake thought he saw a hint of sadness creep onto his face as he turned to look out of the window. For a second, he was bathed in a ray of sunlight, but the warmth did nothing to change his pained expression. Outside the window a bird landed on a branch with its back to him and began to sing sweetly into the winter afternoon. With a heavy sigh he turned back.

"Look, Jake, I don't want to scare you. But you need to know this." Mark paused, making sure he had Jake's full attention before continuing. "Those men…they come from a group."

"You mean there's more of them!" Jake cut him off excitedly.

"Jake, listen!" Mark said sternly. Jake's face dropped like a stone. "Yes, there's more of them. How many? I don't know. And yes, they are looking for us, Jake. For you and me. But they don't want to play draughts with us, they don't want to see if you're OK, or to be our friends. They want to find us so they can kill us. That's what those men were talking about. They were talking about how they are hunting us down, just like they were hunting down that deer, so that they can kill us and take everything we have."

Jake sat in stunned silence, paralysed by what his dad had said. The shaft of sunlight had disappeared and the temperature in the hut had suddenly dropped a few degrees. Outside the window the bird had stopped singing.

"But...but...why would they kill us?" Jake stammered, struggling to find the right words. "They could take our stuff without...without killing us?"

"Because it's easier for them to kill us, Jake. Then we can't fight back. People are different now, they aren't like the people I told you I used to know, or the people you read about in your stories. The world is far, far more dangerous now, and people have become more dangerous with it. The Hunters are scary yes, and they are dangerous, but people...people can be far worse."

Still Jake didn't move. He was trying to process what he was being told. He didn't want to believe what his dad was saying.

"Did...did they kill that man? The man we found when the Hunters chased us?"

Mark nodded solemnly, trying to gauge Jake's reaction and seeing if he had understood what he'd been told. His quickly darkening expression told him that the realisation was beginning to hit home.

"So...if they are hunting us," Jake went on, "then...then what should we do? We can't let them kill us!"

Mark nodded again, relieved that his message was getting across.

"I know, Jake. And they won't. Trust me."

"But what are we going to do? Should we hunt them? Kill them before they can kill us?" Jake looked uncomfortable with the idea.

"No," Mark said sternly. "There's more of them than us and, like I said, we don't know how many there are in total. We know they are looking for us, but up in the trees we are well hidden. If we stay here and don't venture far from the camp...then hopefully they'll think we've gone and they'll move on themselves." Jake frowned.

"How long will it be until they move on?"

Mark didn't answer for a moment, unsure of how to respond to the question. Eventually he shook his head.

"I don't know," Mark admitted with a sigh. "I don't know, Jake. We just need to be extra careful for a few weeks, all right? Make sure we keep quiet and out of sight. When they're gone, then things can go back to normal again."

Jake nodded his understanding and Mark smiled back at him. He felt guilty at having to be so stern, but knew it was important that Jake understood the danger they were in. He turned back to the board between them, eager to change the subject.

"Now, are you going to make your move or not?"

A puzzled expression crossed Jake's face and then quickly vanished when he realised what Mark had meant. He looked down at the board, sticking his tongue out in concentration again as he studied the pieces.

They continued to play for another half hour, Mark winning the next two games and Jake winning the third. The score was tied at two each and they were reaching the end of the decider. Each of them had two pieces left.

Jake studied the board long and hard as he tried to find a way to win, his attention solely fixed on the game in front of him. Slowly he reached out his left hand and moved his draught over one of Mark's, placing his chip almost within striking distance of the final piece. Then he sat back, staring at the board and waiting for his dad to make his move and set the game up for a grand finale.

But the move he was expecting never came.

"Dad," Jake said softly. Then louder, when he got no response. "Dad!"

"Shh!"

Jake looked up sharply and saw Mark crouching by the window, carefully scanning the floor below the hut. Jake froze, straining to hear what had spooked him. He suddenly noticed how still the forest outside had become, the rustling of the leaves the only sound to be heard. Then, gently carried on the passing breeze, he heard the sound of whistling.

Gradually the whistling got louder and Jake began to make out a tune he had never heard before. Fear crept slowly up his spine, the conversation from earlier sharp in his memory. Mark didn't move from his position at the window. His eyes were still fixed on the floor below.

Suddenly Mark shot a hurried look back at Jake, mouthing something under his breath. Jake nodded to show he had understood and crept carefully to the mattresses at the other side of the treehouse. He went to Mark's bed and slid his hand under the pillow, feeling his fingers brush against cold metal. Slowly he withdrew the gun, which felt strangely heavy in his hands, before creeping back over to the window and putting it in Mark's outstretched hand.

Outside the whistling was getting fainter and Jake tried to peer out of the window to catch a glimpse of what was causing the noise, but Mark turned and glared at him as he slid the gun into his pocket.

"Stay away from the window," he breathed, and started to make his way over to the hatch in the floor.

Jake watched as his dad gently pulled open the hatch and threw the rope ladder down the hole. He turned and started to climb down the rungs, first his legs and then his body disappearing as he descended. When his head was about to vanish through the hole, he stopped and looked back up.

Their eyes met, and Jake knew from Mark's face that something bad was about to happen. Then, just like that, he was gone, leaving Jake helpless and alone.

Chapter 10

Mark landed on the floor silently, the soft grass cushioning the impact of his feet. He looked to his right and saw a shadowy figure casually strolling away from him through the trees. Whoever it was hadn't noticed him, and judging by the broad shoulders and large gait, he suspected it was a man. Mark followed, keeping out of sight behind the thick trunks of the conifers.

Within the forest, it was beginning to get dark. A thick blanket of grey cloud completely blocked out the sunlight that earlier had been warming the afternoon, and now a chill breeze blew through the tree trunks, making the branches sway ominously and the pine needles shiver.

Mark stalked through the trees, never taking his eyes off the figure ahead of him. He was wearing a thick coat with fur on the collar, the leather on the back faded and bleaching. A heavy pair of camouflage-patterned trousers adorned his legs, ending in a sturdy pair of walking boots that left large, deep footprints in the grass. He was walking at a leisurely pace, still whistling contently to an oddly cheerful tune.

Mark knew that this must be a member of the group that had settled on the far side of town. From this distance he couldn't tell if it was one of the men he had seen the day before, but the person ahead looked shorter and so Mark assumed that it wasn't. The men from yesterday had spoken about someone called Gabe and Mark wondered if that was who he was now following.

Ahead of him the man stopped whistling, his attention suddenly distracted by something to his right. Mark stopped too, straining to see what had caught his eye, but the forest looked unchanged. He waited, hearing his heartbeat thump loudly in his ears with every breath.

Eventually the man moved to the right and crouched by a small pile of stones that lay neatly arranged in a circle around a blackened patch of grass. Mark swore silently under his breath, realising immediately why he had stopped. He had found their fire pit.

The man examined the ground around the stones, looking for any signs that the pit had been recently used. Mark had stopped making fires ever since their encounter with the body in town; he had been too afraid of the smoke or the light giving away the location of their camp. He realised now that he should have made an effort to hide the remains of the fire as well.

The man started to scan the trees around him, looking for any other signs that someone had been in this part of the forest. Mark quickly ducked behind one of the conifers next to him, holding his breath and straining to hear for any sign of movement. The man stayed still for a full minute, trying to pick out anything else unusual in his surroundings, but the woods seemed perfectly normal, and the only thing he could see were the branches as they waved gently back at him in the wind.

Eventually he stood up from the fire pit, satisfied that the small pile of stones had long been abandoned, and continued through the trees.

Mark followed, keeping further back than before, and soon he could hear running water as they approached the stream that ran close to their camp. Up ahead the man had stopped, stooping down to drink greedily from the fresh water and wash the sweat from his face. Mark used the noise of the stream to get closer, and tried to see if he was armed.

He couldn't make out a gun, but there was a large bowie knife hanging loosely from his waist. Mark felt his heartbeat quicken as he got to within twenty metres of the stream.

The man finished his drink and began to walk casually along the bank of the stream, watching the water rush between the rocks. Mark could hear him whistling again and knew that he was headed to where the stream fell sharply away over the cliff.

Gradually the trees began to thin until they disappeared completely and the man was forced to stop by the sudden drop in front of him. The town lay ahead, the dark, silhouetted buildings looking ghostly and foreboding in the pale light of the wintry afternoon. Mark was carefully peering out from behind another tree, taking deep, slow breaths in an effort to control his breathing.

This was where he had sat with Jake before they went into town, where he had tried to console his fears about the monsters he was so afraid of. Mark had told him that they would be safe in the suburbs, that the monsters wouldn't get them there. The memory caused a pang of guilt to strike him across his chest.

At the cliff's edge, the man was looking out over the town, admiring the impressive view in silence. He took a cigarette from his pocket and placed it between his lips before lighting it and taking a long drag, blowing the smoke carelessly over the drop. Mark looked on impatiently, waiting for him to finish and move on again, away from their home and back into the forest.

There was no need to do anything drastic, he reassured himself. Just let him pass.

Suddenly a stick snapped somewhere in the trees behind them, the crack loud enough to be heard over the rushing of the stream. Mark spun around. His heart was racing and his hand moved instinctively for his gun. He had been preparing to come face to face with another intruder.

He nearly choked when instead he saw Jake standing only a few metres behind him.

Jake looked up, not daring to move after giving himself away. Mark waved desperately at him to get out of sight and quickly he dived behind a tree to his right. On the cliff's edge the man had turned and was scanning the trees suspiciously. Mark pressed himself against the tree that he was hiding behind and looked on nervously, praying for the man to turn back to the view.

But he didn't.

Instead he flicked his cigarette over the edge and started walking back towards the forest. His hand started to reach for something in his coat. A strong sense of nausea began to crawl up Mark's throat, but he forced it back down as he reached for his own gun, knowing that he had to act now, before it was too late. His voice cut through the quiet, rooting the man to the spot.

"Move again and you're dead!"

The man froze, the only movement coming from his eyes as they darted from side to side in search of the voice.

"I've got a gun aimed right at you, and if you move I swear I will shoot you." Mark's voice was firm and unwavering, offering no argument.

"O-OK," the man said nervously, slowly putting his hands above his head. "Just take it easy!"

"Do what I say and you won't get hurt." Mark looked back and saw Jake peering around the side of a tree. He gave him a quick glare and waved at him to hide again.

"OK, OK! I'll do whatever you say." The man's eyes were still desperately searching the trees.

"Turn around and walk back to the edge of the cliff."

"What?"

"Now!" Mark shouted in frustration. The man jumped in surprise.

"OK! OK! I'm doing it, calm down!" He turned around and walked back to the edge of the cliff with slow and careful steps. Mark crept out from behind the tree with his gun trained on his back. The man must have heard him move because he tried to turn his head to get a look at his attacker, but Mark stopped him short.

"Don't even think about it! Look straight ahead and don't turn around."

The man obeyed, knowing he had no other choice. Mark stole a glance behind him and saw Jake still watching them, his face a mix of fear and wonder. Mark grimaced before refocusing his attention.

"Do everything that I tell you and I might let you live.

OK?"

The man nodded slowly, his gaze now fixed straight ahead. Mark had got to within five metres of his back.

"With your right hand I want you to take out your gun, and throw it over the edge. If you move too quickly – I'll kill you. If you turn around – I'll kill you. Got it?"

The man nodded again, no longer protesting. Above his head his hands were starting to shake. Carefully, he moved his right hand into his coat and slowly lifted out a small, black pistol. He tossed it over the edge of the cliff, the weapon hardly making a sound when it struck the ground far below. Mark didn't move.

"Now your knife."

"My knife? Come on ma…"

"Now your knife!" Mark shouted, letting the rage creep into his voice.

Reluctantly he pulled out the long, slender bowie knife, the blade made of sharp steel and nearly a foot long. He threw it over the edge of the cliff, watching it descend into the forest below. He put his hands back above his head.

"OK man, I'm unarmed. I'm not going to hurt you,

OK? So just take it easy." Mark ignored him.

83

"Take off your coat."

"My coat? But it's freezing. I need my coat!"

"Your coat, now! Slide it off your shoulders and onto the floor. Don't turn around!"

The man shook his head and swore under his breath, but slid his arms from his sleeves and let the coat fall to the ground. Mark looked for any more weapons or telltale bulges under his shirt, but he looked unarmed.

"Look, man, I'm doing what you say. Just tell me what you want and we can sort something out, OK?"

Mark stole another glance back at Jake and saw him still watching from the trees, unable to tear his eyes away from the encounter. He looked back at the trembling man in front of him and felt his heart pounding in his chest. He didn't want Jake to see this.

"What's your name?" he demanded.

"Jack," came the reply. "It's Jack."

"What are you doing here?" Mark asked, readjusting his grip on the gun.

"Jus…just passing through, man," Jack's voice was shaky. "On my way to the next town. Couldn't find anything h…"

"Don't lie to me, Jack!" Mark cut him off sharply. "You think I'm stupid? I've seen the others. I know you're part of a group!"

Jack winced at the shouting. The shaking returned to his hands.

"What group?" he protested. "I don't know what you're talking about!"

For a moment, Mark didn't move, unsure of what to do. He knew that Jack, if that was his real name, was lying. There was no way that a completely random traveller was passing through the forest at the same time that a group had set up camp on the other side of town. He also knew that Jake was still watching from somewhere behind them.

Slowly he walked towards the edge of the cliff and placed the end of the gun to the back of Jack's head, the thin, black barrel nestling comfortably between his thick, dark hair. Jack shuddered: his whole body trembled and his knees started to grow weak. Mark put his mouth close to Jack's ear.

"If you even think about lying to me again, that view is the last thing you are ever going to see." His voice had turned strangely calm, the anger replaced with a soft, menacing tone. He waited a moment before continuing.

"How many are there in your group?"

Jack shuddered and his voice grew thick with fear.

"Ten! There's ten of us! Please man, just calm down!"

Mark's blood froze in his veins and he felt his stomach drop to the floor. There were ten of them! He swallowed back the feeling of nausea that had resurfaced in his throat and strengthened his grip on the gun. He tried to concentrate on keeping the shock out of his voice.

"Why are you here?" he asked quietly.

Jack shook his head again. His hands were now shaking uncontrollably.

"We're just looking! Looking for food and supplies. That's all!"

"You kill people?" Mark asked bluntly, trying to catch him off guard.

"No man! Of course not!"

"Bullshit!"

Mark pushed the gun harder into the back of Jack's skull, his finger hovering dangerously over the trigger. His own voice began to shake.

"I found the body that you left in town! Why the hell are you here?"

Jack started to choke. His body crumpled as his knees began to give way.

"Calm down, man, please!" he begged. "I'll tell you, I'll tell you, just…just don't kill me, please!"

Mark said nothing, just stared at the back of Jack's head with the gun still pressed into his skull. The silence was unbearable and forced him to start talking again.

"Our – our leader's got us looking for someone, OK? A kid. A kid and his dad! They don't know about you, man, and I swear I won't tell them. I swear! Just let me go!"

Mark swallowed. What Jack said hadn't come as a surprise, but hearing it still made his throat turn dry and his stomach tie into knots. He tried to focus on his voice again.

"Kid? Are you crazy? I haven't seen a kid in years."

"They're probably dead, man," Jack rambled on, tears now readily flowing down his cheeks. "One of the guys saw the kid fall through a floor and then the Hunters chase them, but our leader is still making us look for them.

Please, man, please don't kill me!"

Mark stood in silence as he tried to work out what to do. His mind was racing, a million questions flying through his head. He took a final glance back at Jake, who was still standing beside the tree.

Jake's eyes were open wide, one arm hugged tightly around himself as he watched. Again, Mark felt something rise in his throat and this time his eyes began to moisten too. He felt himself start to choke, but forced himself not to, tearing his eyes away from Jake and back to Jack in front of him, who was now muttering unintelligibly under his breath.

He had made his decision.

"Get on your knees," Mark said quietly.

"What?" Jack's shaking suddenly stopped.

"Get on your knees," he repeated slowly.

"No, man. No, come on, man! I won't say anything. I won't say anything, I swear!"

"Get on your knees."

"They don't know about you! They're not looking for you. I won't tell th…"

"Get on your knees!"

Jack started shaking again and a heavy sob racked his body. He fell onto his knees, his arms dropping uselessly to his sides, and his head lolled forward as he started to cry openly.

"You don't have to do this, man!" he spluttered from between his tears. "Please don't do this! I won't say anything, I swear. I swear! Please don't kill me!"

He carried on muttering, his begging getting quieter and quieter until eventually it stopped altogether, replaced instead by quiet sobs that made his body tremble and shudder.

Mark nestled the gun back into Jack's hair, resting it gently into the shallow indent in his skull. His breathing slowed and a strange calm descended over him, the pace of his heart slowing to a crawl in his chest. His hand steadied, the gun it held now rock still as it bored into the back of Jack's head. Slowly he moved his finger to the trigger.

Chapter 11

The sound of the kettle clicking bounced around the kitchen, causing the angry bubbling of the water inside to settle. Mark dashed across to one of the wooden cupboards above it, pulling open the small metal handle which was slippery from the steam. He reached inside for a sachet of cold relief and felt his heart drop when his fingers closed around the last remaining packet. He pulled it out and gave the empty cupboard a forlorn look. The store had run out the last time he had been there and he highly doubted they would have managed to get anymore in the last few days. Carefully he ripped the packet in half and poured powder into both of the mugs that were sitting on the side.

It had been a week since Mark had come home from work to enjoy a weekend with his family. Since then he hadn't been back to his office and had only left the house to get food and medicine from the nearby shops. At first, it had seemed like Leah, the older of Mark's two daughters, had come down with a simple case of the flu, but it had quickly become apparent that whatever she was suffering from was far more serious. She had begun coughing up blood the night Mark had got home and each day she seemed to cough up more and grow steadily weaker. The next day Claire hadn't been able to get out of bed and she too was coughing up blood and seemingly getting worse.

Mark poured boiling water into the two porcelain mugs, stirring the murky solution until the powder had completely dissolved. He picked up the mugs from the side and walked out into the hallway, climbing the stairs and heading into Leah's room.

Leah was lying in a ball under her covers, the white linen stained with a fresh patch of red. Mark sighed. He had changed the sheets every day, but Leah had coughed blood onto every fresh pair he had put on.

He placed the mug on her bedside table and tried to work out if she was asleep. Her breaths came in gentle wheezes, like something was stuck in her throat, and Mark couldn't stop himself from wincing at the sound. Leah hadn't reacted when he had come into the room, but that could be down to her severe lack of energy. Mark tried to pretend that it wasn't, that instead she was getting some rest, and so decided to leave her undisturbed and crept quietly back out of the room.

Once in the hallway he closed the door quietly behind him and shook back his tears. Every time he went in he found himself hoping that she would be better, that he would see some sign that the worst had passed. But his hopes were always dashed by the time he had opened the door and found her condition was worse.

With his free hand he quickly rubbed his face, trying to make himself appear more alert. He had barely slept all week, kept awake at night by his crippling anxiety, but he didn't want Claire to see how exhausted he was.

He took a few steps down the landing and pushed open the door to their room, feeling the cruel surge of hope rise from his stomach.

Claire was lying on her side, her body turned away from him so that she was facing the wall. She turned at the sound of the door creaking open and Mark felt his hope fall back through the floor. Her blonde hair lay in a messy pile around her, knotted and greasy from where she'd been unable to wash. Her face was deathly pale, centred round a bright red nose that was raw from sneezing and outlined by sunken cheeks. She looked so thin, Mark realised, and she was shivering slightly despite her thick duvet. But what struck Mark the most was her eyes; her irises had turned dark-red and were sat amidst a thick web of bloodshot veins.

"Is Leah OK?" she asked, wincing as she tried to sit up. Mark rushed quickly to her side, placing the mug on the bedside table and running a hand through her hair.

"She's sleeping. I just checked on her."

It wasn't a direct answer to her question, but it was the most promising answer Mark could give without lying. Claire nodded slightly, deciding not to pursue the point. For a moment, they sat in silence. Claire was staring at the stained bed linen, her breathing coming in heavy rasps. Mark sat watching her, feeling utterly helpless.

"Is there anything I can do?" he asked eventually. Claire blinked quickly, stirring from her thoughts before giving a gentle shake of her head.

"Apparently they've closed the borders," she said. "Every continent is now reporting cases of it, and millions more people are catching it every day."

Mark looked down at the floor and rubbed his arm nervously. She must have been listening to the radio, because he had heard the same news on the TV downstairs. All over the world people were falling ill and governments were trying desperately to stop the disease from spreading. They had closed the country's borders this morning, but it was far too late to make a difference. It was reported that over seventy per cent of the population were sick, and that statistic grew by the day. The National Health Organisation had said the disease was an aggressive mutation of Influenza, something akin to the Spanish flu. So far their only advice had been for those that were infected to stay inside, get lots of rest and keep up their fluids. The advice was basic at best, the kind of thing you said to make it seem like you had an idea of what you were doing, but it hadn't stopped the death count from rising to the millions. Mark knew they were nowhere near to finding a cure.

"They'll find a way to stop it," Mark lied, more for himself than for her. "You shouldn't be listening to the news anyway, you need to be resting."

"Why hide it from it?" she said with a sigh. "Burying my head in the sand won't stop what's happening."

Mark looked away again. He was afraid to talk in case he gave away how scared he was.

"Is Abby still OK?" Claire asked tentatively.

Mark nodded. Abby, his youngest daughter, had shown no signs that she was sick. Her and Mark were sleeping downstairs, so as to reduce their chances of catching the disease, and he had been amazed by how well she had coped with the situation. She missed her mum and sister, and it frustrated her that Mark wouldn't let her see them, but understood why they needed to be quarantined. She could sense that her dad was upset, even though Mark was careful not to cry in front of her, and sometimes he wondered if he was looking after her, or if it was the other way round.

"You need to keep her safe. Keep her away from us and make sure she doesn't get sick. She's going to need you more than ever when I–."

"No!" Mark stopped her before she could finish, the first of his tears escaping and running down his cheeks. "There's still time. They'll find a cure, some way to stop this."

He looked at her through sparkling eyes, fighting to keep his hope alive. Claire looked back at him with sad eyes, either too weak to argue with him, or not wanting to break his spirits. Slowly she lifted a hand to his face, holding his cheek and wiping away his tears.

"Just keep her safe."

After he left the room he went to the bathroom and cried for half an hour. Then he splashed his face with water and went downstairs. Abby was sitting on the sofa, holding a plastic bottle to the mouth of one of her teddies. Mark knew that the teddy was sick and that Abby was giving it medicine. She jumped up when she saw her dad and ran over to him.

"How's Mummy and Leah?" she asked quickly.

"They're fine darling," Mark lied. "They're missing you."

Abby nodded. Sometimes Mark was sure that she could see right through him.

From somewhere outside there came an ominous howling. Mark turned and walked to the window that looked out over their back garden, a small lawn scattered with pink bikes and scooters. Bear was sitting with his back to the house, his puffy white fur looking bedraggled and worn. He leant back his head and let out another low howl.

Bear had started acting strange a few days ago. Mark wasn't sure if it was a reaction to Leah and Claire being sick, or if he could sense the pandemic that was happening around him. Animals seemed to have a sixth sense when it came to these things. Whatever the case, he had started pining at the back door, desperate to be let outside, and howling endlessly throughout the night.

"Bear misses Mummy and Leah too."

Mark turned and saw Abby next to him, standing on her tiptoes to try and see out of the window. Mark smiled briefly.

"Come on. Let's watch some cartoons."

They headed back to the sofa and laid down on the soft cushions. Mark turned on the TV and put his arms around Abby, holding her tight to his chest as she watched animations chase each other round the screen. Mark felt suddenly exhausted and pulled a blanket over them before closing his eyes.

When Mark woke, up his head was buzzing, a sharp pain lingering behind his eyes. Abby was curled up next to him, lying under his arm as she slept. He didn't know when he had drifted off, but somehow the sleep had made him feel worse. He stood up from the sofa, being careful not to wake Abby, and rubbed the sleep from his eyes before creeping up the stairs.

He stopped outside Leah's room, failing to fight down his expectation. He still felt half asleep when he pushed open the door, the crack of light falling over the floor and onto the small bundle tucked up in the bed. Instantly Mark sensed that something was different, that something was missing that had been there before, and for the first time he felt his hope grow a little bit larger.

He walked quietly over to the bed, his footsteps cushioned by the soft carpet.

"Leah," he whispered gently.

Leah didn't move. Her mug was still on the bedside table, completely untouched. Mark reached out and placed a hand on her shoulder, then quickly withdrew it when he felt how cold she was. His breath caught in his throat and suddenly he was wide awake. He had realised what was different, what was missing that had been there before.

Leah's gentle wheezing was gone.

Chapter 12

Jack was still sobbing quietly, unable to see the ground in front of him for the tears in his eyes. His hands shook uncontrollably and inside his body his stomach was writhing. The back of his throat was full of something thick and heavy and he felt so sick that he thought he was going to start retching.

He tried to concentrate on his breathing and felt each breath going in and out of his body with a shudder. Terror gripped every part of him and he squeezed his eyes shut, waiting for the hammer to fall, and tried to think about anything except what it would feel like. What it would feel like to die. The sound of his breathing racked in his ears, drowning out everything else.

He waited…and waited.

The sound of his breathing still filled his ears.

Slowly he opened his eyes and saw green grass on the floor beneath him. He hadn't heard the gunshot, nor felt the bullet penetrate the back of his skull, but then he wouldn't have, would he? He didn't dare to move in case he shattered this strange illusion he found himself in. The illusion that somehow he was still alive. His body was still shaking with fear and he started to wonder if he was already dead.

Still nothing happened.

Eventually he turned around, expecting to be facing into the barrel of a gun, a bullet flying towards him out of its end to take his life. But instead he saw the stream trickling gently through the rocks as it fell over the edge of the cliff, and the deep, dark greens of the forest as the grey clouds chased each other above the canopy, the branches gently waving back at him as they rustled in the breeze.

Jack felt his relief overpower him, and held his head in his hands as sobs racked his body once more.

Chapter 13

Mark and Jake watched Jack from the safety of a bush that was nestled amongst the trees.

Peering out from between the leaves, they saw him curl into a ball on the ground and start to weep loudly. Mark watched on with an unreadable expression on his face, one hand still clutching the small, black pistol. Jake looked on in awe.

After a few minutes the weeping stopped and Jack slowly uncurled into a sitting position. He took his time looking out towards the town as he recomposed himself, hugging himself from time to time and wiping the tears from his face.

Eventually he stood and crossed the stream hurriedly whilst glancing nervously around him. Mark let out a sigh of relief, his grip gently easing on the grip of his gun as he watched Jack disappear into the trees.

He crawled out from under the bush and brushed down his clothes, returning the gun to his pocket as Jake crawled out after him. Through the trees he could see the sun had reappeared above the clouds and was starting to set; the light streaking the grey clouds with violent purples and reds. Inside his head he felt his mind whirring as it tried to process everything that had just happened.

Jake stood next to him in silence.

After a while Mark turned his back on the sunset and walked back to the camp. Jake followed closely and kept shooting nervous glances back to the stream to see if Jack would reappear. When they were halfway to the tree house, they stopped and Mark stooped down to pick up the stones that encircled their fire pit. One by one he tossed them into the surrounding forest, the rocks landing with the sounds of cracking twigs and gentle thuds when they hit the floor. There wasn't much that he could do about the blackened grass, so instead he left it as it was in the hope that it looked abandoned. As he stood staring at the patch of dead grass, he noticed Jake still standing in silence. He was biting his lip and swaying on the spot nervously.

"Are you all right?" Mark asked, surprised by how hoarse his voice sounded.

Jake lowered his head.

"I'm sorry," he muttered quietly. "I – I just didn't want to be alone."

Mark looked at him in confusion, unable to discern his meaning.

"What are you sorry for, Jake?"

"I should have stayed back in the hut. I should have waited for you to come back. If I hadn't followed you, I wouldn't have stepped on that stick, and then that person wouldn't have seen us."

Mark, despite everything that had just happened, felt himself start to laugh. Jake looked up in surprise.

"It's not your fault, Jake. It was an accident. I'm not mad at you. And that person never saw us. I made sure of it."

"But. But if I had stayed in the hut…"

"It doesn't matter," Mark cut him off quickly. "I shouldn't have left you alone. It's as much my fault as it is yours."

Jake looked unconvinced that he was not to blame and fixed his dad with a strange look, as if he was contemplating something that he didn't quite understand. Mark looked back at him, waiting for the question. He didn't have to wait for long.

"Why didn't you shoot him?" Jake asked after a few seconds.

Mark looked away and ran his eyes over the trees around them. The forest had fallen still, and the gentle trickle of birdsong that had been present all day had started to fade as night drew closer. The last rays of the sun clung to the tops of the trees, the light that filtered down to the floor getting fainter by the minute. Slowly Mark turned back to meet Jake's expectant gaze.

"Let's sit down," he said softly, and they both sat down on the cold, wet grass. He waited a minute before continuing, listening to the trees whispering to each other as he worked out what to say.

"Do you think I should have killed him?"

Jake looked down at the floor and began picking at the grass with his hands. He took some time before answering and when he did he seemed unsure of himself.

"Was he one of those men? One of the men that shot that deer?"

"He didn't shoot the deer, but he is one of the men from that group," Mark confirmed. Jake curled his tongue as he concentrated.

"You said that they want to kill us. To kill us and take our stuff. But we can't let them do that." Jake looked at his dad for approval before continuing. Mark nodded back in way of an answer; his expression was still unreadable. "So...so if they try to do that then...we should kill them. So they can't hurt us."

Mark nodded, unsure of whether he should be horrified or glad. He felt both. It hurt him to hear Jake talk like this, to speak of killing others, but at the same time it was a relief that Jake was finally understanding the threat that people posed. .

"Yes, Jake," he said solemnly. "That's true. If we don't do anything, they will kill us. It's important you understand that."

Jake still looked confused. His curiosity was not yet satisfied.

"So...so why didn't you kill that man?"

Again, Mark thought long and hard before giving an answer.

"Because I didn't have to," he said simply. "We aren't like them, Jake. We don't kill people for fun or because we want to take what they have. The only reason that we would ever kill someone would be if they were going to hurt us. And back there, when that man was kneeling on the floor like that – he couldn't hurt us. Do you understand?"

Jake nodded slowly, but still looked unconvinced.

"But he can come back. With the others."

"Yes," Mark conceded. "And he probably will. But if I had shot him then they would have come looking for him anyway. Maybe there are others close by that would have heard the gunshot. Either way, at some point they will come looking for us. It wouldn't have made a difference if I had killed him – so I let him live. That's what makes us different from them. It's important that you understand that too."

Jake nodded and Mark saw a hint of understanding appear on his face as he turned the words over in his mind. Mark looked away, wondering if he should feel guilty for the lie he had just told.

He couldn't have killed him in front of Jake; that was the main reason he had let Jack live. Jake's memory of their first ever meeting with a person – something he had dreamed about since he had first heard stories of other people and of friends and families – would be of the man he thought was his father executing someone in cold blood. There was no way that Mark could do that to him.

So he had let Jack live.

Besides, what he had told Jake was technically true. If Mark had killed Jack, his group would know something was wrong when he never returned, and eventually they would come looking for him. Maybe, because Mark had let Jack go, he wouldn't tell the rest of his group about being held at gun point, either out of shame or fear. But Mark doubted it. Whatever decision he made was likely to turn out badly.

It had been the right thing to do, he reassured himself.

It had been the right thing to do for Jake.

He just hoped that he wouldn't end up regretting it.

Beyond the trees the sun finally fell below the horizon, plunging the forest floor into darkness. Already Mark could feel the temperature beginning to drop and he saw Jake shiver with cold as he wrapped his arms tightly around himself.

"Come on," he said quietly. "Let's get back."

Both of them stood to leave, Mark tossing the last of the stones into the forest as Jake headed back to the hut. When he turned to follow, Mark felt a strange sensation run down his spine, as if an icy finger was gently running down his back.

He turned quickly and peered into the dark, but there was nothing. Just the silent tree trunks, silhouetted against the night. He turned back around and hurried to catch up with Jake. He must still be on edge from earlier.

He caught up with Jake and placed a reassuring hand on his back. Jake looked up at him, his face barely visible in the gloom.

"So what do we do now?" Jake asked, wrapping his arms more tightly around himself.

"We get back, we eat something, and we rest."

"But won't they come looking for us?"

"Yes, but not tonight. Not yet. And even if they do, they'll never see our treehouse in this light. We need to sleep. Both of us. We have a long day ahead of us tomorrow."

They reached the tree which held their home and ascended the ladder in silence. Jake led the way, struggling awkwardly with the rungs without the use of his right hand. Mark followed closely behind. When they were inside, Mark pulled the ladder up and placed it on the floor by the hatch.

"What are we doing tomorrow?" Jake asked, as he picked up a blanket and wrapped himself in it. Mark shut the hatch and pulled the bolt firmly across.

"We need to go back into town." Mark looked up in time to see Jake shudder. "I know I said we wouldn't go back for a while, but things have changed." Jake swallowed, but nodded his understanding.

"What are we doing in town?" he asked tentatively.

"We need to find them, Jake. We need to find out where their camp is."

Mark had moved across to his backpack and was already stocking it with provisions. He wanted to leave as soon as the sun came up. Jake watched him nervously.

"And I'm coming with you?" he asked.

"Yes," Mark replied firmly. "I know it's scary, but I'm not leaving you on your own. You're staying with me."

"Good," Jake nodded defiantly, his voice taking on a steely expression. It was the answer he had been hoping to hear. Mark smiled softly.

"What are we going to do when we find their camp?" Jake continued.

Mark stopped packing and looked up.

"I don't know yet," he admitted slowly, with a shake of his head. "I don't know."

It was true. He had no idea what they would do once they found the camp. If the group was as much as ten strong – and Mark had every reason to believe that it was – then he couldn't just charge in there with a five-year-old boy and try to kill them all then and there. The thought alone was suicide. But at the same time he couldn't just stay here either and wait to be found.

He needed to do something. Anything to get an advantage. Maybe if he could find out where the group were camped then he would have a better idea of what that something was. Besides, all of a sudden it seemed to be safer in town.

"What about the Hunters?" Jake's voice roused him from his thoughts.

"Try not to worry about the Hunters, Jake. Right now we need to focus on those people. OK?" Jake nodded in reply.

After he finished packing they sat in silence for a while, listening to the first nocturnal creatures waking up for the night. Mark stared at Jake, who was huddled under his blankets, and felt a cascade of emotions rip through his body. He had always feared this day would come. Feared that something would happen that would threaten to ruin the life that they had made for each other. Now finally that day had arrived, that something was here, and Mark knew he would have to do everything that he possibly could to protect them. Even if it was the last thing on earth he wanted to do.

"I have something for you, Jake," Mark said quietly, trying not to choke on the lump that had formed in his throat. "Just in case anything happens."

Jake looked up at him from his cocoon of blankets.

Mark had wanted to wait. Wait until Jake was older and the timing was right. He never wanted to be forced into making this decision because he had no other choice.

Inside Mark was in turmoil. His heart was at war with his mind, his instincts with his inner conscience, which said it was wrong for a five-year-old to be capable of such a thing. But deep down he knew that it couldn't wait any longer.

It didn't matter to those men how young he was, and if something happened to Jake because Mark thought he wasn't old enough for the responsibility then he knew he would never forgive himself. Besides, Jake had already experienced far more than a five-year-old should and it was for this reason that Mark hoped he was ready.

Slowly Mark stood and reached up to where the wall of the treehouse joined to the roof. At the top of the wall, there was a small lip beneath the ceiling and his hand searched around for what he knew was hidden there. His fingers brushed against metal and his hand closed around the sturdy grip.

Jake looked on curiously, trying to see what he was doing. Mark turned and walked across the hut before crouching down in front of him. He looked him in the eye, a sad expression on his face, and held out the object in his hands.

Jake looked down and gasped as the moonlight crept through the window and glinted off the dark metal. Slowly, and with trembling hands, he took hold of the gun.

Chapter 14

The sunset fired streaks of red and purple across the evening sky, making the last hour of day seem brighter than usual.

In his chair, Gabe sat next to the gently crackling fire, looking upwards through the canopy at the impressive palette of colours. A sharp bang made him jump in his chair and brought his attention back to the camp around him. Crouched down by the fire, Daniel was banging loudly on the side of one of the metal pots, the well-known signal that dinner was finally ready.

Around the campsite the men all dropped what they were doing and headed quickly over to the sound of the banging. One by one they took their seats and huddled up against the warmth of the flames as they waited for Gabe to take one of the sizzling steaks that was cooking over the fire.

Once they each had a piece of the deer meat the group ate in silence, the only noise the crackling of the twigs as they burned and the smacking of lips as they chewed noisily on the venison. Dave, who was often the first to finish his meals, was the first to speak.

"Anyone seen Jack?"

He was met with a series of shaking heads and shrugs.

"He was with us this morning," Paul said, with a mouthful of steak. "Probably just got lost in the woods, he'll be back soon."

Dave grunted in reply and sat with his hands stretched out towards the flames. Above the canopy the sunlit streaks in the clouds were beginning to fade, meaning the campsite was beginning to darken.

Gabe stared into the heart of the fire, rubbing the rough stubble around his chin in thought. Jack should have come back by now. The rest of the scouting group had returned hours ago, all of them reporting the same, hopeless news.

Nobody had found anything.

Between them the group had covered a lot of ground, but everywhere they had searched had seemed like normal forest, with no sign of it being disturbed by the boy or his father. Gabe had joined one of the scouting parties, to make sure the men searched the area properly, but he too had found no trace of the couple.

Doubt began to slowly creep into the back of his mind, but he forced it away quickly. It was far too early to even think of calling off the search. Jack might yet bring back some good news, and even if he didn't then it wouldn't matter. The forest was large. Far larger than they could hope to cover in a day.

Gabe looked up sharply at the sound of one of the men coughing, and his gaze fell upon Joseph. He looked a mess. His face was a mass of cuts and bruises, one eye a dark red where it was bloodshot, and the other squinting out nervously from between swollen eyelids. His nose sat at an awkward angle, obviously broken from one of the blows, and dark gaps were scattered between his teeth where they had fallen out.

Gabe felt his blood rush as he admired his handiwork and couldn't keep himself from smirking. He turned back towards the flames. Joseph would think twice before trying to undermine him again.

On the other side of the circle Dave suddenly sat up and began peering into the forest.

"Jack's back," he said over his shoulder. "Hey Jack!

Where have you been?"

"Got a bit lost," came the reply from within the trees.

As one the men turned to see Jack just as he stepped out of the darkness and into the light of the fire, his head hung low over hunched shoulders as he approached the circle and his face looked pale and blotchy.

"Grab something," Dave said, pointing towards the last slice of meat.

"No thanks," Jack replied, rubbing his arm nervously. "I'm not hungry."

Dave shrugged and turned his attention back to the fire. The rest of the group had barely acknowledged him and continued to tuck into their meat while it was still warm. All except for Gabe, who watched intently from across the flames.

He had sensed it immediately. Something was wrong. Jack seemed different, nervous, as if he was shaken. He stood awkwardly on the edge of the group, still yet to sit down and join them and not looking as if he was going to either. It was unlike any of the men to not be hungry, especially after walking all day, and it was very unusual for Jack to get lost.

Gabe ran his eyes over him, trying to read his body language, and stopped when he reached his belt. He could have sworn that Jack had a knife this morning.

Gabe took a deep breath, trying to quell the sudden surge of adrenalin that rushed through his body.

Jack did have a knife this morning, Gabe was certain of it. He had seen him polishing the handle before they had left and only a month earlier he had been bragging about what a find it was to the rest of the group.

There was no way that he would have left something so precious in the forest. Not a chance. Something had happened to him while he was out in the woods, Gabe was sure of it. He needed to find out what it was.

"Let's take a walk, Jack," Gabe said suddenly, standing up from his chair. "I need to talk to you about something."

Jack turned to face him, his eyes wide with panic before he quickly gathered himself and tried to act casual.

"Sure, Gabe. What do you need?"

Gabe walked slowly around the circle and when he reached him he put his arm around Jack's shoulders to steer him away from the fire.

"I just need to ask you about something. It's nothing to worry about, but it's something that's been bothering me."

They started to walk away from the men huddled around the flames and soon they were outside of the circle of tents and heading deeper into the forest. Gabe could sense Jack's confusion and saw him shooting nervous glances back over his shoulder. Behind them the warm light from the fire was getting smaller and smaller.

"What is it, Gabe?" Jack asked, shifting uncomfortably under his arm.

"How come you got back so late, Jack?" Gabe replied, his voice taking on a caring tone. "We were starting to get worried."

Jack gave him a sceptical look, clearly wary of Gabe's sudden interest in him.

"I told you, boss. I got lost. Went pretty far out into the woods and it took me a while to find my way back."

"Sure, sure," Gabe nodded, still leading Jack away from their camp. "It happens. At least, you're back now. Did you find anything while you were out there? See anything unusual?"

Jack looked down at the floor and shook his head.

"No, boss. I couldn't see any sign of them. But I'll go out again tomorrow. Something will turn up."

"Oh, I don't doubt it will, Jack," Gabe laughed softly. "No doubt at all. It's only a matter of time until we find something."

"Yes," Jack laughed nervously, then, more sure of himself, "yes, exactly, boss."

"Just, just one thing that's bothering me, though." Gabe stopped walking and turned to face him. Behind them the light from the fire could no longer be seen.

Jack waited for him to continue, unsettled by the strange stare on his face, but Gabe maintained his silence, and it was Jack who was the first to talk.

"What is it, boss?"

"Where's your knife?" Gabe's voice was as hard as stone, the caring tone from moments before completely gone.

Jack tensed instinctively and swallowed. Around them the forest was in complete darkness and he could barely see Gabe standing in front of him. He glanced back towards the campsite, but was met with a wall of black. He suddenly realised how alone they were.

"My knife?" he started, trying to keep the shaking from his voice. "It's in my tent."

"No, it's not," Gabe's response was immediate. "You took it with you this morning."

"Oh, that one?" Jack felt his voice falter slightly. His insides were churning. "I lost it when I was out in the woods. Must have fallen off my belt." He laughed nervously, but quickly stopped when Gabe didn't join in. His stare was unflinching.

"I'll only ask once more," Gabe said coldly. "Where – is – your – knife?"

"I told you, boss," Jack said, his voice now starting to shake. "I just…just lost it."

Gabe stared at him with an unmoving expression. A minute passed in silence, the tension becoming more intense. Jack felt his heart begin to beat faster and faster. His throat was dry and he felt like he was going to be sick when a thick lump of bile crawled slowly up from his stomach.

Still Gabe didn't move and Jack felt himself start to sweat. The silence was unbearable and he desperately needed to break it, but something about the way Gabe was looking at him told him that he shouldn't speak.

Finally, as he was about to burst under the tension, Gabe's face broke into a smile and he began chuckling softly. He took a step towards Jack and placed his arm around him again.

"Oh Jack," he said softly.

Gabe turned him around and brought his free hand to the back of Jack's head, getting a tight grip on his hair before slamming his skull into the nearest tree.

"Do you think I'm stupid?"

Jack's face hit the bark with a thud, the shock only numbing the pain for a second. Gabe pulled his head back again, pulling hard on his hair. Jack screamed, but the sound came out weak and hoarse, before Gabe slammed his face back into the tree with a wet smack. Gabe pulled back his head again and screamed into his ear. "WHERE–IS–YOUR–KNIFE?"

Jack spluttered on the blood that was filling his mouth. He spat it out before trying to speak, but more blood quickly took its place.

"OK, OK, I'll tell you!" he spluttered. "Please, Gabe, I'll tell you."

Gabe moved his head sharply forward again, but stopped short of driving him into the tree. Jack cried out and flinched as the bark came towards him. Gabe threw him down to the ground and watched with disgust as he coughed and spluttered desperately, then bent down and grabbed him by his coat, forcing him back against the tree that was now splattered with blood.

"Talk!" Gabe demanded.

"I got caught," Jack said, wincing in pain with every word.

"Who caught you?" Gabe asked, tightening his grip on the coat.

"A traveller!" Jack went on. "Just some traveller. I was at the top of this slope and he crept up on me. He had a gun on me and he made me throw my knife and my gun over the edge."

"What did he look like?" Gabe's curiosity momentarily numbed his rage.

"I didn't see him. He didn't let me turn around."

"What the hell do you mean, you didn't see him!" Gabe shouted, his rage returning in an instant.

"I didn't, Gabe, I swear! He made me have my back to him the whole time, I swear it, boss! He had a gun on me!"

Gabe brought down his forehead hard onto Jack's nose, feeling the bone crunch satisfyingly beneath the force. Jack screamed in pain as blood began to pour from his nostrils.

"Idiot!" Gabe screamed. "What did he say to you?"

"He, he wanted to know what I was doing there," Jack managed, between mouthfuls of blood. "He said...he'd seen others. Others of the group, and wanted to know about us."

"What did you tell him?"

"Nothing, Gabe, I swear!"

"Liar!" he screamed into his face.

"I'm sorry," Jack pleaded, his voice breaking into sobs. "He had a gun on me. He was going to kill me!"

"Was the boy there?" Gabe asked, disgusted by the mess in front of him. "Did you see the boy?"

"What?" Jack sounded genuinely surprised. "No. He was just a traveller. He said he hadn't seen a kid in years. You've got to believe me, Gabe, please!"

Jack broke down completely, his voice disappearing amidst a torrent of tears. Gabe let go of his coat and watched as he slid slowly down the tree, clutching his ruined face in his hands as he wept.

Idiot, Gabe thought. It was him. The father. It had to be. They had searched the place high and low and found no sign of anybody else other than the traveller they had shot when they first arrived, and now Jack was claiming another one appears from nowhere. Not a chance.

Gabe realised that he should be happy. This meant that they were alive, that their searching was not in vain, but right now he felt far from happy. Jack would have told them everything. Why they were here, how many they were, what they were looking for. He looked down at Jack, who was still weeping on the floor, and spat on him in disgust.

"Oh Jack," Gabe said quietly. "You've really screwed things up for me. I don't know why he let you live, but he should have done us all a favour and ended you right there and then."

On the floor Jack continued to weep. Gabe sighed and rubbed the blood from his forehead.

"But still," he continued, more to himself than anything. "It's not all bad. They're alive. That's good. They're alive and can still be caught, assuming you haven't scared them off."

He crouched down beside Jack and leant over him.

"Tomorrow, you are going to take me to where you found them. OK? The exact spot that you found them."

He waited for a response. Eventually Jack took his hands away from his face and nodded, trying to compose himself.

"Good," Gabe said, standing up and taking a look at the dark around him. He wanted to search for them now, but he could hardly see the trees in front of him and knew that any attempt to find them at night would be useless. He would have to wait until morning; the moment it was light enough to see by they would set off.

Gabe turned his back on Jack, no longer listening to the heavy, ragged breaths that had replaced the sobbing.

A smile tugged at the corner of his lips as he realised that it would be the last time Jack tried to lie to him.

As he headed back towards the camp, his rage beginning to fade, Gabe's thoughts returned to the mysterious boy and his father.

He was getting closer. So close that he could feel the thrill rising slowly within him, building and building into something so intense it would soon become unstoppable. His heart beat faster just at the thought of it and blood surged through his veins as he imagined the final chase, closing in for the kill. He was so close that he could almost reach out and touch them. And tomorrow he'd be even closer.

Chapter 15

They descended the ladder in silence; two formless shapes moving swiftly in the darkness.

When they reached the floor, the larger shape began moving through the trees, heading downhill in the direction of the town. The smaller shadow followed quickly in its wake. Around them the forest was as still as a graveyard, not yet awoken from its nocturnal slumber. In the sky above them, the morning sun was yet to be seen, a layer of heavy clouds in its place that were threatening to release their contents onto the earth below.

When the town came into view, Mark stopped and looked out through the trees at the desolate buildings. At one time, the town would have been lit up by pale oranges and yellows, each of the floors in the tall, lifeless skyscrapers blazing with light even at this hour.

Now the towers were dark and silhouetted against the grey backdrop of the sky; the buildings at their base all shrouded in shadow. But even though he couldn't see the town, Mark could still sense the ominous, unnatural feeling that emanated from the vacuum in front of him. He shivered and turned to check that Jake was still following before continuing downhill.

Last night Mark had barely slept. All night he had lain awake worrying, playing out in his head the hundred different scenarios that the morning might bring. When eventually he had drifted off to sleep, he had been woken shortly after by another of Jake's nightmares, and had spent the rest of the night wide awake by his side.

A chill breeze blew through the forest that made him grip his coat more tightly around himself. It was a cold morning and it seemed to get colder as they headed downhill. The clouds above them were beginning to brighten, signifying that the sun had finally risen and the day had now arrived. Behind them the forest stirred as the first of the birds started up the dawn chorus. Ahead of them the town lay still and dead.

They were headed for the far side of town, where the main road started through the forest and away to the next city. Mark suspected that the group's camp would be close to the road; it was far quicker than setting up in the middle of the forest and a group that size had no need to move covertly.

The thing that Mark was unsure of was if they had set up their camp in the town itself, or just outside it. It might not make a difference, but he wanted to know how close he could get without being seen.

Reaching the far side of town would take them at least a couple of hours and he suspected that they might be sleeping rough tonight. He had packed enough in his backpack for them to stay in town for at least a few nights if it came to it, but if luck was on their side then they would be home by the evening.

The trees began to thin as they reached the bottom of the hill and soon they found themselves standing at the edge of the old storage yard that marked the town's boundary. The yard was deathly quiet; the only sound coming from the wind as it whistled ominously between the rusting storage units.

Jake shot nervous glances around him as he looked for any sign of danger. He moved his hand to his right coat pocket and closed his fingers around the small bundle inside. The heaviness of the gun reassured him and a determined expression settled on his face.

They started to skirt through the suburbs, keeping close to the edge of town, as they had done many times before, but this time they stayed out of sight of the surrounding forest.

As the day brightened, the shadows began to fade and the silhouetted buildings became clearer and more detailed. The clouds still hung heavily above them, but enough light managed to filter through to let them see clearly by.

Mark kept his eyes peeled as they moved, looking for anything unusual or out of place that would give them a clue to the group's movements. For the first hour, he saw nothing. The lack of discovery made him both nervous and relieved.

It wasn't until the second hour that they saw their first sign.

They were headed down a quiet street, a row of detached houses to either side. At the end of the street, lay a small cul-de-sac, the turning circle at its centre overgrown with a thick mass of thorny scrubs.

As they rounded the circle, Mark noticed that the doors on each of the houses were hanging loosely from their hinges. The wooden panels were cracked and splintered where they had been hit with force and some had even been knocked clean from their frame and now lay on the floor.

He gestured for Jake to be quiet, before approaching the house nearest to them and walking slowly through the shattered door frame, his ears pricked for any signs of danger. The corridor beyond seemed relatively untouched, the wallpapers yellowed and peeling from years of decay. It was only when they went into one of the rooms that led off the corridor that they saw the damage.

The room had been ransacked: the faded leather sofas and chairs had all been tipped over and the cushions were thrown messily over the ripped-up carpet. A wooden bookcase lay smashed to pieces, the books that had once filled it now scattered everywhere.

In silence, they checked the rest of the house, being met by the same carnage in every room they entered. Mark hadn't been to this street for some time, but he was certain that it hadn't been like this when he was last here.

They left the house and carried on, moving slower and more cautiously now that they knew at least some of the group had been here. More streets passed and Mark scanned the houses in each one for any further signs that they had been broken into and searched.

Soon they found themselves in streets that he had not been to for years and he realised that Jake had never been to this part of town. Jake must have realised too, as he was looking around with interest at the strange houses and buildings that surrounded him.

The unfamiliarity made Mark feel uncomfortable. The ruins here seemed somehow more sinister; a potential new danger hiding behind each door.

He found himself shivering involuntarily and turned to look behind him as a tingle ran up his spine. He remembered a similar sensation from when he had sat by the fire pit with Jake after their close encounter with Jack the day before and struggled to identify what it meant. It felt like something that he hadn't felt for years. It felt like he was being watched.

Jake turned too and stared at the empty street behind them before looking up at Mark with a puzzled expression. Mark shook his head before turning and continuing down the street, trying to ignore his growing sense of unease. A chill breeze whistled hauntingly through the gaps between the houses and he realised suddenly how quiet it had become.

They must be getting closer.

At the end of the street, they turned right and headed down a narrow alley, continuing to glance nervously back at the way they had come. At the other side of the alley, they emerged into a small square of houses that were centred on a rusting play park that was almost totally obscured by tall, overgrown grass.

Shattered windows at the houses' front stared emptily at the playground, that at one time would have let parents watch their children as they played happily in the park. Now the only movement came from a swing which swung gently on the breeze, the chain squeaking loudly in protest with each revolution.

With a pang of guilt Mark realised Jake had never played on a swing.

They headed for another alleyway on the other side of the square and began to move around the tall grass in its centre. Halfway around the square they stopped. Something had grabbed Mark's attention out of the corner of his eye.

He didn't need to have been here recently to know that this was new.

The front garden of the house beside them was something close to a meadow; the tall grass framed by a line of bushes that had grown unkempt for years. But leading through the middle of the front garden and round to the side of the house was a trail of flattened grass and flowers that formed a well-worn path.

Mark looked down at the floor around him, but could see no continuation of the trail; the path stopped abruptly when it reached the cracked concrete.

Jake had noticed it too and tugged at Mark's sleeve as he pointed at the trail. Mark nodded and beckoned for him to follow as he stepped carefully onto the trodden ground, following the path exactly so as not to leave new prints. Jake copied him and together they made their way across the garden.

At the side of the house, they found the trail continued, the vines that fell across the path having been hacked back to the wall, and they followed it to the backyard. Ahead of them they saw the trail continue across a lawn and disappear through a gap in the fence at the end of the garden.

They stopped and looked around them for any more clues. Everything else in the garden seemed normal, but the back door of the house had been kicked in, the glass that had been in the window now scattered over the floor.

Mark felt his throat tighten. They needed to go inside.

They headed into the house, the glass crunching beneath their feet as they stepped over the broken door. They found themselves in a kitchen, the cupboards hanging open and the meagre contents strewn messily over the floor.

Mark headed upstairs, knowing that the rest of the house would be in the same state. The stairs creaked loudly underneath his weight and he gripped the banister tightly in fear that they might give way. Jake followed closely behind.

At the top of the stairs, he headed down the landing towards the front of the house, moving into what had once been a bedroom. The mattress had been thrown onto the floor, the bed sheets left in a tangled heap by its side, and the far wall was covered in green where a thick layer of mould had taken residence.

He walked over to the window, trying not to look at the mess around him, and looked out over the small square of houses. The jungle of grass swayed gently in the breeze, the swing still protesting loudly as it rocked back and forth, but everything else lay still, the derelict houses as lifeless as ever.

He turned away, still unsettled from the sensation he had felt earlier, and saw Jake picking something up from the floor. He was holding the object delicately, as if it would break at any moment, and carefully wiped the dust from it with his fingers. Mark saw Jake's eyes grow wide with wonder as he stared at the small wooden frame clutched in his hands.

Beneath a large crack in the glass were four faces that were smiling back at him, the eyes above the smiles sparkling with happiness. A man and woman stood either side of a small boy and girl, the two children holding an ice-cream cone in their hands. The sun shone down on them warmly from a pale blue sky, the sunlight sparkling off the deep blue water that lapped gently on the beach behind them.

Mark felt a sharp pain lance across his chest.

Jake was utterly immersed in the picture, eyes staring in wonder at the family on the beach. Behind him Mark turned quickly away, his throat suddenly dry and hoarse, and looked back out the window at the square below.

He waited in silence, watching the swing rocking back and forth in the rusting play park. Deep inside him he felt a growing pang of guilt and he felt his eyes start to sting. He heard Jake place the picture back on the floor and quickly buried the feeling deep inside him. He kept his eyes straight ahead when he turned to leave the room.

They headed for the back of the house and went into another bedroom, that at one time must have been the boy's in the picture, and made straight for the window that looked out over the garden. Mark tried to keep his attention focused on the view outside instead of the room around him.

Beyond the garden fence he could see the trail disappear again as it headed between two more houses, ending suddenly as it reached the pavement of the next street. A few streets further on he could see the dark green of the forest and in the distance off to his right he could see the long strip of road that ploughed mercilessly through the trees.

Follow the path, Mark thought to himself. Head out into the next street and see what we can find. They had to be getting closer.

They headed back down to the garden, the stairs creaking loudly again as they descended. Outside the garden looked still and Mark stepped carefully over the door. He looked up at the dark, grey clouds above him and let out a deep breath.

Suddenly something creaked to their right and Mark turned sharply to see a large wooden gate opening out from the fence. His heart stopped, his blood turning cold in his veins, and his breath caught at the back of his throat. A second later his hand shot to his side and wrenched the gun from his pocket.

A person appeared in the gate, taking a step into the garden before looking up and freezing to the spot, eyes opening wide with surprise in unison with his mouth.

Mark didn't think, only reacted, and brought the gun up to aim. He pulled the trigger instinctively. The sound of the gunshot made him jump and beside him he heard Jake yell in surprise.

Ahead of them the person grunted, moving a hand to the hole that had appeared in his stomach. His face turned pale as he looked down at the blood flowing out from between his fingers, then he dropped to one knee and looked up at Mark in shock.

From behind the person three more men burst through the gate, shouting at Mark and Jake as they pointed their guns towards them.

Two of them were armed with pistols, the barrels aimed at Mark's chest, and the other sported a large hunting rifle which had turned quickly towards Jake.

Mark froze, not daring to take another shot. His eyes were fixed on the end of the rifle.

"Drop it!" the man with the hunting rifle shouted, aiming down the scope at Jake. "Drop it or I kill him!"

Mark let go of the gun, raising his hands in the air as the weapon bounced on the patio. One of the men with a pistol walked up to him and grabbed the gun from the floor, putting it in his pocket as he backed quickly away. The third one turned and knelt down beside the person whom Mark had shot.

"Calm down!" Mark said quickly, struggling to control the panic building in his stomach. He looked at the man with the rifle in desperation. "Don't hurt him. Please! We can work this out."

"He's badly hurt, Dave!" shouted the man who was kneeling over the victim of the gunshot. "Come on, Steve, stay with me now!"

"Shut up!" Dave replied over his shoulder, keeping his rifle trained on Jake. "Keep it down or you'll attract them!"

"I didn't mean to shoot him," Mark started to explain quickly. "He came out of nowhere, I just panicked! Just don…"

"It's them." The man who had picked up Mark's gun cut him off. "Gabe was right!"

Mark turned to look at who was speaking and winced when he saw his face. It was a total mess: the man's eyes were swollen and bloodshot and his nose was sitting at an unnatural angle. Cuts covered his cheeks and forehead and his skin was a blotchy array of deep purples and greys. Behind him, still lying on the floor, Steve had started to whimper.

"What's the matter with him, Greg?" Dave said over his shoulder.

"He's been hit in the stomach and the wound's

bleeding pretty badly. I can't stop it."

"Is he going to make it?"

Greg shook his head, looking down at his friend helplessly.

"Not if we don't stop the bleeding."

"Leave him," the man with the ruined face said coldly. His eyes hadn't moved from Mark.

"What the hell are you on about, Joseph?" Greg said, the disbelief plain in his voice.

"Leave him," Joseph repeated.

Steve began to groan in protest, a strange gurgling sound coming from his mouth as he tried to speak. His breathing was becoming more ragged by the second and his entire body had started to shake.

Dave shifted uncomfortably and risked a glance behind him. The expression on his face made it clear that he didn't like what he saw.

"We can't just leave him, Dave," Greg said, desperately trying to staunch the bleeding. "What are we going to do if one of the trucks breaks?"

Mark watched as the men began to argue with each other, his eyes jumping between them. He needed to find a way out – and quickly. The gunshot could have alerted more of them, or if not them, then the Hunters, and he knew that if they were taken back to the men's camp then it was over.

He looked at Jake to his right and saw him looking down at the floor, his hands shaking above his head.

It couldn't end like this. He couldn't let it end like this.

Mark swallowed down the panic that was rising in his throat and looked desperately around him. He needed something. Anything to give them a chance. They couldn't fight their way out against four of them, even if one was wounded, and if they tried to run then the men wouldn't hesitate to shoot them. He turned to look at Jake again and saw a glimmer of hope.

They hadn't taken his gun.

He looked back at Steve, who was still shaking on the floor. Greg was knelt by his side, trying in vain to stop the blood from draining out of him. Somewhere from deep within Mark's mind a thought began to emerge, at first weak and hazy and then becoming clearer and clearer. He looked back at Jake and felt his resolve harden. It was the only chance they had.

"I can help him!" Mark said loudly. The men stopped arguing and turned to look at him. Joseph spat on the floor and readjusted his grip on his pistol.

"What?" Dave said, eyeing him suspiciously.

"There's a doctor's surgery a few streets that way," Mark pointed back through the house. "Get me to it and I can help him."

Dave took a long, disbelieving look at him, trying to work out why their captive was trying to help them. None of the men answered and Mark sensed that he was running out of time. The silence became unbearable.

"Please," he begged. "I'll do whatever I can to save your friend. Just let the boy go!"

Jake turned quickly to look at him, his eyes filling with tears and a look of horror on his face. Mark's eyes didn't move from Dave, who was still holding the rifle.

"Bullshit," Joseph spat. "Just leave him. Let's take these two back to Gabe."

"He's right," Greg chipped in, his gaze also fixed on Dave. "There's a doctor's only a few streets from here. I came across it a few days back. Gabe will go crazy if we don't bring back Steve. You know he's the only one who can fix the trucks."

Dave shifted uncomfortably as he considered his options, trying to work out which action would least anger his leader. Mark couldn't take his eyes off him and could hardly breathe as the silence began to stretch. With each second that passed he felt their chances of escape slipping further and further away.

Please, he begged silently. It can't end like this. Next to him Jake had started to cry.

Suddenly Dave looked up and fixed him with a stare. He walked over to Jake and grabbed him by the coat, pulling him up sharply. Jake whimpered and tried to push him away, but Dave barely seemed to notice and placed the barrel of his rifle under Jake's chin, pushing it upwards so that his head was forced back. Throughout the whole movement he had kept his eyes locked onto Mark's.

"This better not be some kind of game you're trying to play," Dave said venomously. "If you try to run – he's dead. If you try to fight – he's dead. And if you can't save him…" he pointed back at Steve lying on the floor; he moved his face close to Mark's and said the last three words slowly, "he…is…dead."

Mark stared past him, looking instead at Jake with the rifle to his chin, and tried to quell the anger that the sight brought on. He forced himself to try and remain focused, but already he could feel panic taking his anger's place and threaten to consume him. Jake looked back at his dad with eyes full of tears. He was shaking uncontrollably.

They wouldn't let him go, Mark knew that. He knew that begging for their lives would be useless. He also knew that it didn't matter if he saved Steve or not; the men would take them both back to their camp and kill Jake in front of him. They would make him watch Jake die before eventually killing him too.

But Mark had no intention of trying to save Steve, nor did he have any intention of begging for their lives or letting them take away the one thing he cared so much about.

They had one last hope, one final chance to get away. A chance that would very likely result in both their deaths.

Mark watched as Dave pushed Jake ahead of him, pulling a pistol from his pocket and placing it to Jake's head as they began to move.

I'm sorry, Jake, Mark whispered silently, as he too was forced to move forward. I have no other choice.

Chapter 16

"Here."

Gabe stopped and looked out over the town that was sprawled out messily below him, taking in the impressive view from the cliff. He took a step closer to the edge so he could look down at the trees below and was surprised by how high up he was. A sense of vertigo suddenly hit him, causing him to take a step back before he became dizzy. He shook his head to try and dispel the feeling and shot a quick glance at Jack behind him.

Jack was looking at the surrounding forest, rubbing his arms nervously. His face was badly swollen and covered in weeping cuts from the beating he had received, and during their trip from camp he had barely spoken. As Gabe surveyed the results of his beating, he felt his confidence return, the vertigo quickly replaced by a sudden rush of adrenalin.

"Right here?" Gabe confirmed, and watched Jack nod in reply.

Gabe turned away and surveyed the small clearing by the edge of the cliff. A large rock stood at the edge of the trees beside a small stream that rushed out from the forest and into the clearing before plummeting over the cliff's edge. It all looked very natural and undisturbed. There was no sign of a camp or fire as far as he could see.

A thought suddenly occurred to him and he couldn't stop a cold smile from creeping onto his face. He turned to face the cliff's edge and pulled a gun from his belt, aiming it in front of him at about waist height.

"So you were on your knees. And he was standing behind you like this? With the gun to the back of your head?"

He turned to Jack and smiled cruelly. Jack shuddered and looked quickly away, not wanting to remember the experience. Gabe let out a laugh before shaking his head and spitting at the ground in disgust.

"Where did you find the fire pit?"

"This way," Jack mumbled, and started to head back into the woods. Gabe followed, curiously eyeing the stream that ran beside them. It was peaceful in this part of the forest, and Gabe was surprised to hear birdsong from the canopy above. Ahead of him Jack turned left and began to walk away from the stream. Gabe gave the water one last look before following closely behind.

"Here it is," Jack said, pointing at a blackened patch of grass that had appeared on the floor. He began scanning the trees around him again while Gabe squatted down to examine the black circle. He couldn't help but be disappointed by what he saw.

There was no doubt that there had been a fire here – the grass was as dead as a doornail and in some places charred to a crisp – but amidst the charring he could make out dots of green where new growth was already sprouting and there was no layer of fresh ash that he had been expecting.

He cursed quietly under his breath. There had been no fire here for a while.

"That's strange," Jack muttered. Gabe turned to look at him.

"What?" he said sharply.

Jack took a moment before answering.

"There were rocks here," he began, pacing around the grass, "a circle of rocks to form a fire pit."

Gabe looked back at the edge of the burnt patch. Jack was right. The grass was still flat around the edge, the ground beneath indented where small, heavy objects had only recently been placed.

He stood up and started to look for any sign of the missing stones, while Jack scoured the trees around them. A minute later Jack stopped by a tree that stood a few metres away and stooped down to pick up a large, grey rock that was nestled within the tree's roots. He brought it back to Gabe and turned it over in his hands for him to see. One of the rock's sides was charred black.

Gabe felt relief wash over him and let out a deep breath. There may not have been a fire here recently, but if the stones had been moved since Jack was here yesterday then someone must still be trying to hide.

The peace, the stream and now the fire pit. It was the perfect place for a home.

Gabe was close. Now that he knew where to look for the camp, it was just a matter of finding it.

Jake's legs were shaking.

He was being held up by a thick, hairy arm, the foul smell of sweat and body odour filling his nostrils and catching in his throat. He found himself struggling to breathe as his chest was crushed under the arm's force, but the group didn't stop to rest and he was forced to keep going. The cold metal of the gun barrel felt strange and unnatural pressed into the side of his head.

Dad had been right. The people they had found did want to hurt them. Even though they hadn't done anything to hurt them.

At the front of the group, Jake could see Mark helping to hold up Steve, the man who he had shot. Jake could hear Steve mumbling to himself as they walked and Joseph, who was close behind him and pointing a gun at Mark's back, had kept scolding him to be quiet so he wouldn't attract the Hunters.

Jake shuddered. He was scared. Scared about what the men would do. He remembered Dad saying that they would kill them both if they got the chance. At first, Jake had thought that his dad was being silly, but as he looked around at the big men with their guns and stern expressions, he realised that he had been the one in the wrong.

Jake didn't want to die.

Maybe if Dad saved the person he had shot then the men would let them go, Jake tried to reassure himself. Dad was always good at helping when he was hurt or sick. He had helped his wrist get better and knew that it needed to be put into a cast, and when he got colds Dad gave him a drink that helped his sore throat go away. Maybe he would know how to help Steve too, and they would let them go home.

Jake stumbled on a crack in the road and felt himself begin to fall forward. The arm around his chest tightened and pulled him back. The gun pressed harder into his temple and he winced in pain. He started to panic again and the pain in his chest grew worse as he began to struggle.

"Let go of me!" he shouted, tears filling his eyes.

He was silenced by a sharp slap that struck the side of his face. Jake gasped in shock as a vicious stinging ripped across his cheek. A few seconds later he started to cry.

"Hey!" Mark had turned around when he'd heard Jake struggling. "Don't hurt him!"

"Shut up and keep walking," Joseph snarled threateningly. Mark gave Jake a despairing look.

"Calm down, Jake. Don't cry. It's going to be OK." Behind him Joseph laughed and spat on the ground.

Jake tried to calm himself and felt his breathing begin to slow. The tightness in his chest slowly receded and although his cheek still stung he found his tears had stopped.

It's going to be OK, he repeated to himself, I just need to be brave. But already he felt himself starting to panic again. A thought suddenly struck him. When he woke up feeling scared because of one of his nightmares, Dad would tell him to try and think of something else, something happy to keep his mind off of what was scaring him.

Like the picture!

In spite of his situation, he felt a warm feeling permeate his stomach. He wanted to think about the picture he had found.

He had seen pictures of families before, mostly in the books he read or in old magazines, but they had just been cartoons or drawings rather than real people. The family he had seen in the picture were different.

For a start, they weren't a drawing, but a real family that at one time had lived together in that house. It had struck Jake how every one of them had been smiling. All of them had looked so happy, their eyes sparkling with joy – even the dad.

He wondered where the picture had been taken. He guessed that the water in the background must have been the sea, because he could see waves and it was too big to be a lake. Jake had never seen the sea, but he had seen pictures of it and Dad had told him all about it. If it was the sea, that meant the family were standing on a beach. The beach looked warm and the family didn't look as if they were scared of the Hunters there. Jake wished that he could to go to that beach.

But it wasn't the beach that had really interested him, or even how warm it had looked. What had really caught his attention were the woman and girl in the photo – the mother and daughter.

Dad never talked to Jake about his mum. Whenever he had asked about her he would suddenly go very quiet and just say that she wasn't around anymore before quickly changing the subject.

Jake assumed that she was dead – everyone else that Dad had known was – and the thought made him sad even though he had never known her.

Sometimes he wondered if she might still be alive. Maybe her and Dad had gotten separated once and couldn't find each other again, or hadn't liked each other any more so she had gone away. Maybe she was out there somewhere, looking after her daughter – his sister. He had always wanted to have a brother or sister, someone his age that he could play with when Mark left him back in the hut or was busy doing something else. Maybe one day they would all find each other again and be like the family in the photo.

Suddenly Jake shook his head and bit down on his tongue, scolding himself for being so stupid.

He didn't have any brothers or sisters, no siblings for him to play with, and he knew that his mother wasn't out there somewhere still alive and well. She had died long ago, along with everybody else. He would never get to meet her.

He roused himself from his thoughts and tried to take in his surroundings. His dad had never taken him into this part of town and so he couldn't recognise any of the buildings that he could see. It also seemed quieter than usual and he listened as the footsteps of the small group echoed loudly around the desolate street.

Jake felt a weird feeling start to form in the pit of his stomach and the back of his throat turned dry as he strained to hear anything above the ghostly echoes. One by one, he felt the hairs on the back of his neck stand up and a cold shudder wriggled down his spine.

Stop being scared, he told himself sternly. Stop being stupid! Dad won't let them hurt us!

He scrunched up his face and tried to keep his anxiety at bay, but it was useless. He looked up and felt the dreadfully familiar feeling of terror start to consume him at what he saw.

Ahead of them the tall silhouettes of the skyscrapers were creeping closer and closer.

Mark's shoulder screamed in pain, demanding him to let go of the weight it was supporting, but he ignored it; gritting his teeth and heaving the wounded Steve back onto him instead.

Throughout the walk Steve had gotten worse. He was still shaking uncontrollably and now his face was as white as a sheet from the cruel combination of shock and blood loss. With every step his breathing had become slower and more laboured and now Mark had to strain his ears to hear his light, shallow wheezing.

But they were almost there. The doctor's surgery was only two streets away and Mark was painfully aware that they were running out of time. He could feel the barrel of the gun boring into his back, Joseph looking for any excuse to pull the trigger, but what was far worse was knowing that Jake was just behind him, a gun pressed firmly against his temple as he was forced to follow.

The thought made his throat tighten and his chest ache. He shook his head firmly. Not now, he scolded himself, not yet. Right now he needed to focus.

With a grunt he shifted Steve back onto his shoulder and pressed on down the street, running his eyes quickly over the rooftops.

At the end of the street, they turned left and came into view of what he'd been dreading to see. About fifty metres ahead lay the doctor's surgery. He let out a deep breath as he fought down a surge of panic.

"Almost there," he said, with a look behind him. "It's just down this road."

Joseph glared back at him, his ruined face scrunched up in a mixture of anger and pain. He motioned with the gun for Mark to keep moving. Before he obeyed Mark stole a glance at the back of the group, at the trembling figure of Jake. He looked terrified and Mark had to turn away before he choked on the lump in his throat. It was with a great effort that he started moving forward again.

They didn't have much longer.

As they moved towards the surgery, Mark felt himself shudder involuntarily and his arms turned prickly with goose bumps. Out of the corner of his eye he saw Greg, who was helping him carry Steve, shudder too and look nervously around at the houses. Jake began to whimper quietly somewhere behind him and he heard Joseph readjust his grip on his gun. Clearly the uneasiness was felt by the entire group.

They carried on in silence, their footsteps deafeningly loud in the quiet street. A chill wind blew at them from the road ahead, making Mark gasp and Steve moan softly on his shoulder.

Once the breeze had passed he looked back up and felt his heart sink. He had thought that it would have taken them longer, but he had been wrong. They had arrived at the doctor's surgery.

Greg moved forward, leaving him to support Steve's full weight. He hurried up to the thick, wooden doors, a rusting plaque hanging loosely on a nail at its front, and pushed down on the handles as he shoved the doors forwards.

The doors didn't budge. Mark had to stifle a sigh of relief.

Greg turned around and made eye contact with Dave, communicating silently. Then he walked back to Mark and took Steve from him, straining under the weight.

"Kick it down," came a stern voice from behind him.

Mark turned to face the voice and was met with the sight of Jake crying quietly to himself. He turned quickly away before the sight became too much.

Time was running out.

Slowly he walked up to the door of the surgery and tried the handles again. It was definitely locked and the doors felt thick and heavy. It would take at least a few kicks to knock them down.

He took a step back and after a moment launched the heel of his foot into the centre of the doors. His leg jarred on impact, sending a spike of pain through his thigh, and the echo of the kick bounced deafeningly around the houses.

But the doors didn't budge.

Slowly Mark drew his leg back again and this time kicked harder. Again, the spike of pain and the loud crash as his heel slammed into the wood, but still the doors didn't move.

He stood back for a second and pretended to catch his breath. As he panted, he pricked his ears and pleaded to hear something other than his own breath. The silence had never seemed so cruel.

A third kick. The same result as before. Time was almost up.

A fourth kick. This time the doors gave slightly under his heel.

It would only take one more kick to knock them down. Two if he was lucky. He had to buy himself some time. He pricked up his ears again, but the silence was total.

Slowly Mark turned and walked back towards Jake and the small group of men. He knew it wouldn't work, but he had to try.

"Let him go now," Mark said, failing to keep his voice from shaking. The men looked at him in confusion for a moment, then Joseph started to laugh. "Not a chance in hell. Now hurry up!" Mark turned to face him.

"Please," he pleaded. "I said I'll help your friend if you let Jake go. We're at the surgery. I can help him – but not until you free Jake."

Joseph scoffed, his face twisting into something between amusement and anger. He moved over to Jake, keeping his eyes on Mark's, and placed the gun to the side of his head. He smiled cruelly.

"Hurry. Up."

Mark almost choked, unable to keep down his panic anymore. He tried to speak, but found that his throat was too tight and the air had gone from his lungs. Jake began to cry openly, the sobs racking his body and filling the empty street.

Mark stood helplessly in front of the group, unable to speak or move. All of them were looking at him, growing more and more impatient as they waited for his next move. All except Steve, who had started slipping in and out of consciousness.

He had literally seconds left.

"Three."

Joseph started counting, his finger moving onto the trigger.

Mark shuddered, tears now flowing from his eyes. Jake tried to shy away from the gun, but was held too firmly in place. This time Mark did choke, unable to beg or plead. It would be useless anyway.

"Two."

The finger tightened on the trigger, the barrel pressing deeper into Jake's skull.

Jake screwed his eyes shut, crying and shaking uncontrollably. Mark looked on, unable to tear his eyes away. Close your eyes, Jake, he pleaded silently. It will all be over soon. He almost broke down, but somehow held himself together. He needed to be strong. Be strong for Jake, for just a little bit longer. He held his breath and waited for the final number and the gunshot that would follow.

I'm sorry, Jake. I'm so, so sorry.

The silence lasted an eternity.

"On…"

"Shit!" Greg's voice made Mark flinch. As one the group turned to him and saw that he was looking across the street, his face turning deathly pale. Joseph looked at Greg in confusion and turned to see what had caught his attention. He swore too and quickly removed the gun from Jake's head. Mark looked to the other side of the road and felt his breath shudder out of him.

Across the street, stalking silently from out of the houses, were four Hunters. Their gleaming yellow eyes were fixed on the small group of people in front of the surgery and their tails were held delicately in the air behind them. When they reached the middle of the road, they stopped and sunk their bodies to the tarmac, low growls emanating from deep within their chests.

Dave turned to see what the others were looking at and froze on the spot. Jake, who was still held tightly in his grip, had stopped crying.

"No one move," Joseph said quietly.

No one did. None of them wanted to give the Hunters their cue to strike. The tension in the air grew thicker as both groups waited for the other to make the first move. On Greg's shoulder Steve had stopped shaking. His gentle wheezing was the only sound that could be heard.

Why are they waiting? Mark thought. Why haven't they attacked?

Suddenly he felt a rush of wind to his side and Greg screamed loudly as something big knocked him to the floor. Mark turned to see Greg pinned to the ground, a Hunter clawing ferociously at Steve who was lying motionless on top of him.

Across the street the Hunters leapt forward, bounding across the road and up the path to the surgery. Joseph was the first to open fire, emptying his bullets into the line of beasts. Dave threw Jake to the side and fired too, but the Hunters barely flinched and continued darting forward.

Mark moved quickly, running forward to grab Jake from the floor and pulling him back towards the surgery. Dave went down as two of the Hunters pounced on him, pinning him to the floor and tearing chunks of meat from his chest. He screamed, a horrible, gurgling sound that turned quickly to choking as blood filled his lungs.

Mark flung Jake onto his shoulder, the adrenalin in his blood eradicating his earlier pain, and sprinted towards the entrance to the doctor's surgery, not even noticing Greg who was still screaming beneath the Hunter that was tearing Steve to pieces.

Without hesitating he charged into the surgery doors, the already weakened wood cracking beneath his weight. The sudden impact made him stumble, but somehow he kept his balance and ran through a reception and down the first corridor he could see, the dim light from the skylights providing just enough light to see by. Behind him he heard the clatter of claws on the tiled floor as the Hunters raced after him.

He reached the end of the corridor and saw a fire exit which he bundled through and found himself back out in the daylight. Without stopping he ran headlong through an overgrown garden and onto the street that ran behind the surgery.

He needed to get off the road.

Mark ran to the first house he saw, which stood directly next to the surgery, and ran straight through the front door which was already hanging off its hinges. He ran past the stairs, into the back of the kitchen, and pulled down on the handle of the backdoor.

Locked.

He looked right and saw the wall of the house had collapsed. He leapt over the shattered bricks and into the next garden. Behind him he heard the Hunters as their claws skittered and scratched on the kitchen floor.

He ran down the garden, over the fallen fence at the bottom and into the yard of the house that backed onto it. The doctor's surgery was to his left now and he could still hear the men screaming as they tried desperately to fight off the rest of the pack.

He ran down the side alley of the house in front of him and found himself back on the street they had walked down earlier. He turned right and sprinted down the pavement leading away from the surgery.

He risked a glance back and immediately regretted it. Two of the Hunters were closing in on him. He turned and barged into the house to his right, knowing he didn't stand a chance if he tried to outrun them on the street. Quickly he headed down the hallway and for the garden at the back of the house, but stopped when he saw the collapsed ceiling at the end of the hall.

It was a dead end. He could hear the Hunters entering the house.

The stairs were to his left. He sprinted up them two at a time and turned to run down the hallway when he reached the top. The door ahead of him hung open and he flung them both through it, slamming the door behind him. He found himself in a bedroom and looked desperately around for somewhere else to run.

There was nowhere. He was trapped.

A large double bed lay in the middle of the room and he sprinted around it, throwing Jake to the floor and pushing him under the bed. Jake looked up at him, his eyes wide with terror and hands shaking uncontrollably.

Mark reached into his coat pocket and took out his gun.

A loud crash came from the doorway and a large crack appeared down the centre of the wooden door. Mark rested his arms on the bed and pointed the gun at it.

The second crash took the door down and the body of a Hunter fell through it. It got to its feet and shook itself vigorously, its tail thrashing on the floor and fur bristling, then locked its eyes onto Mark and bared its teeth menacingly.

Mark aimed – and fired, emptying the magazine into the Hunter's face as it pounced. He heard the soft click that told him the gun was empty and dropped it as he fell to the floor, waiting for the Hunter to land on top of him. He heard a loud thud when it slammed into the wall next to him and braced himself for the sharp pain of fangs sinking into his skin.

But the pain didn't come, and instead the Hunter lay motionless on the floor. A pool of blood began to form beneath its head.

Mark looked up and saw the dead Hunter, but had already started searching for his gun before he could feel relieved.

The gun was still on the bed, but the magazine was empty. He started searching desperately for any ammo in his pockets, but knew he wouldn't find any. The other Hunter slowly rounded the doorway, a deep menacing growl rising from its throat. It stopped to stare at him before lowering its body to the ground, preparing to pounce.

Suddenly the sound of loud gunshots filled the room and Mark watched the Hunter fall to its side with a yelp of pain. It got up and turned to face into the hallway, snarling loudly. More shots rang out and its face turned into a mass of blood as it was torn to pieces. It fell to the ground and began writhing helplessly on the floor.

Mark stared in disbelief, his mind unable to process what he had just seen, but before he could make sense of it he had already pulled Jake out from under the bed and was moving around it to leave the room. When he reached the foot of the bed, he froze. In the doorway stood Joseph.

Joseph glared at them, his face a bright crimson between the dark, purple bruising. He started to reload his gun while walking towards them.

"You bastard!" he shouted, his voice shaking with fury. "You lying bastard!"

He finished reloading the gun and pointed it at Mark, his hand shaking violently.

"Do you think that was clever? Leading us into a trap? Did you honestly think that you would get away? They're dead because of you. You killed them! And now you are going to pay for it!"

His voice had gotten louder with every word, flecks of spit flying from his mouth as he screamed. He was now standing directly in front of them, blocking their way to the door and their only chance of escape. Mark was crouching helplessly on the floor with Jake cradled in his arms.

"Give me the boy," he said menacingly.

He reached forwards to grab Jake, but Mark pulled him away. Joseph stepped back and pointed the gun at him.

Without warning he pulled the trigger, the sound of the gunshot exploding in Mark's ears. Mark fell to the floor, clutching his shoulder and screaming in pain. Joseph reached forward again and wrenched Jake away despite his desperate attempts to cling to his dad. Jake struggled to get away and shouted in protest, but quickly fell silent when he felt the gun being pressed into his temple again.

"You're going to watch this!" Joseph spat at Mark as he moved his finger to the trigger. "You're going to watch him die!"

"No!" Mark screamed, trying to get up and lunge himself towards them. "Please, please don't!"

His eyes met Jake's. He knew it was too late.

Suddenly Joseph's head jerked backwards and a thin red line appeared across his throat. The line split, and blood spurted outwards, spraying onto Mark before pouring down onto Jake's head. The hand holding the gun went limp and fell to the floor and Joseph's body slid backwards as more blood gushed from his throat.

Jake fell forward and crawled desperately towards Mark. When he reached him, he hugged him tightly and started to shake.

Mark looked up, squeezing Jake tightly to him, and saw someone standing over Joseph's body.

The left hand held a knife, its blade streaked with dark, red blood from Joseph's throat. Long, thick hair that was wild with knots fell either side of a stony, weathered face; the expression blank and unreadable. Indecipherable eyes watched coldly as Joseph writhed on the floor, the flow of blood steadily ebbing from his throat. Her head turned to look silently down at them.

It was a woman.

"Come on," she said quietly, with a voice that was dry and hoarse. She held out her free hand towards them.

Mark looked at her, this strange woman that had just saved Jake's life; then down at Joseph, who had stopped writhing and now lay as still as the Hunters; then at Jake, whose arms were still wrapped

127

tightly around him and whose breathing was gently slowing to short, shallow gasps.

He looked back up at the woman and reached out to take her hand.

Chapter 17

They left the house through the front door and turned right before heading down the street. Behind them the snarling of the Hunters and screaming of the men faded quickly as they moved away from the surgery.

The mysterious woman led the trio, Jake following behind her and Mark bringing up the rear. At the end of the street, Mark turned to check behind them and realised he could no longer hear the men screaming. The last, haunting echoes had been carried away by the breeze until once again the street was still.

Nothing had followed them.

He turned back around and saw the woman had stopped and was looking at him impatiently. She beckoned for them to follow before continuing down the street. Jake tugged gently at Mark's sleeve and looked up at him in bewilderment. Mark looked back and shrugged, equally as confused.

They headed off in pursuit of her, trying to close the already growing distance between them. She moved quickly, her footsteps barely making a sound as she navigated expertly through the desolate streets, stalking through the ruins like a spectre.

Mark struggled to keep up and felt the pain in his shoulder starting to rear its head, his earlier rush of adrenalin now starting to fade. Beside him Jake was almost sprinting to try and keep up, his head still covered in a thick layer of Joseph's blood

They passed through several streets like this, none of them talking as they put as much distance as they could between them and the Hunters. Mark realised that they were heading towards the outskirts of town, back in the direction that he and Jake had come from that morning.

"Hey," he said, keeping his voice low and quiet. "Where are you going?"

The woman turned back and fixed him with a strange stare.

"Somewhere safe," she answered bluntly. Her voice was as coarse as gravel.

Mark nodded, then started shifting uncomfortably. He wasn't sure how to ask the next question. She looked on impatiently.

"Why did you save us?" he said finally.

Her look turned to one of surprise.

"Later," she said quickly. "Not here."

She turned and headed off again, putting an end to their conversation. Mark stared at the back of her head in confusion, but found he felt compelled to follow the ghostly stranger, despite having no idea as to where she was taking them. He turned to look at Jake, who was catching his breath beside him. It was clear that he felt the same way.

They hurried to catch up with her, the sudden effort making Mark clutch his shoulder in pain.

"This safe place," he panted. "Where is it exactly?"

"Not far," she replied bluntly. "Just a few more streets away."

Mark nodded, debating whether he should suggest they go back to their camp instead. On the one hand he didn't know if where she was taking them was safe, but on the other hand he still didn't know who this stranger was, and just because she had saved their lives didn't mean she couldn't still do them harm.

It was possible that she could be leading them into a trap, but he reasoned that it was unlikely. If she wanted to hurt them, she could have just let Joseph kill them and save herself the trouble, but maybe she thought they had a camp somewhere and wanted the spoils for herself?

Either way, it would be best if Mark didn't mention their home until he knew who they were dealing with.

For the remainder of the journey, they travelled in silence. The woman still stalked ahead of them, keeping her eyes peeled for any sign of danger. Mark watched her suspiciously, wincing with every step as the pain from his shoulder crept slowly up his neck. He tried to keep himself from thinking about the events that had just unfolded and focus on the situation at hand, but eventually his mind succumbed to his recent memories and he shuddered as he realised how close their recent encounter had been.

He couldn't lose Jake, he began repeating in his head. Whatever happened, he couldn't lose Jake.

Mark realised that he must be in shock; that his mind was trying to cope with the stress of their latest brush with death. He couldn't even begin to imagine how Jake must be feeling.

He tried to turn his attention to their surroundings and saw that they were passing through a large, open street. To their right stood a small park that was overgrown with weeds; at one time a bustling picnic spot where children would play while parents talked the day away aimlessly.

Ahead of them the woman suddenly turned and began heading away from the park, to an old, decrepit building that loomed sadly over the green, open space. Mark stopped and looked up at the building, recognising the decaying façade in an instant. She was taking them to the town's public library.

In his head, he found himself trying to map out the building. It had been decades since he had been here and he only vaguely remembered a high ceiling above endless rows of bookshelves. But he could remember enough to know that the woman had been right – this was definitely a safe place. There were plenty of places to hide inside the building – it was practically a maze in there – and the windows were far too high for the Hunters to reach.

The sight of Jake looking back at him roused Mark from his thoughts and he quickly hurried towards the library, feeling better now that he knew their destination.

Up ahead the woman was heading for the side of the building, completely bypassing the steps that led up to the library's main entrance.

Mark and Jake followed, guessing that the front door was barricaded so as to block the easiest way in, and when they rounded the corner they followed her up a metal staircase that clung to the side of the building. The stairs squeaked loudly beneath their weight, but showed no signs of breaking, and at the top they entered the library through a sturdy fire door.

The first thing that struck Mark was the cold. The inside of the library was freezing, the old walls doing nothing to keep out the bitter chill of winter.

He found himself standing on the second of the two levels the library had, the higher of which skirted around the building's edge like a balcony to provide the perfect view over the ground floor. It meant that he could see everything on the floor below them and he couldn't help but feel sad at the sight with which he was met.

The endless rows of bookshelves which he could remember now lay scattered everywhere, the majority lying in heaps where one had fallen and initiated the subsequent cascade of an entire row. Across the floor were strewn thousands and thousands of books, their loose pages blowing loosely around in the cold draughts that skirled through the building.

He couldn't believe the state it had become and found the mess a painful reminder of just how long ago it had been since the world had collapsed.

A movement to his right made him turn and he saw the woman walking deeper into the library, staying on the upper level and heading for the back of the building. They followed her along the narrow walkway. To their right stood more rows of bookshelves, and a wooden banister guarded the drop to their left. A thick layer of dust covered everything in sight, their footsteps leaving dark imprints on the pale grey floor.

Near the back of the library the balcony suddenly opened out into a sitting area that was backed up by more rows of bookshelves that spanned as wide as the entire room.

The woman walked through the sitting area and headed straight for a gap in the row behind, her shadowy figure disappearing between the wooden shelves. Mark grabbed Jake by the hand, who was looking around in wonder at the endless amount of books, and pulled him through the opening, where they found her waiting impatiently by another gap.

She led them along a specific route through the labyrinth of dark passages amongst the bookshelves, navigating the maze with ease and making sure that she was always within their sight. After a while the darkness began to recede and the bookshelves gave way to a small space that had been cleared of debris to make room for a small bed and a fire.

The woman turned to face them and held out her arm to indicate that they had arrived. Mark looked around the small camp in front of him, impressed by how well hidden it was.

"I'll be back in a minute," she suddenly muttered, and before they could reply she had disappeared back between the bookshelves, leaving them alone.

After a few seconds Mark felt the gentle tugging at his sleeve again.

"Dad," Jake whispered. "Is that…is that a woman?"

"Yes, Jake," Mark whispered back, turning to meet his excited gaze.

"Is she...is she going to hurt us?" he asked cautiously.

"I don't think so, Jake," he replied, placing a hand on his shoulder. "I think we're safe for now."

It was true. Mark didn't think the woman was going to hurt them; though her sudden disappearance had made him uneasy. He squatted down and looked Jake in the eye.

"But don't tell her about our house. OK? We don't know if we can trust her yet."

Jake nodded enthusiastically, trying and failing to hide the excitement on his blood-covered face. Mark grimaced and took off his backpack, wincing sharply from the sudden pain in his shoulder.

From his backpack he retrieved a water bottle and an old cloth. He wetted the cloth and began to gently wash the blood from Jake's hair and face. Jake stared off into the distance as the water and blood ran from his cheeks and Mark wondered again at how he must be feeling.

"Are we staying here tonight?" Jake asked slowly.

Mark was surprised by the question and then realised that he didn't know the answer.

"I think you should." The woman's voice made them both jump.

Neither of them had heard her return, but there she stood in the entrance to the maze, a bundle of sticks under one arm and a small stack of books in the other. She placed the small collection in the corner of the camp, next to some hewn logs that were arranged in a pile, before brushing her hands down her trousers to get rid of the dust. Once she was finished she looked back up at them.

"They'll be looking for your camp by tomorrow."

Mark was taken aback and tried to keep the alarm from his face.

"We don't have a camp," he lied. "They'll be wasting their time."

The woman sat down with her back to one of the bookshelves, picking up a small stick from the little bundle and placing it between her teeth. She started chewing thoughtfully as she returned his stare, looking almost amused by what he had said.

She knew, he realised with horror. She knew about their camp.

He was about to say something to try and confirm his suspicion, but before he could she shrugged and turned her attention to the floor.

"Suit yourself," she said. "But if you don't have a camp then you should definitely rest here for the night."

Mark's bewilderment grew, the confusion eating away at him. A million questions careened through his mind, the answers of many he couldn't begin to guess at, but he kept himself from asking them in fear that he might give away how clueless he was. Behind him Jake had sat down on the floor, unable to take his eyes away from the mysterious stranger.

She turned to face him, sensing that he was staring at her, and gave him an awkward look.

"What's the matter, kid?" she asked. "Never seen a woman before?"

Jake looked away quickly, his face turning red with embarrassment. The woman looked taken aback and shot Mark an enquiring look. Mark stared back at her, his face rife with suspicion.

"Who are you?" he asked slowly.

"Got any food in that bag?" she asked in reply, nodding to the backpack that lay on the floor.

He nodded slowly and reached for the backpack, retrieving some dried meat from inside. He held it out to her and she grabbed it quickly before taking a large bite. She scrunched up her face as she chewed the tough, dry meat, and gave the rest a disapproving look before taking another mouthful. Mark looked on impatiently as he waited for her to finish.

Once the meat had gone she sat back against the bookshelf and let out a deep sigh.

"Thanks," she said, placing her hands on her stomach. "I haven't eaten in three days."

Behind him he heard Jake shuffle. Mark knew what he was thinking, but he wasn't prepared to share any more food with the stranger until he knew her intentions.

"Who are you?" he repeated, determined to not let her escape the question.

"You should let me look at your shoulder," she replied, leaning forward and peering at the hole in his jacket.

He quickly covered the wound with his hand, wincing in pain at the sudden movement. The woman shook her head and gave him an irritated look. Jake watched the encounter in silence, absorbing every moment.

"Who are you?" Mark said again, through teeth gritted with pain. "Who are you and what do you want from us?"

The woman sat back with a huff and folded her arms across her chest. She looked from Mark, to Jake, and back to Mark again, at the two sets of eyes that stared imploringly at her.

They looked afraid, she realised. Scared and afraid of everything that was happening to them. Finally, she succumbed to the stares.

"My name's Rae," she said slowly. "And I want you to help me kill those bastards."

Chapter 18

Gabe sat down heavily in one of the chairs around the fire and stared into the flames that were just beginning to devour the pile of twigs from which they had sprung. To his left he could hear the sound of tearing as Mike and Daniel skinned a couple of rabbits that had been caught in their traps. It wouldn't be long before they would be cooking on a spit over the fire, roasting nicely for when the scouting group that had gone into town to gather supplies would return.

He watched as the fire grew and engulfed the rest of the kindling. On the other side of the flames he saw Jack get up and place the first of the logs into the pit. The flames wasted no time and began to lick greedily at the crackling wood.

They had searched the forest around the abandoned fire pit for over an hour and, apart from a few more charred rocks that were scattered around the trees, their search had turned up nothing.

Gabe couldn't understand it. They must have a camp somewhere, but there weren't many places to hide one amongst the trees. He had begun to wonder whether the fire pit had been a decoy, something to draw their attention away from the father and son's true location. But if it was a decoy then why try to hide it by throwing away the rocks?

He rubbed his eyes as they started to sting from the smoke from the fire.

Maybe the father and son had been spooked. The encounter with Jack had most likely scared them and as a result they may have dismantled their camp and were now constantly moving in an effort to remain hidden. It was most likely, Gabe reasoned, and he felt another surge of anger towards Jack for the setback. Fortunately if they were moving around then it wouldn't be long before one of his men stumbled across them.

Tomorrow he would go back to the abandoned fire pit and search the place more thoroughly. There would be more clues as to where the father and son had gone and if they weren't moving around then he still suspected that their camp would be close to that spot.

They were definitely getting closer, he reassured himself. It was just a matter of time.

A movement to his left distracted him and he turned his attention to Daniel and Mike, who had just finished skinning the rabbits. Daniel stood up, a skinless carcass in each hand, and walked over to the fire before dropping them in a pan to begin cooking them over the flames.

The fire crackled and spat, the flames reaching up and licking at the pan hungrily as the meat on top began to sizzle. The smell of roasting rabbit filled the campsite, making Gabe realise just how hungry he was. A few moments later Paul and Cal appeared, giving the roasting meat an approving look as they slumped down into their chairs.

"Still no sign of them yet," Paul announced to the group.

"It's only just getting dark," Mike replied, joining the circle and resting his chin on his stump. "They'll be back soon."

Paul shrugged uncertainly.

"Yeah, well they better have found something good in there. My shoes are falling to pieces."

They watched the rabbit cook in silence, the meat sizzling over the heat. Above them the sky was getting darker and the evening breeze took on a sinister chill as night began to fall.

Gradually the small group shuffled their chairs closer to the fire, trying to keep warm as the temperature plummeted. At the edge of the circle, Paul kept glancing towards the dark outline of the town, but as the evening dragged on he could still see no sign of the scouting party.

"They should be back by now," Paul muttered, slowly getting out of his chair to better scan the trees around the edge of the camp. "I'm going to go and look for them."

The rest of the group grunted in reply, none of them wanting to leave the warmth of the fire.

Paul started walking to the edge of the camp, leaving the smell of cooking meat and the roaring red flames behind him. He wouldn't go far, he thought to himself as he crossed the perimeter of the camp, instantly regretting leaving the warmth. He would just check the edge of town to see if there was any sign of them before turning back.

He left the safety of the trees and headed across the small patch of land that marked the barrier between the town and the forest. Ahead of him the dark silhouettes of the houses loomed menacingly and he couldn't help but feel slightly uneasy as he approached them.

Most of the groups that went out to search an area would return before it got dark, though it wasn't exactly unusual for parties to return later if they had found something or got lost on their way, but as Paul took his first steps into the shadowy alleyways of the town, he couldn't stop himself from feeling that something was wrong.

It was probably their situation, he reflected, as he came out from an alleyway into a wide open street. They had been tracking this father and son for weeks now and they had barely found any trace of them. This wasn't the first time that Gabe had grown an obsession in hunting a traveller down, but lately his behaviour had become far more unpredictable.

Take Joseph and Jack, for instance. He had never seen Gabe give any of the men as severe a beating as the one he had given Joseph, and although none of them had seen it, it was obvious that he had done the same, if not worse, to Jack.

He began heading down the dimly lit street, searching for any sign that the scouting group were nearby. The realisation hit him suddenly from out of the dark.

Gabe was getting desperate. They had all been too scared to notice, but now Paul realised that he had been running out of ideas of how to keep the group going for a while. Now that he thought about it seemed so obvious. Gabe was losing control.

He stopped halfway down the street and looked at the quiet desolation that surrounded him. The sky had turned to jet black, leaving only the silvery moonlight for him to see by. The wind whistled gently through the cracks and alleyways, making the leaves of the creepers and vines that covered the houses rustle gently.

There was still no sign of them.

He was about to head back to the warmth of the fire when something in the distance caught his ear. He held his breath, listening to the rustling of the leaves as he stared into the dark ahead. There it was again.

It sounded like footsteps.

It could be nothing, he thought to himself, as another breeze blew down the street. The wind liked to play tricks when it whistled through the ruins, but gradually the footsteps got louder and now Paul was certain that someone was heading his way. He crouched behind a car to his left, the paintwork peeling to reveal the corrosion beneath, and pulled out his gun, which he aimed into the dark. A shiver ran up his spine as he listened to the footsteps getting closer.

A figure began to emerge from the darkness, running quickly towards him and shooting nervous glances back the way it had come. As the figure got closer, Paul saw that it was a person, and gradually he began to recognise who the person was. He let out a sigh of relief and put his gun back in his pocket.

"Greg!" Paul exclaimed, as he stepped out from behind the car. Greg, who had been running towards him, jumped in fright, then relaxed when he recognised his greeter.

"Paul," Greg panted heavily, "they're gone! I…I couldn't do…anything. They got them, Paul!"

"Whoa, whoa! Calm down," Paul said quickly, looking nervously at the darkness behind Greg. "Catch your breath, all right? You're safe now."

Greg shook his head abruptly, still panting heavily.

"There were so many." The words came quickly. "They came out of nowhere and then–"

"Greg!" Paul said firmly, causing him to look up. "Calm down! Where are the others?"

"Dead!" Greg shouted in exasperation. "They're all dead!"

He hunched over and started shaking uncontrollably. Paul looked down at him in disbelief, struggling to make sense of what he was saying. A vile sickness started to build in the back of his throat as the realisation kicked in. He shot a nervous glance at the street around him again and found that the shadows didn't seem so empty anymore.

"Let's get back," Paul said, putting his arm around Greg and leading him quickly back towards the forest. "Let's get you some food by the fire and you can tell us what happened."

Gabe turned his head sharply at the sound of someone approaching from the trees. At the edge of the camp, he could make out two figures emerging from the dark, and as they got closer to the fire he recognised them as Greg and Paul. Greg looked terrified and was shaking uncontrollably whilst he leaned on Paul for support. Gabe sat bolt upright in his chair, instantly sensing that something had happened.

"Damn, Greg, are you OK?" Daniel asked, standing up from the cooking rabbits.

Paul sat Greg in one of the camp chairs closest to the fire before sitting down himself and holding out his hands towards the flames. The rest of the group were staring at Greg, waiting impatiently for him to tell them what was wrong, all except for Mike, who was looking back in the direction that they had come from.

"Where are the others?" Mike asked gruffly, as he turned back to the circle. Everyone's attention was now fixed on Greg.

"They're dead," Greg whispered quietly, his hollow eyes not moving from the crackling flames. None of them responded. There was a sharp intake of breath before a stunned silence settled over the group. Eventually Greg continued.

"It was the Hunters. They came out of nowhere and…they're all dead."

Still no one spoke. The words were still sinking in. Greg continued to shake uncontrollably, occasionally wincing with fear as he relived the memories of the attack. No one tried to comfort him.

Eventually Gabe broke the silence.

"What?" he spat in disbelief, his initial shock quickly turning to anger. The others turned to look at him in surprise. He started to shout.

"What do you mean they're all dead? How the hell did that happen?"

"He tricked us," Greg whispered quietly. "He said he could help Steve…that he could save him. But he tricked us."

He shuddered again at the memory. Gabe looked at him in confusion. He wasn't making any sense.

"Who tricked you?" Gabe asked angrily. "Who tricked you? What the hell are you talking about?"

"The dad," Greg replied faintly. "The dad and boy."

"What?" The anger disappeared from Gabe's voice. It wasn't the response he'd been expecting.

"We found the dad and his boy," Greg repeated. "But he shot Steve. In the stomach." He rubbed his own stomach gently, as if to reiterate the point.

"He was in a bad way. Really bad. Joseph wanted to leave him but the dad said that he could help him. That he knew how to stop the bleeding if we could get him to the doctor's surgery. We got there, but the doors were locked and then…then the Hunters came."

He shuddered again and began to rock gently in his chair. Around him the rest of the group were silent, the crackling of the flames and the spitting of the meat the only sound to be heard. Suddenly the men jumped as Gabe slammed his fist into the arm of his chair.

"Why the hell didn't you bring them here!" he shouted, his face turning red with rage. "What the hell were you thinking?"

Greg winced in fright.

"He was going to die. We had to do some…"

"Idiot!" Gabe cut him off, spit flying from his mouth. "You had them and you let them get away!"

Greg kept his eyes fixed on the fire, offering no response.

"Tomorrow you take me back there," Gabe continued. "You take me back to where you found them so we can catch them again!"

"No!" Greg turned to look at Gabe for the first time since he had returned. His eyes were wide with fear. "No Gabe! There's no way I'm going back there again!"

"Yes you are!" Gabe shouted, as he stood up from his chair. "You, me, and Daniel are going there at first light!" He pointed at Daniel, who shuffled nervously by the fire.

"No Gabe!" now Greg was shouting too. "I'm not going back! They died! Three of us died! And you want to keep looking? I'm not doing it! To hell with that dad and his son. I'm not going back into that town!"

Gabe shook with rage as he stared down at the terrified Greg. He clenched his fists and felt the blood rushing to his hands, saw the corners of his vision begin to blur as his anger became uncontrollable.

"I'm not asking you, Greg," his voice was quivering. "I'm telling you."

Greg stared back. His eyes had started to water, his fear forcing out his tears.

"I'm not going back there, Gabe," he said faintly.

Gabe was on top of him in a flash.

His hand closed around Greg's throat and he slammed the back of his head into the cold, hard ground as the chair toppled to the floor. Beside him Paul began to get up, but he was quickly stopped by a fierce look from Jack.

"Coward!" Gabe screamed. He pulled back his fist and buried it into Greg's face, the hard crunch beneath his knuckles making his blood surge. He pulled his fist back again and hit him harder. Greg cried out in pain as blood spewed from his nose, but continued to protest despite the ferocious attack.

"I'm not going, Gabe. I'm not going back in there!"

Gabe struck him again, feeling more enraged with every punch. His knuckles burned with pain and he could feel his fists becoming wet with blood, but still he continued to pummel Greg's terrified face, which was quickly disappearing into a bloody mess. The wet thuds of the impact drowned out the protests, which had now given way to desperate splutters and gurgling.

The rest of the group sat around the fire in silence. None of them dared to intervene, and instead kept their eyes fixed on the crackling flames, wincing at the sound of every blow.

Still Gabe continued, desperately feeding his rage that demanded he kept on hitting. Greg's arms, which had been trying to protect his head, now lay limp by his sides, and his legs were no longer scrabbling on the floor.

Eventually Gabe felt the strength in his arms disappear and his punching ground to a slow halt. He fell onto his side and breathed heavily, his vision slowly returning to its normal state. His knuckles were on fire and he could feel that his hands were covered in thick, warm blood.

Gradually the anger dissipated and he rolled over to look at the victim of his rage. Greg's face was no longer visible, replaced instead with a bloody pulp that was spewing blood. Gabe's face was emotionless as he looked at what he had done, but inside the satisfaction he felt was stronger than ever.

Slowly he got to his feet, still panting heavily to try to catch his breath. No one dared to look at him as he stepped over Greg and walked back to his chair. The warmth of the fire permeated his skin, helping to dispel the rest of his rage and return some clarity to his thoughts.

Tomorrow he would go back to the abandoned fire pit with Jack to search for the camp, he decided, as he sat back down. There was no point risking getting attacked by the Hunters. He would send Paul, Daniel and Cal to search in town instead, and make sure that if they found the father and son then they would bring them back straight away.

Around the circle the rest of the group shot nervous glances towards Greg's battered corpse, searching for any sign that he might still be alive. But Greg's body remained unmoving and one by one they turned back to the crackling flames that were spitting bright embers up into the night sky, and to the two slowly cooking rabbits that were now black and charred.

Chapter 19

Inside the library it was bitterly cold.

The wind whistled through the ancient bookshelves, fluttering the pages of crumbling books that had long been forgotten and causing discarded paper to skitter across the floor. High above, just below the lofty ceiling, the grimy windows turned dark as the sun finally set over the world outside.

On the building's upper level, from deep within a labyrinth of bookcases, came an orange glow that permeated the darkness. The dry sticks crackled noisily as they were consumed by flames and sent bright embers floating lazily up towards the ceiling before they disappeared.

Atop the fire a rabbit carcass spat angrily as it roasted. When it was cooked through, it was removed from the flames and shared out amongst Mark, Rae and Jake, who were huddled to the warmth.

Mark looked down at his plate of food, carefully rubbing his shoulder that had now been tightly bandaged. Rae had dressed the wound a few hours earlier. First she had pulled out the bullet lodged in his muscle with an old pair of tweezers, then she had taken a bottle of vodka and applied it generously to the hole in his shoulder as a substitute for antiseptic.

That part had hurt.

He had bitten into an old cloth to stop himself from crying out, as a stinging like he had never felt before ripped through his shoulder. It had felt as if an angry hornet had been repeatedly stinging him and the wound had still burned almost an hour later.

Then Rae had pulled out a first aid kit from one of the bookshelves and unwound a roll of bandage from inside. She ripped it with her teeth before wrapping it around the bullet hole, ignoring Mark's moaning as she pulled it as tight as she could.

Once she had tied the bandage off she had picked up her knife and disappeared into the bookshelves, leaving Mark and Jake to stare at each other in confusion as they found themselves alone in her camp. It was a few hours before she eventually returned with a skinned and gutted rabbit tied to her waist.

Jake's eyes had lit up with wonder when she had come back and Mark could still see the warm glow on his face as she handed him his share of the meat.

Mark couldn't help but worry about how Jake must be feeling, but it seemed that somehow he hadn't been overwhelmed with the trauma of the day's events combined with Rae's appearance.

Understandably Jake was fascinated by her and, judging by the look on his face, it was clear that he thought they had finally found a friend. Mark, however, did not share Jake's trusting nature and was not prepared to let his guard down just yet. He was still trying to make up his mind about how to feel about the woman.

For a while, they ate in silence, Rae staring emptily into the flames as she chewed. Mark stared too, stealing occasional glances at her and trying to understand why she had saved them.

Jake was less subtle and barely touched his food. Instead he sat staring at Rae, unable to tear his eyes away from her. After a while Rae stirred, sensing that she was being watched, and turned to meet his stare.

"Are you OK?" she asked bluntly, tossing a bone into a slowly growing pile in front of her.

Jake nodded frantically, picking up his own food and chewing on it quickly. Once he had finished his mouthful, he started to speak.

"Th…thank you for saving me and my dad," he stammered nervously.

"You're welcome," Rae replied bluntly, picking up another piece of meat.

Jake kept staring at her, opening and closing his mouth as he tried to work out if he should ask his next question. After a few seconds she sighed and turned to face him again.

"What is it, kid?" she asked impatiently.

"Wh…why did you save us?" Jake asked, his face twisting in confusion.

Mark looked suddenly up from the fire, interested to hear her response. Rae looked back at Jake, surprised by the question.

"Because you were in trouble," she replied. The look of confusion remained on Jake's face.

"So?" he replied bluntly.

Now it was Rae's turn to look confused.

144

"What do you mean, "so"?"

"So what if we were in trouble?" Jake went on. "You don't know who we are. We could have been with those men. We could have hurt you!"

Again, she looked at him in surprise for a few seconds before an amused grin broke across her face.

"You're sharp, kid," she said approvingly. Mark noticed that the way in which she looked at Jake had changed, as if she were only just seeing him for the first time.

"I knew you weren't with those men," she confessed. "And I also knew that you wouldn't hurt me – unless I gave you good reason to."

"But how did you know?" Jake asked, unconvinced. Mark had been thinking the same thing.

"Because I've been watching you," she replied. Mark sat up straight, his eyes widening in surprise. "I've been watching you and that group ever since they arrived."

Mark's surprise turned quickly to scepticism and he found himself scouring his memory. Could she really have been watching them? If so, how long had she been watching them for? Surely he would have noticed something if she had.

His mind raced with questions that demanded an answer, but he kept his mouth shut, not wanting to put her on the spot and spook her into silence. Beside him Jake was still staring at her strangely, another question clearly on his mind, and it looked as if he was struggling to hold it back. Eventually he could hold it in no longer and the words blurted out.

"Are you my mother?"

Mark felt his heart skip a beat and for a moment he forgot to breathe. His gaze shot to the right and fixed Jake with a look of horror. He hadn't been expecting that at all. He opened his mouth to say something but the words never came. Quickly he turned back to Rae to see her reaction.

She looked almost as surprised as him, but far more confused. Mark opened his mouth again to speak, to say anything to fill the awful silence, but Rae beat him to it. "No," she said firmly, fixing Jake with a hard stare. "I'm not your mother, kid."

Jake looked down at the floor, the disappointment clear on his face, and hugged himself tightly. Mark met Rae's eyes and gave her a quick nod as he put his arm around Jake. Rae nodded back, seeming to understand the situation, before returning her attention to the fire.

The three of them finished their meal in silence.

An hour later Jake was fast asleep underneath a blanket by his side, finally having succumbed to his exhaustion as he was caressed by the warmth of the fire. The meal from earlier had been finished and Rae had taken the remains of the carcass outside and dumped them away from the library. Now she and Mark sat either side of the fire, both lost in their thoughts as they stared silently into the flames.

Suddenly Rae stirred and slowly she got up from the floor. She stepped over to one of the bookshelves that formed the Camp's perimeter and reached through one of the spaces between the shelves into a small gap behind. From out of the gap she pulled a large brown bottle, the top firmly secured with a cork.

She sat back down by the fire and pulled out the cork, then picked up two dented metal mugs and poured a large measure into each. She held out one of the mugs to Mark, who took it cautiously, before throwing back her entire measure in one.

Mark took a sip of the drink and felt a burning sensation, as scotch hit the back of his throat and drained slowly down to his stomach. He felt the warmth permeate his entire body and realised that this was the first drink he had had since before he had found Jake. He took another sip, this one larger than the first, before cradling the mug in his hands and looking up at Rae.

"How long have you been watching us?" he asked plainly. Rae finished pouring herself another measure, then put the bottle to the side.

"A few weeks. Ever since that group arrived," she replied. Her eyes didn't leave the fire.

"What have you seen?" Mark asked, uncertainty creeping into his voice.

"A few things." She took another gulp of scotch. "For a start, I know about your camp. The treehouse. I was surprised at how well you've hidden it. I doubt I would have seen it if I hadn't seen you climbing up the ladder."

Mark winced and took another sip of scotch to hide his reaction. He had thought Rae might have seen him and Jake when they had gone into town, but he could never have guessed that she had been watching them whilst they were in their home.

"What else?" he probed, trying to sound as if he wasn't surprised by what he had heard.

"I saw your encounter with one of the men, by the cliff." She looked up from the fire and fixed her eyes on his. "Why didn't you shoot him?"

Mark turned away to look at Jake, who was still sleeping peacefully by his side.

"I didn't need to," he said quietly, as he watched the slow rise and fall of Jake's chest. He turned back to her. She waited for him to continue, but he had nothing else to say.

"You should have killed him," she said bluntly, when she realised he was finished. Her eyes turned back to the fire. "That was a mistake. It would have meant one less for us to kill."

Mark shrugged, taking another sip of scotch. She was probably right, but he didn't like her use of the word "us". "Why were you watching us?" he asked, watching her expression carefully. Rae was staring blankly into the fire, gently swirling the dark liquid in her mug.

"I wasn't," she replied. "Not at first." She waited a while before continuing.

"I've been following them. That group that have settled here. I tracked them here from the last town they were at. I was following one of them in town when I suddenly heard your kid screaming the place down. I saw you running from the shop with something like three Hunters on your tail. I didn't think you were going to make it, was certain you wouldn't actually, but all the same I followed you to that building you holed yourself up in.

"There was about four of them then, trying to batter the door down to get to you. At one point, I thought it would give, but somehow it held. I waited all night, watching to see what would happen, and the next morning there you both were. Alive. That's when I started watching you – to see what kind of people you were." She took another swig of her drink.

"Why does it matter?" Mark asked. The reminder of the chase made him feel uncomfortable. "Why does it matter what kind of people we are?"

"Because I needed to know if you would help me," she looked up to meet his gaze again. "I needed to know if you would help me kill the men in that group, and that you wouldn't try to kill me in the process."

She downed the rest of her drink and poured herself a third measure. Mark watched her take another long drink.

147

"Who are they? This "group". Why are they here?"

She took a moment before answering and when she spoke her tone was matter of fact.

"Bandits, marauders, drifters. There are plenty of names for them. They travel from town to town, scavenging what they can and stealing the rest from whoever they come across. They kill men, rape women, then kill them as well when they're finished. Surviving isn't enough for them. They need to feel powerful, to be the strongest people left alive, and they achieve that by abusing anyone weaker than them. They're a danger to everyone left surviving, an abomination to the memory of the human race. And that's why you need to help me kill them.

Mark sat in silence for a moment, contemplating what she had said. Rae was staring deep into her mug, as if she was waiting for something to appear there.

"I never said we would help you," Mark said coldly. A weak smile appeared on Rae's face.

"You don't need to say it. They know you're here – and you just killed four of their men. Do you think that's going to make them give up looking for you and move on?"

She waited for him to answer, but he stayed silent.

"Of course it won't," she continued. "They aren't going to stop until they find you." She paused as she took another swig. "Unless, of course, you kill them first," she fixed him with another hard stare. "But there are still six of them left. Six of them. And two of you. We need each other's help."

She looked back at the flames, not bothering to read his reaction. She didn't need to. She knew that she was right. And Mark did too.

"Why do you want to kill them?" he asked, looking for a reaction and trying to go back on the offensive. But she gave nothing away. Instead, she took another sip of her scotch and changed the subject.

"You have a smart kid," she said casually. "How old is he?"

"Five," Mark replied bluntly. Rae nodded.

"Jake. Right?" Mark nodded back.

"How the hell did you raise him out here?" she turned to face him again, her expression one of genuine interest. "I take it he never knew his mother?"

The question hung awkwardly in the air, like a spectral phantom that loomed above the fire and sucked the warmth from the camp. Mark opened his mouth to answer, but stopped before he spoke.

148

For a wild moment, he considered telling her how he had actually found Jake; that Jake was not his son, but a baby he had found that had been born to dead parents. He dismissed the idea with a shake of his head and held out his mug for a refill. Rae obliged, making this measure considerably bigger than the last.

"I'm sorry," she muttered, putting the bottle to the side again.

Mark stared into the dark, murky liquid in his hands; the surface gently reflecting the firelight. A strange feeling descended over him and he found himself swallowing back a lump that had formed in his throat. It had been years since he had sat and spoken with someone other than Jake and he found a host of painful memories wash over him like a wave at the realisation.

Why shouldn't he tell her about how he had found Jake? What difference would it really make? The pain gave way to guilt, which swelled as he looked towards Jake, who was still sleeping peacefully. He forced down another lump in his throat and knew that if he didn't tell this stranger, then he may never tell anyone at all.

He took a long drink of his scotch to prepare himself.

"I found him," he whispered quietly. On the other side of the fire Rae stirred from her thoughts and looked up at him in confusion. "I found him," he repeated, louder this time.

"What?" she asked, not understanding what he meant.

"Jake," Mark continued, his voice beginning to shake. "I...I don't..."

He drew in a deep breath and tried to compose himself. Rae put down her mug, sensing that this was important, and stared at him intently.

"One morning, about five years ago, I headed into town. It was early morning, the sun was just coming up, and everything seemed normal – just like any other time. I was heading for the towers in the middle of town, the skyscrapers that tower over everything else. You must have seen them."

She nodded to show that she had and waited for him to continue.

"When I was about halfway to the centre, well away from the forest by now, I heard screaming, loud, high-pitched screaming, but I thought I must have been hearing things because I hadn't seen anyone for months – years even. But then I hear it again and now I'm certain it's real, so I try and find out where this screaming is coming from."

He took another sip of his scotch. Rae was still watching him intently.

"I follow the sound to this cul-de-sac and I could hear the screaming is coming from one of the houses. So I go round to the back of the house and get in through one of the windows. I could tell that it was coming from upstairs, but as I climb inside the screaming suddenly stops and everything turns deadly quiet. I could sense that something bad had happened."

He stopped and winced at the memory. Rae was now hanging on every word.

"I took out my gun and went upstairs, and when I reached the top of the staircase I saw a body in the room ahead of me. A man's body. He'd been ripped to pieces and I knew straight away that he was dead. But I…I could still hear something. Something else was in the room."

He took another sip to steady himself, then carried on.

"I went into the room and I saw it. A Hunter – but it hadn't seen me. Instead it's crouched over something and I know that it's killed another person. Before the Hunter saw me I got behind it and shot it in the back of the head, killing it before it had a chance to attack. That's when I saw the other body. The body of a woman, also torn to pieces."

He shuddered, but forced himself to keep going.

"I was about to leave, when…when I saw something move on the ground by the woman. Something tiny. And that's…that's when I saw him."

His voice was cracking and his eyes were wet with tears; but he managed to maintain his composure.

"She'd just given birth. He couldn't have been more than a minute old. He was so small. So small and defenceless. I couldn't…I couldn't…"

He took a sharp intake of breath as tears started to run down his face.

"I couldn't just leave him there to die. So I took him."

Mark looked up at her through glistening eyes and saw her sitting in stunned silence. Through his tears it looked as if she was sparkling in the firelight. For a while, neither of them spoke, there were no words that seemed appropriate, until finally Rae broke the silence. "Amazing," she said, her voice barely audible. Then louder. "That's amazing." She shook her head in disbelief. "It's…" But she had no idea what to say.

Mark looked back at Jake and tried to wipe the tears from his eyes.

"He's still my son," he said quietly. "I may not be his biological father – but he's still my son. I brought him up as my son, and I love him like my son."

He felt his heart overflowing as he watched Jake's sleeping face in the glow from the fire.

"Does he know?" Rae asked eventually. Mark shook his head and returned his gaze to her.

"I don't know how to tell him," he shrugged helplessly. "Or if I should."

Rae nodded slowly, offering no advice. Then she started to shake her head again. She was still struggling to come to terms with what she had just heard.

"How did you know?" she began. "How did you know what to do? Did you have kids before?"

She winced as she realised the insensitivity of her question. Mark looked quickly towards the fire.

He opened his mouth to speak, but found that he couldn't. He felt another wave of emotion building inside of him. All he could manage was a shake of his head.

Rae nodded in reply, not wishing to probe any further.

"Did you have kids?" Mark asked quietly, wanting to turn the focus away from him.

"No," she replied quickly. "Never wanted them."

They sat in silence for a while, both of them deep in thought. Mark went to take another sip of his drink, but realised the mug was empty. He held it out to Rae for a refill.

"Most people wouldn't have done that," she said, as she refilled his mug. "I certainly wouldn't have. You saved his life. In a world like this…that's incredible!"

She tried to look him in the eye to show her sincerity, but he looked away quickly.

"Is it?" he asked.

He was met with a confused look, then a shake of the head.

"What do you mean?"

"I mean is it incredible?" He looked at Jake again. "You said it yourself, "In a world like this"."

Mark looked up at her with imploring eyes, as if he was searching for something that she might have.

"He has dreamed about meeting people for so long. Since I first told him that other people existed! And then the first person he does

151

meet tries to kill him. You are probably the only person he will ever meet in his entire life that doesn't want to hurt him or take him away from me. He'll never have a friend his age. He'll never have someone he can talk to that isn't me. He'll never fall in love. He'll never have a family. He will only ever have me. And one day I'll die and then he'll have nothing."

He stopped, breathing heavily as he let his words sink in. Across from him Rae didn't respond.

"And he has nightmares," he continued. "Every night he has nightmares. He wakes up screaming. Covered in sweat and crying his eyes out in fear. He's terrified of the Hunters, of losing me. He's only five. Five! And I gave him a knife. A knife which he's used. And now…now I've given him a gun."

Mark stared at her with desperate eyes, searching for some kind of reaction that would justify what he'd done. Rae looked back, not knowing how to respond.

Eventually, with tears running down his face, he looked down at the ground in shame.

"These past few weeks he's nearly died more times than I can count. If you hadn't showed up today, he would be dead."

His voice had taken on a resigned tone. He looked around helplessly as he searched for the right words and swallowed back another lump that had formed in his throat.

"What kind of life is that?" he asked, looking back up at her. "Have I saved him? Or have I just…" He took a deep breath. "Or have I just made him suffer."

Rae stared at him with an expression that was equal parts shock and confusion. Her mind raced to process everything that she had just heard, still not quite believing that the story could be true. Then her expression hardened and she shook her head in defiance.

"No," she stated firmly, fixing him with another hard stare. "You saved him. He would be dead if it wasn't for you. You care for him, don't you? You said it yourself. You love him as if he were your own son. He would never have known what that love felt like if you hadn't saved him in the first place."

The look in her eyes said that she was certain. Mark shied away shamefully from her gaze.

"I was going to kill myself," he said quietly, his voice empty and hollow.

Confusion returned to Rae's face.

"The day I went into town; the day I found Jake. I was heading for the towers at the centre because I was going to climb to the top. And once I got there I was going to hang myself."

Another stunned silence.

"Why?" Rae failed to keep the surprise from her voice.

"Because I didn't see the point anymore." He looked up at her to show his sincerity. "I was alive, yes, and surviving well. I had a camp, I had water, I could get food when I needed it – but what was the point?" He held up his hands helplessly.

"I hadn't spoken to another person in years. Hadn't even seen another human being. And if I did ever see anybody again then they would probably rather kill me than talk to me. I used to sit every day, looking out over this town, and I would just think. Think about how things were. Think about how things had changed. Think about everything I had lost. And one day…one day I didn't want to think any more."

He picked up his mug and took another long sip. The fire was still flickering lazily away, the log on top smouldering in the heat.

"If I hadn't found Jake," he continued, "then I would be dead. I saved him…to save me. You tell me what right I had to do that."

For a long time, Rae was silent, not for the first time unsure of how to respond. Gradually her gaze returned to the fire as they both sat deep in thought, mulling over their conversation.

Mark was shaking his head slowly, trying to discern how he felt for finally telling someone the truth about Jake. He found that the same questions continued to torment him; the confession had provided no answers. He wasn't surprised. He hadn't expected it to. And he knew that he would torture himself over what he had done for the rest of his life.

He had just needed to tell somebody.

The sound of Rae's voice broke the silence; the noise startling Mark and bringing his attention back to the camp. It took him a moment to realise what she was talking about.

"My husband," she said quietly, her voice suddenly seeming soft and gentle. "They killed my husband."

Chapter 20

The sun beamed warmly down on him, the hot rays caressing his skin and reflecting brightly off the sand. Somewhere in the distance, he could hear the waves lapping gently against the shore, the crashing surf surging quickly forwards, before gently receding back down the beach.

Mark tried to focus on the sound, but found it was drowned out by the endless noise around him; the noise of hundreds of people talking and shouting as they engaged in excited conversations with each other or indulged in simple games. Above the commotion a flock of seagulls cawed noisily in the light blue sky as they fought for the best positions to swoop down and pick off anything that wasn't being watched.

A movement to his right made him stir and he opened his eyes to see his wife's face staring lovingly back at him. He felt a warm feeling suddenly smother his insides and he couldn't help but smile back. She turned away from him, propping herself up on her arms so she could look out towards the water. Mark took his time admiring her slender figure before putting his head back down and closing his eyes again.

He lay like that for a while, enjoying the warmth of the sun and his wife lying next to him. It was a good day, he decided. A perfect day.

From somewhere behind him the sound of tinny music came creeping over the beach, the familiar tune causing heads to turn and children to scramble excitedly as the ice-cream van arrived. Mark smiled as he heard his wife sit up sharply, knowing what she was thinking before she even spoke.

She muttered something to him as she stood up from their little camp in the sand, turning to smile at him before stepping over a line of sand castles and heading off towards the water. Mark sat up and watched her go with sleepy eyes.

She reached the sea, her footsteps sending large splashes up into the air with every stride. The water close to the shore was packed with adults and children alike as they dived between the waves and threw inflatable balls to each other above the surface. She headed deeper into the water and for a moment Mark lost sight of her as a large wave crashed onto the beach.

He waited for her to reappear, but after a few moments found he was scanning the crowd for any sign of the distinctive blonde glow of her hair.

There. He saw her again. But his smile quickly disappeared as he saw how far away she was from the shore.

He stood and walked slowly down towards the water, trying not to lose sight of her again. Why was she so far away? And why was she still going further? Above the blonde hair there suddenly appeared two arms that began to thrash angrily at the surf.

Mark began to move more quickly as an uneasy feeling crept into his stomach. Around him the sun beds and picnic blankets began to fall away, replaced instead with mile upon mile of endless sand, and above his head the seagulls began to circle menacingly, cawing and screeching as the flock grew more enraged.

Yet still his wife seemed to be moving away, pulled relentlessly by the current that was dragging her further out to sea.

He started to run down the beach, his uneasiness transforming into panic. His feet sank into the sand and every step became harder as the sand somehow got deeper and deeper. Ahead of him the waves crashed noisily against the shore and his breathing got faster. In the distance, she continued to disappear.

Suddenly, his calves screaming in pain with the effort, he broke through the sand and stumbled into the sea, but just as soon as he felt the cold water wash over his feet the sky and sea began to fall away, leaving nothing in front of him except an endless black, and his wife who was still fighting desperately to get back to him.

He started to sprint, his feet flailing helplessly in the dark as he tried to hurtle forward. He felt himself moving, travelling away from the shore and further into the void, but his wife moved further still, the distance between them getting larger no matter how fast he ran.

Terror consumed him and he screamed into the emptiness, a pained, angry scream that was swallowed by the void and kept the darkness around him silent and complete. He screamed again, thrashing at the air helplessly while still sprinting forward.

Inside his chest he felt his lungs beginning to burst and his vocal chords were tearing as every ounce of his body strained with effort. But no matter how hard he tried to save her, she continued to get further and further away, before finally she disappeared completely into the dark.

Mark sat perfectly still, listening to the silence that lay heavy throughout the house. Outside the sun had set, leaving the sky a jet black and the garden outside in deathly shadow. A fence panel lay flat on its side. Bear had hurled himself into it the day before, battering it down and sprinting off into the town beyond. Mark hadn't bothered to look for him.

The bundle lay still in his arms, unmoving beneath a woollen blanket. Abby had started coughing only a few days ago, but the disease had moved through her quickly. Mark had sat with her in his arms until the end and hadn't moved since she had stopped breathing a few hours ago. He had no reason to. Claire had died only the day before.

Outside the front door he heard a dog barking wildly as it sprinted past. He wondered for a moment if it could be Bear, but didn't get up to check. Abby was still warm and if he tried hard enough he could pretend she was just asleep.

It was another few hours before he could no longer pretend. Her body was now cold and slowly Mark stood up with her still held in his arms and took her outside. Two mounds of dirt lay in the corner of the garden, one slightly fresher than the other. Carefully he placed Abby down by one of the flowerbeds and picked up the spade that was leaning on the fence.

For a while, he worked on autopilot, his body going through motions while his mind was elsewhere. He had no idea how long he had been digging for, but suddenly he was looking at a deep hole in the ground, his shirt stuck to his back by his cold sweat. He thought his face had been sweating too, but he realised he had been crying.

He walked over to the bundle by the flowerbeds, shivering at how cold it felt, and walked Abby over to the hole in the ground. He kissed her lightly on the forehead before placing her in her grave. He started crying again as he buried her.

Once he was finished he looked up at the dark night sky, at the black clouds chasing each other endlessly. Around him the town was still and silent, the stench of death hanging thick and heavy above the empty buildings. The loneliness was like nothing he had ever felt before and he buried his face in his hands as he fell to his knees. He wept loudly for the rest of the night, crying uncontrollably next to the three mounds of earth that marked where all their lives had ended.

Chapter 21

Mark woke with a start, his breathing coming thick and fast. He sat up and looked in panic at the darkness around him. Slowly his eyes adjusted to the gloom cast from the dying embers of the fire and bookshelves started to appear, all of them identical apart from their varying states of decay.

He looked to his left and saw Jake lying on the floor, still curled up into a tight little ball under the blanket in which he slept. Gradually Mark felt his breathing return to normal and his panic began to recede. A thought occurred to him and he quickly checked to see if he had woken up Rae, but she was nowhere to be seen.

He pulled back his blanket and stood up from his makeshift bed on the floor, knowing that now he was up he wouldn't be able to go back to sleep. He took one last look around the camp before starting to make his way through the maze of bookshelves.

It had been the first dream he had had in years, he thought, as he rubbed the tiredness from his face, since before he had found Jake even. Usually when Mark slept it was through complete exhaustion, and he would fall into a black pit of nothingness until he was torn back to reality by the slightest movement or sound. It was one of the very few things other than Jake that he found himself grateful for.

He came up to a junction in the bookshelves and paused before turning right. If he had remembered correctly, then in a moment he should come out into the seating area on the large, open balcony that looked down over the ground floor.

It was probably the conversation from last night, he reflected, as he felt his way through the dark. Some of Rae's questions had stirred up memories that he hadn't thought about for years and, even though it had just been for a fleeting moment, the memories had brought with them a whole host of emotions that he had tried so hard to bury.

Sometimes the memories still came to him – he guessed it was impossible for them not to – but his mind kicked in the moment they emerged and suppressed them almost instantaneously. Sometimes he felt guilty for blocking out his past, especially the memory of his family, but he couldn't bring himself to think about them too often. He was scared about what might happen if he relived the pain of losing them.

He had also never told Jake about his family, or about certain other things from his former life; not even a hint that they had ever existed. It would only serve to confuse him, Mark had reasoned, and Jake was confused enough.

He emerged from out of the bookcases and onto the landing that hung over the ground floor. The rest of the library stretched out ahead of him, the still, cold air hanging thick with frost. High windows stared darkly back at him from below the ceiling, allowing only a murky haze of light into the abandoned building. It was just enough to see a few feet in front of him and allowed him to avoid tripping on the carpet of rotting books beneath his feet, but the far side of the building was still shrouded in darkness.

As he approached the railing of the balcony that looked out over the ground floor, he sensed something move in front of him and he froze to squint into the dark.

"Couldn't sleep?"

The sound made him jump, but he quickly recognised Rae's dry, cracked voice. He sighed with relief and continued towards the wooden banister. As he got closer, he saw Rae's silhouetted figure appear to his left, one arm leaning on the banister as she turned back away from him. Mark joined her and rested his arms on top of the rail.

"Yeah," he replied quietly. His voice was swallowed up by the vacuum in front of him, as if he were back in the dream. The likeness made him shudder.

"Me neither," she replied.

For a while, they stood in silence, both lost in their own thoughts that had been conjured up from the night before. Rae had gone on to tell Mark how she had been married to her husband for almost twenty years and that they had managed to stay alive by moving from town to town and scavenging what they could. She had told him how she had loved her husband, and that she doubted if she would have been able to cope with losing everyone else that she loved if it hadn't been for him.

She had also told Mark how the men that were now hunting them had captured him. How they had taken him back to their camp before torturing him and slowly beating him to death.

"So what's our first move?" Mark asked. Beside him Rae stirred from her thoughts.

"Do you know where their camp is?" she asked.

"No," he replied. "That's what we were looking for yesterday."

Rae nodded slowly, her face unreadable in the dark.

"Then that's where we go," she said decidedly. "You need to see what we're up against. If we're lucky, then most of them will be out searching for you two, which means that they'll only leave one or two behind to guard the tents. Fortunately I know a place in town where you can see straight into the camp, so I reckon we go there to see how many they've left behind and then decide what to do."

Mark nodded. A tingle of nervousness had started creeping up his spine.

Six of them left. If they did leave one or two to guard the camp, then they could lower that number to four by the end of the day.

Mark wanted this ordeal to be over as quickly as possible, for the group to disappear, so he and Jake could return home and continue to survive as they had always done; but now that he knew they wouldn't leave of their own accord, especially after he had led four of the group to their deaths, he would have to force them to go.

Mark was more than aware that that would probably mean having to kill every last one of them.

The light that came through the windows began to brighten as he tried to prepare himself for the task that lay ahead, unveiling the gloomy shadows of the broken tables and stands below.

Mark looked down at the carnage and tried to remember what the library had looked like before it had fallen into disrepair; back when the tables were full of studying students and avid readers, and the stands were stacked with the latest best sellers.

But the memory was too weak. All he could see was a graveyard.

He turned to face Rae with a grimace as a jolt of pain shot through his shoulder.

"We'll go after Jake gets up," he said hoarsely. "I want to let him sleep a bit longer. He's still in shock from yesterday and he needs to rest."

Rae turned sharply to look at him, wearing a puzzled expression.

"You want to take Jake?" she asked in astonishment.

"After what happened yesterday?" Mark felt himself bristle.

"I'm not leaving him," he said firmly, fixing her with a defiant stare. Rae looked back in bewilderment, struggling to understand his reasoning.

"He'll be safe here," she replied slowly. "They don't know about this place. They don't even know that I exist. If we were at your camp, then I would agree with you, because they know it's there and they'll be searching everywhere for it, but here...they won't be looking here, and Jake will be far safer here than in the middle of their campsite."

Mark stared back at her with a fiery expression, annoyed that she had challenged him on what was best for Jake – but begrudgingly he knew that she was right.

The men didn't know about this place and taking Jake into the middle of their camp was extremely risky. Mark just didn't want to leave him on his own, not after yesterday. Jake wouldn't like it either, he hated being in town at the best of times, but Mark would never forgive himself if they took him with them to the camp and something terrible happened.

He turned away from Rae and looked out towards the other side of the building, the light now strong enough to reveal the far wall. He had to do what was best for Jake, and the more he thought about it the clearer the answer became.

"OK," he said slowly, hanging his head in resignation.

"We'll leave Jake here."

Chapter 22

The weak sun drifted through the high-vaulted windows of the library, doing little to warm the frosty air that filled the room. Motes of dust swam lazily in the shafts of sunlight, blown around by the draughts of wind that whistled through the building. On the upper floor Jake ambled through the forgotten aisles, coat hugged tightly around him against the cold as he scanned the titles of book after book.

He was alone. Mark and Rae had gone in search of the men's camp soon after he had awoken.

At first, Jake had begun to panic at the prospect of being left on his own again, but Mark had explained to him that it was far safer if he waited in the library for them to return. The men wouldn't be looking for them here, he had explained, and the Hunters couldn't get in either because the windows were too far from the ground.

Jake had agreed to stay behind then, even though he still didn't want to. He was worried about what might happen to his dad if he went to camp, but as the day had worn on he had become more relaxed and eventually he'd decided he would set out to explore the ancient library.

Since then he had seen more books than he ever knew existed and was busy exploring every aisle to see what wonders they contained.

His footsteps echoed softly around the library's high walls as he moved between the bookshelves, but Jake barely registered the sound as he lost himself in the endless blurbs and titles. He stopped and picked up a book from the floor that was still mostly intact, wiping the thick layer of dust from the cover to reveal the fading picture beneath.

The image was of lots of buildings which were all brightly lit and had hundreds of people milling about beneath them. Jake's eyes grew wide with wonder as he meticulously studied the picture and he wondered if he could see his dad in the crowds at the bottom of the buildings, but the picture was too faded to make out any of the people's faces, and eventually he returned the book to the floor before carrying on down the aisle.

Down the next row Jake's mind begin to drift away from the books in front of him, and he found himself wondering if Dad had found the group's camp yet, and when Rae and he would get back to the library.

Jake had enjoyed the meal the three of them had had last night and he had tried desperately to stay awake so he could continue to watch their new friend. But exhaustion had eventually got the better of him and in the end he couldn't stop himself from drifting off to sleep. He decided that tonight he would make sure that he stayed awake so he could talk more to Rae.

At the end of the aisle, he emerged at the top of a staircase that led down to the floor below. The wooden stairs creaked heavily with every step as he descended and he felt a tingle of excitement race up his spine when he looked out over the large expanse that he was still yet to explore.

He would try to find a new book to read, he decided, as he ran his eyes across the heaps of books that littered the floor. One he hadn't read before so he could tell Dad all about it once he was finished.

With his newfound ambition Jake set off in search of the book, rummaging through the dusty piles for something that caught his eye, but the books down here didn't have any pictures on their front and he found himself struggling to read words he had never seen before in their complicated titles.

He was about to give up and head off to the bookshelves when a picture suddenly flashed up at him from the dull, lifeless pile.

The picture was of a woman; a pretty woman staring lovingly down at a small baby which she cradled in her arms. Jake picked up the book and ran his hand gently across her face, feeling sadness well up inside of him.

It was a shame that Rae wasn't his mother, he thought suddenly. The thought caught him off guard and only added to the strange feeling that was building in his stomach.

Of course Jake had known that she wasn't, even before he had asked her, but part of him still wanted to believe that one day he would get to meet his mother. But how could he meet someone if they were dead? In some of the books, he had read it said that you got to meet people who had died when you died too. Did that mean the only way that he would get to meet his mother was if he died as well?

Jake hadn't thought about it before and he wasn't sure if he liked the idea of having to die to see his mother. For a brief moment, he considered asking his dad about it when he got back, but he quickly decided against it. Dad wouldn't like it if he asked about his mother again, and he definitely wouldn't like Jake talking about dying.

Jake put the book back on top of the pile from which he had found it and continued to explore the silent graveyard, trying to put the thought of his mother out of his mind.

He looked around him, wondering where he should go next. There was so much to see and for a minute he just stood turning on the spot, admiring his surroundings. He looked towards the library's entrance and tried to imagine what it would look like with people coming and going. He felt himself smile at the daydream, but his attention was brought crashing back to the present by a loud bang.

Jake spun around and froze, his concentration fixed on the back of the library. The space ahead of him was dark and foreboding, the floor cast in shadow by the balcony above.

He was sure that the sound had come from that direction and now he could see clouds of dust whirring energetically in the air that hadn't been there before, as if the dust was suddenly awake after a long and peaceful sleep. Everything else was still; the bookshelves standing tall and silent while they rotted in the shadows.

Jake pricked up his ears, straining to hear any sign of what had caused the bang, but the library had fallen silent except for the skittering of paper that was being blown across the floor.

He shivered: an involuntarily spasm that ran from the top of his head to the tips of his toes. Something wasn't right, and he realised his hand had moved instinctively to his pocket; his fingers sliding in and closing around the cold, hard metal within.

Dad had given him his gun back before he'd left, freshly reloaded with some bullets that Rae had given him. He had said that he wouldn't need to use it, that it was just to make him feel safer, but now, as he stared into the darkness at the back of the building, Jake thought that he might need to use his gun after all.

He started to back towards the stairs, the books on the floor cushioning his footsteps, while he watched for any signs of movement from the shadows. He reached the bottom of the staircase without incident and put his foot carefully up onto the first step. He winced as the loud creaking of the wood filled the silent building.

He waited, his face scrunching up with anxiety and his breathing intensifying. Please be nothing, he begged. Please just be an old bookshelf finally collapsing to the ground. Still nothing moved in the darkness ahead of him. The silence in the library was complete.

He felt his breathing slow again and his hand moved away from the gun in his pocket as his nerves settled.

It was nothing, he reassured himself as he started back up the stairs. He was just being paranoid.

The loud groaning of the wood filled the library again and Jake listened as the sound echoed back from the corners of the building. He was about halfway up the staircase when he heard something else join the creaking. His foot stopped in mid-air before he could climb any further.

The creaking stopped instantly and in its place came a low, menacing growl that sent shivers racing up his spine. Slowly Jake turned towards the darkness underneath the balcony and felt his hands start to shake as the growling got closer.

He quickly backed up the stairs, wincing with every creak that now sounded deafening. The growling grew steadily louder and Jake felt himself beginning to panic.

He reached the top of the stairs and dived behind the banister next to him, turning to peek nervously through the gaps in the wooden slats. The floor below was still unmoving. As Jake waited, he felt the hairs on the back of his neck begin to prickle one by one.

Suddenly one of the shadows began to move.

A large shape emerged from the darkness, followed closely by a cloud of dust that had been kicked up in its wake. The shape had appeared from between two bookshelves and as it stalked slowly into the light Jake recognised the unmistakeably grey fur of a Hunter. Its tail thrashed lazily behind it, making the dust swirl in turbulent eddies as it advanced across the floor. As it approached the centre of the room, the Hunter's head began to swivel from side to side, scanning the room for any signs of life.

Jake swallowed and returned his hand to his pocket. Slowly he pulled out his gun, squeezing the grip tightly in his shaking hand. On the floor below him the Hunter had tilted its head back and begun to sniff the stale library air. Jake saw the wagging of its tail become more feverish with every sniff.

He had to hide, Jake thought quickly. Hide until Dad came back.

He tore his eyes away from the Hunter and searched around him frantically for a hiding place. Empty bookcases stared back at him; the gaps between the fallen shelves had left large gaps which could be seen straight through.

He turned and looked towards the maze which hid Rae's camp. It would be easy to hide in there, but would he be able to reach it without alerting the Hunter? He shuddered at the thought of being followed into the maze. He didn't want to be trapped in there with a Hunter chasing him.

Quickly he scanned the rest of his surroundings, feeling more and more despairing as he realised there was nowhere he could hide. He glanced back down at the Hunter and saw it rummaging its muzzle through the pile of books he had been searching through only moments earlier.

Tears began to build up behind Jake's eyes and he was forced to fight off his sudden urge to curl up into a ball and cry.

Come on, Jake, he scolded himself, desperately trying to muster up the courage he needed to find a way out. Dad wouldn't give up if he were here. He took a desperate last look around him again.

There!

The fire exit they had used to get in.

Jake felt a surge of hope sprout in his chest, momentarily relieving the tightness in his stomach. The door wasn't too far away from where he was and he could probably reach it without drawing the Hunter's attention. Once he was outside it wouldn't be able to find him and he could wait safely for Mark and Rae to return.

He took a deep breath, preparing himself for the short dash across to the door, but as he was about to make his move he hesitated.

Dad had told him that under no circumstances was he to leave the library. He had said that if anything went wrong then Jake should hide and wait for him to get back – but surely this was different. Dad had no idea that a Hunter could get into the library, and Jake had no idea how long it would be until he would return.

He looked back up at the door, unsure of what he should do.

He would just wait outside. If he stayed at the top of the staircase that led up to the fire exit, then he would still be safe. He gritted his teeth, feeling determined once more, when suddenly he felt another shiver crawl down his spine and his mustered courage suddenly vanished.

For a moment, he held his breath and something in the back of his mind told him that he shouldn't move. Slowly, he turned his head to look back at the floor below.

The Hunter was looking straight at him.

Jake whimpered and could do nothing to stop his entire body from trembling as he stared into the Hunter's piercing eyes. Its tail had stopped wagging and was now poised high above a bristling, grey body which had slunk low to the floor as it prepared to propel itself forwards. But what terrified Jake the most was its face, which had slid slowly back to reveal two rows of jagged, bloodstained teeth.

Jake wanted desperately to cry. He wanted to lie down and cry his eyes out. He wanted his dad to be there; to take him away from the Hunter and back to their house where it was safe.

But he couldn't. He couldn't do anything. Instead, he was locked in place by the Hunter's gaze. Completely paralysed by fear.

Then it moved.

The Hunter darted to its right, heading straight for the staircase that led up to him.

Jake screamed and found suddenly that he was running; sprinting madly for the door that led out of the library.

He heard loud creaking as the Hunter tore up the stairs, its claws ripping into rotten wood.

Jake didn't look back. In his chest, he heard his lungs screaming for air, but he forced himself to keep running. He had to make it outside. He would be safe if he just made it outside. Behind him he heard the Hunter's claws scratching angrily on the floor.

He reached the fire exit and wrenched it open, struggling with the door's heavy weight. Daylight streamed into the library, the bright light making him squint, and he lunged through the small gap in front of him and onto the metal railing outside.

A strong breeze hit him in the face, the air somehow warmer than inside the building, but he had no time to enjoy the sensation and immediately he heard something heavy smash into the gap behind him.

Jake spun around and found himself face-to-face with the snarling Hunter. The beast's head was jammed in the doorway, its teeth gnashing viciously as it tried to pull itself through the gap.

Jake screamed, to try and block out its snarling more than anything else, and brought up his hands quickly, the gun gripped tightly between them aiming straight at its mouth.

He pulled back hard on the trigger and almost dropped the gun in fright as he jumped at the deafening sound that pounded against his ear drums. The gun kicked back like a mule and Jake's hand went with it, causing him to cry out as pain lanced up his wrist.

In the doorway, the Hunter yelped and jerked its head back sharply when the bullet hit home. With the obstruction now gone the heavy door was free to swing shut and the sound of the lock clicking into place could just be heard before the Hunter slammed its body against the other side.

For a moment, Jake stood still, his eyes fixed on the fire exit. Then it slammed into the door again and he saw the surface dent.

Quickly he turned and began leaping down the stairs, his feet pounding against the rusting metal. Once he reached the ground he started running. He ran across the street, into the nearest house and out into the garden on the other side

He kept running, the long grass whipping at his coat as he sprinted through the overgrown lawns, too terrified to look back and see if the Hunter was following. His legs screamed in pain and his wrist was throbbing from where the gun had bent it back, but still he kept running, urged on by the fear that had taken control of his body.

He ran through another garden and into the back of a house, slamming the door shut behind him and running up the set of stairs he found in the hallway. He ran into the first bedroom he saw and slammed that door shut too, his vision a blur as his eyes filled up with tears.

In the corner of the room stood a double bed and Jake threw himself under it, dropping the gun next to him as he curled up into a ball. A lump formed in the back of his throat and his cheeks were wet where tears were streaming down them.

He had no idea where he was, he realised suddenly. The Hunter was still out there and he had absolutely no idea where he was. How was he going to get back to the library? How was he going to warn Dad that it was no longer safe in there?

Deep sobs racked his body as the hopelessness of his situation sunk in. He wrapped his arms tightly around himself and cried helplessly on the floor.

He was lost. Lost in a town full of nightmares and with no idea how to get back home. For the first time in his very short life, Jake was completely and utterly alone.

Chapter 23

It had taken them an hour to reach the block of flats that stood near the edge of town. They had moved quickly and quietly, neither of them uttering a word as they stalked through the abandoned streets.

Along the way Mark found himself looking at buildings and landmarks that he hadn't seen for over a decade, and was shocked at how unrecognisable they had become over the years. Those that hadn't completely collapsed into ruin were well on their way to doing so and all of them had been reclaimed by Mother Nature, the bricks and mortar buried deep beneath a thick shell of vegetation.

He doubted he would have been able to navigate his way through this part of town, such was the change in the landscape, but Rae seemed to know exactly where she was going and took barely any notice of the memorials around her.

They finally stopped when they reached the entrance to the flats. Rae turned to face him – he realised it was the first time she had acknowledged him since they had left the library – and pointed towards the upper storeys of the building. He looked up at the shattered windows above them, then nodded back to her to show that he understood.

The heavy security door that had once marked the entrance to the flats was nowhere to be seen, allowing them to step out of the watery daylight and into the murky gloom of the building.

The interior was almost completely concrete and their footsteps echoed ominously off the walls as they made their way up the winding stairs. Cracks covered every surface around them, all of which were overflowing with weeds and grasses, and where graffiti had once stained the walls there was now a thick layer of moss and lichen.

At the top of the stairs, they came out onto another concrete landing that was just as run down and overgrown as the ones they had seen on their way up.

Rae headed for the door that was directly in front of her, taking no notice of her surroundings, and entered the apartment behind it.

Once inside she walked down a narrow hallway and into a small living area, heading straight for the large window that dominated the far side of the room.

Mark followed, glancing quickly around him at the decaying apartment. He could tell this wasn't the first time that Rae had come here.

He joined her by the window and looked out over the buildings below.

The tops of the houses glittered white with frost, which was slowly receding as they bathed in the winter sun, and were separated by thin lines where paths ran between them. Several streets away from them the rooftops suddenly ended, replaced instead by the thick trunks of the conifer trees where the forest began.

"Do you see it?" The sound of Rae's voice almost startled him. He returned his attention to the trees and squinted to see any sign of the camp.

"No," he replied, with a shake of his head. In the distance, the trees stared emptily back at him.

Next to him Rae took off her backpack and took out a small pair of binoculars from its front pocket. She raised them to her eyes and pointed them towards the forest, adjusting the focus while she concentrated on a single point. Mark waited patiently, trying to work out where she was looking.

"Here," she said suddenly, handing the binoculars over to him. "Look at the trees straight ahead of you, so that the road is off to your right. Then follow the trees to the left and keep going until you see it."

He obeyed, finding the start of the trees and dragging his vision to the left. The wavy branches and dark, thick trunks flashed by, the interior of the forest almost impenetrable despite the daylight.

He stopped when a flash of white caught his eye, and it took him a moment to realise that he was looking at the side of a tent. He scanned further to the left and more tents sprang into view. He adjusted the focus and suddenly he could see the entire camp at the end of the binoculars.

"I see it," he said solemnly.

He counted around ten tents, some strung up between the trees and others pitched up and pegged to the ground. They were arranged in a jagged circle, all facing inwards towards a large circle of chairs and a large pile that at night must house a fire.

"They set up camp there when they first arrived and haven't moved since. Just out of town, they have three trucks parked up at the side of the road. That's how they move from place to place. Siphon off petrol from abandoned cars and load it into the trucks. The roads are still quite driveable."

Mark nodded, only half listening to what she was saying. His attention was mainly focused on the bundle of tents he could see through the binoculars.

As far as he could see, there was no fencing or walls around the campsite and it appeared that no attempt had been made to adopt any form of camouflage. Instead the camp sat in stark contrast with the forest around it, an obvious eyesore in the landscape.

Good, Mark thought to himself. They clearly weren't expecting anyone to try and attack them.

"Can you see any of them?" Rae asked.

"No," he replied. On the other side of the binoculars the camp lay still, the only movement coming from the gentle flapping of the tents in the breeze. Next to him Rae sniffed.

"Wait!" he said suddenly. He could have sworn he had seen something move to his left.

He shifted his gaze and focused on what had caught his attention. Emerging from the tree he could see a man strolling casually into the campsite.

The man looked skinny, and Mark did a double take at the sight of his left arm, which appeared to end abruptly above the elbow. Mark certainly didn't recognise him as one of the men that he had already seen.

He watched as the man reached the centre of the camp and sat heavily down in one of the chairs. Mark let out a low sigh; he hadn't realised he had been holding his breath.

"I can only see one of them," he said, handing the binoculars back to Rae so that she could look. "He's sitting in one of the chairs in the middle. The others must be out searching for us."

A spike of panic cut through his body as the thought of Jake, alone in the library, rose in his mind, but he quickly suppressed it and tried to refocus his attention on the task ahead.

"Perfect," Rae replied, a cruel smile playing over her lips as she fixed the one-armed man at the end of the binoculars in her sight. She lowered the binoculars and returned them to her backpack, which she then slung over her shoulder as she made for the hallway.

"Come on," she said, as she re-entered the stairwell. "We don't know when the others will be back."

Mark followed and together they quickly descended the concrete stairs and walked back out onto the road. Rae turned right and headed down a dark, narrow alley that acted as a cut through to the next street.

Mark followed close behind, feeling the adrenalin rush already as he prepared himself for what would happen when they reached the camp. He tried to use the rush to stave off his anxiety, which was slowly building as the thought of Jake alone in the library continued to plague his mind.

Half an hour later the houses around them became sparser and the pace with which they were moving began to slow instinctively. Mark could sense that they were getting close to the camp. Ahead of them he could now see the forest, which loomed menacingly over the last few, crumbling houses of the town; the imposing treetops casting the tired buildings into shadow.

Mark looked for any sign of tents at the edge of the forest, but so far all he could see were trees. Rae turned back to face him and pointed to a row of houses ahead of them that were slightly to their left. Mark felt his mouth dry out and his heart rate quicken.

The camp was just on the other side.

They headed for the small row of houses, concentrating on keeping their footsteps quiet, and snuck through an alleyway that was situated in the middle of the row. Behind the houses sat a row of gardens and they climbed silently into the one on their right.

The overgrown vegetation provided perfect cover and they stalked through the miniature jungle, hunkering down behind a bush when they reached the foot of the garden. Mark peered out from between the leaves, being careful not to rustle them, and felt his heart jump.

Ahead of them lay a stretch of barren land, a clear border between where the town ended and the forest began. It also formed a path that led straight to the campsite that was scattered messily amongst the trees in front of him.

He took a moment to compose himself.

"So how are we doing this?" he whispered, looking for any sign of movement from within the tents.

"I'll go in from that side," Rae said, indicating the leftmost tent. "And you go in from the other. That way if he spots one of us then the other can sneak up on him from behind."

Mark nodded in agreement. He could feel a sense of nausea creeping into his throat, but he forced it down and focused on where he had to go. He wanted to get this over with.

"You ready?" he asked, his legs poised and ready to move. Next to him Rae nodded slowly, her hand moving to grip the handle of her knife.

"Go," she said quickly, and disappeared around the bush.

Mark moved too, keeping low and moving quickly over the small shrubs that littered the stretch of no man's land. His eyes were fixed on the camp, looking for any sign of movement, but he could see nothing and he quickly cleared the open space and entered the forest. He moved up to the outermost tent on the right hand side and crouched down behind it, straining his ears to listen for anyone moving.

The camp was quiet and he had now lost sight of Rae. Quickly Mark darted to the next tent, his footsteps silent as they ghosted across the forest floor. Behind the second tent he stopped again and listened, but the camp was still eerily silent. The only thing he could hear was his blood thudding in his ears.

He risked a peek around the corner of the tent and saw the one-armed man he had seen through the binoculars sitting in one of the chairs at the Camp's centre. Something moved to his left and Mark turned to see Rae crouched down by one of the trees.

She had noticed him too and, whilst looking across at him, put her hands together and rested them on the side of her head.

Mark stared back in bewilderment, completely confused by the gesture. He held up his hands to show that he hadn't understood.

Rae pointed towards the man, who was still sitting quietly in the chair, and this time Mark looked more closely at the motionless body, at the steady rise and fall of its chest. He quickly stifled his surprise and nodded back at Rae to show that he now understood. Mark could hardly believe their luck. The man was fast asleep.

They crept out from behind the tents and were met instantly by the sound of gentle snoring. Mark visibly relaxed, his shoulders slightly slumping as he turned to look at the camp around him. In contrast, Rae seemed to have become tenser; a serious expression was fixed firmly on her face and she was staring daggers at the man asleep in the chair.

"Tie him up."

Rae's whispering caught Mark off guard and he was even more surprised when he found himself catching a coil of rope that had been thrown towards him.

He looked down at the frayed length of rope, running the cord through his hands before shooting a puzzled look at Rae, but she took no notice of his reaction and was already walking slowly towards the occupied chair.

Her next move left him even more bewildered.

Rae rounded the chair in which the man was sleeping so that she was standing in front of him. Then she drew back a hand and slapped him hard across the face, pulling something around his mouth at the same time.

The man awoke instantly, sitting up sharply and staring at her in surprise. His right arm grabbed at the arm of his chair and he tensed as he prepared to throw himself towards her, but stopped when he saw the glint of the gun barrel pointing towards him.

"Don't move," Rae demanded fiercely, pushing the gun into his forehead and making him squirm.

He replied with a strange muffling sound and Mark realised that she must have wrapped duct tape around his mouth when she had struck him.

For a moment, nothing happened and with a start Mark understood what Rae was waiting for. He quickly moved forward and crouched down behind the chair to tie the man's legs together. He then went to do the same for the hands, but did another double take when he could only find one.

He remembered what he had seen through the binoculars, the left arm ending just above the elbow, and for a moment found himself dumbfounded as to what to do next. He settled on tying his one whole arm to the back of the chair, making sure there was no way it could come loose.

When Mark was finished, he stepped back and looked at Rae for their next move. Her actions so far had taken him completely by surprise. He hadn't realised that she had wanted to interrogate him.

Rae stared down at the one-armed man over the end of her gun, her face beginning to twist and contort as her eyes bored into him. The man stared back, his breathing coming in short bursts through his nose as he tried to read the face of his captor. Mark walked off to the side of the chair, standing back to watch the silent confrontation. An uneasy feeling started to build in his stomach.

Suddenly Rae moved; to Mark's astonishment she dropped the gun, the pistol landing at her feet with a gentle thud. The man looked down at the weapon, he, too, confused by the action, but his eyes widened quickly with terror when he looked back up. Mark hadn't seen where Rae had drawn the knife from, but he could see it now as it sliced through the air, landing with a sickening thud in the man's left thigh.

Screaming came from behind the duct tape and the man's eyes nearly popped from his skull. Rae let go of the knife, leaving the blade stuck in his leg while his muscle twitched and spasmed. Mark looked on in horror, unsure of how he should react.

Rae spat on the man in front of her, grabbing hold of the knife again and twisting it viciously before wrenching it out. The man howled with pain beneath the duct tape, the sound only reaching the outside world as desperate, muffled grunts. She held the knife to his chest and he whimpered, shaking his head as tears started to flow freely from his eyes.

But she did not relent.

Instead she grabbed a fistful of his coat with her free hand and cut the fabric with her knife as he continued to whimper. Once the skin beneath was exposed she slashed the blade hard across his chest. A thin, angry line appeared on his skin that began weeping with blood.

Mark's eyes continued to widen as he watched the violence unfold, unsure of whether he should intervene; but the look on Rae's face told him to stay well away from her. He winced as she began pummelling the man's chest and face with her fists.

The beating continued for an entire minute and when Rae finally stopped she was panting heavily, blood flowing freely from her knuckles. In front of her, the man was dipping in and out of consciousness, his face now covered in a mass of blood. It was completely unrecognisable as the face Mark had seen only moments before.

Rae moved one of her hands forward again and Mark winced as he waited for the next blow to fall, but instead she grabbed a corner of the duct tape at the man's mouth and tore it away.

Mark expected to hear him scream, but instead a fountain of blood spewed out from his mouth when the duct tape was removed and several teeth fell into his lap as his head slumped forward. Mark felt like he was going to be sick.

Rae put her hand under the man's chin and pulled up his head so that he was looking at her. One of his eyes was barely visible beneath an already swollen mass of purple and the other struggled to focus on her stony expression. Her lifeless eyes stared fiercely back into his.

"That's for my husband," she said coldly.

She let go of his chin and the man's head slumped back down to his chest. Rae rolled up his sleeve, then picked up her knife from where she had dropped it on the floor and held it to his one good arm, which was still bound tightly to the chair. She pressed the metal firmly into his skin, then sliced the blade quickly across his thin, pale wrist. The skin turned a deep crimson as blood began spurting out.

She turned her eyes back to the man's face and watched calmly as his life slowly drained away.

It took them half an hour to search the rest of the camp. They raided each of the tents, taking whatever weapons, ammunition and supplies that they could find. By the time they had finished, Mark's backpack was almost bursting and he could feel the weight pressing down uncomfortably on his wounded shoulder as he walked to the forest's edge.

The trip had been a success; they now had one less member of the group to deal with and they had gained munitions in the process, but anxiety still gnawed tirelessly at the back of Mark's mind and all he felt was a desire to get back to the library as quickly as possible to see if Jake was OK.

Ahead of him he saw Rae sitting at the edge of the forest. She had her back to him and was staring out towards the derelict houses. When Mark reached her, he stopped and stood beside her.

"You OK?" he asked quietly. For a while, Rae didn't move and Mark wondered if she had heard him.

"I'm sorry you had to see that," she said eventually, her eyes still staring straight ahead. Mark waited for her to continue.

"It's fine," he said after a while, shifting uncomfortably in the awkward silence.

"I can't stop thinking about what they did to him," she said, her voice shaking almost imperceptibly. "I've seen what they do. To the ones they bring back."

Her voice trailed off as she lost herself in her thoughts. Mark opened his mouth to say something, something reassuring or that would bring her some comfort, but he closed his mouth again when he realised there were no such words.

"Come on," she said, standing up quickly and turning to face him. Her eyes were red and her cheeks were slightly wet from where a few stray tears had escaped.

She turned back to the town and started walking towards the first of the houses.

"That Jake of yours will be wondering where we are."

Chapter 24

Gabe stood on the edge of the cliff, watching the tops of the trees far below him as they swayed precariously in the breeze. Above him the sunlight broke through the dark, grey clouds which clung to the tops of the derelict skyscrapers in the town's centre, striking his face and brightening up the tree tops below. The sudden warmth made his blood boil.

Four of his men were dead. The realisation was yet to hit him.

It wasn't that Gabe hadn't lost men before – it was impossible not to in a world such as this – but never had he lost so many in such a short space of time, and never had it been to the hands of just one man.

A surge of anger began to build within his stomach, causing him to grind his teeth together. His gaze turned cold and defiant as it locked onto the town beyond the trees.

He would find them, he affirmed to himself as he turned his back on the view. He would find them.

He started to walk back to the abandoned fire pit, the sun disappearing behind the thick branches of the trees as he entered the forest. Ahead of him he saw Jack crouched over the blackened patch of ground, running his eyes over the floor around him in search of any kind of trail.

They had left their camp as soon as it was light and headed back to where they had been searching the day before. Paul, Daniel and Cal had gone into town to find the place where the others had been slaughtered and would search the area for any sign of the elusive father and son. Gabe doubted that the search party would find anything useful – the father and son would have got as far away as they could from the trap they had sprung – but in the chaos of the Hunter attack they might have left something behind that hinted at where they were hiding.

"Nothing."

Jack's voice brought Gabe back to the forest. He had stood up from the floor and was looking at the trees around them helplessly. Gabe joined him in surveying their surroundings.

He knew that they wouldn't find them anywhere near this place, most likely having abandoned it after their confrontation with Jack, but they couldn't have picked up their entire camp and taken it with them. It must still be around here somewhere; cleverly hidden amongst the trees. He was just missing something.

"Let's take a look around," Gabe said, heading off through the trees to his left. Jack shrugged and set off in the opposite direction, and as he disappeared into the forest Gabe felt himself relax. He had wanted some time alone.

The forest around him was deathly quiet and his footsteps crunched on a hard layer of frost as he stalked between the trees. His eyes swam from side to side as they scanned his surroundings, looking for any sign of a hidden entrance that they might have missed, or an oddly shaped bush that might prove to be something more, but nothing seemed out of place and eventually he found the events of the previous night creeping into his thoughts.

He felt his blood rush through his veins as the image of Greg's face disintegrating beneath his fists suddenly appeared.

Gabe hadn't meant to kill him. When his rage had eventually subsided and the clarity of his thoughts had returned, he had been genuinely surprised that he had gone as far as to beat Greg to death.

His knuckles were badly cut from the impact of the blows and his hands ached even now, but despite the discomfort Gabe found that he had no regrets about what he'd done.

It had felt good. So good. Better than anything he had felt for a long time.

His anger had been unbelievable and Gabe could still feel the unquenchable pit of rage as it roiled and churned in his stomach, consuming him from within and taking complete control over his body. Each punch had felt better than the last, the violence the only thing that could satisfy his temper.

A warm smile broke across his face as he reflected upon the memory and he felt goose bumps prickle his skin.

But he had been lucky.

Gabe had needed Greg to show the rest of the group where he had been attacked by the Hunters, and if it hadn't been for Paul knowing the whereabouts of the doctor's surgery which Greg had mentioned, then they would have had no idea where the ambush had taken place.

But Paul had known the location of the doctor's surgery, and as a result the only consequences of Greg's death had been positive. The men now feared Gabe more than ever before, and with that fear came a power over the group that meant they would do whatever he said. None of them had even been able to look him in the eye since last night and this morning they had done everything they could to stay out of his way.

Gabe relished the feeling. As long as that fear remained, then so would their obedience.

He stopped walking at the same time as his thoughts ground to a halt. The forest around him had remained unchanged for the duration of his walk and the empowerment which he had felt moments ago began to wane at the prospect of another fruitless search.

He let out a long sigh and tilted back his head, rolling his neck lazily over his shoulders to try and unravel the knots that had formed. The sky looked grey and lifeless through the gaps in the canopy.

What was it that he was missing?

He closed his eyes and felt the cool breeze blow gently over his face. The forest around him was silent and for a moment he felt as if he could have been the last person left on Earth. In the branches above him, a thrush began to sing heartily, the gentle warbling disturbing the quiet and causing him to open his eyes.

He watched as the bird flitted calmly between the trees, hopping from branch to branch before stopping to lift its head and chirp casually into the afternoon. Gabe's face took on a look of disgust and he wondered whether he should reach for his gun and try to shoot it.

It was too far away, he decided, as the bird flitted into the next tree and out of sight. It would just be a waste of bullets.

He was about to head back to the fire pit and search in a different direction when an idea suddenly occurred to him. For a while he stood in silence, turning over the thought in his mind.

Was that what he was missing, he asked himself, as he turned his gaze back towards the canopy? The thrush that had been perched there was nowhere to be seen.

Surely it couldn't be that simple.

Gabe began to scan the canopy around him, searching for any sign of something that looked odd or out of place in the treetops, then he turned and started walking back to the fire pit, stepping clumsily over the blanket of frozen pine needles as he kept his eyes on the branches above. The treetops swayed gently in the afternoon breeze and above them the sky was clearing as the grey clouds began to scuttle away.

It must be, Gabe thought, scanning the treetops frantically. It has to be.

There!

He froze. He had almost missed it, but the quickening of his pulse told him that something had definitely caught his eye. Slowly he turned his gaze back to one of the trees which he had just been looking at.

The base of the tree was thick and barren, with no obvious way of climbing up it, but about halfway up the trunk suddenly exploded into a cluster of branches.

Gabe watched as the branches swayed steadily from side to side and tried to work out what had caught his attention. He tilted his head to the side, trying to take in the tree's movement, and found himself focusing on where the branches began to fan out from the tree trunk.

He suddenly realised what had seemed out of place.

Not all of the branches were moving.

It took his eyes a few moments to adjust to the illusion, but gradually the shape of a small, wooden hut began to appear amidst the waves. The hut was nestled comfortably in the tangle of branches; its dark green exterior blending perfectly with the pine needles.

Gabe could scarcely believe what he was seeing.

Carefully he sneaked up to the base of the tree, afraid to take his eyes away from the treehouse in case he couldn't find it again. He only looked away when he was close enough to touch the bark in front of him and he quickly began to search for a way to climb up to the branches.

He saw the ladder dangling in front of him instantly and swore in disbelief at the thin rope and wooden rungs that camouflaged perfectly with the backdrop of the tree.

"Jack," he shouted loudly over his shoulder, following the ladder with his eyes that ran up the tree trunk and disappeared into the bottom of the hut. "Jack, get over here!"

Through the trees he heard the sound of someone running and Jack suddenly burst into view as he came racing towards him.

"What is it, boss?" he panted, as he reached the base of the tree.

"Here," Gabe said, holding out the ladder in his hand.

Jack looked at the object in confusion and Gabe watched his expression carefully as his eyes followed the ladder up the tree. Surprise broke quickly across his face and he shook his head in disbelief.

"Unbelievable," Jack muttered slowly, turning to look back at Gabe.

"Yes." Gabe nodded his agreement and passed the ladder to him. "Go check it out."

Jack shot him another puzzled look which quickly turned to spitefulness when he understood Gabe's meaning. But he didn't argue. Instead he took hold of the ladder and began climbing up the tree, drawing a cold smile from Gabe who was watching him ascend.

Jack stopped when he reached the top of the ladder and carefully poked his head through the hole that had been cut into the bottom of the hut. When he had decided it was safe, he clambered up through the hole, disappearing momentarily from Gabe's view. A few seconds later his head reappeared.

"All clear," he shouted down to the floor below.

Gabe nodded and stepped onto the first rung of the ladder, unable to stop a sense of excitement from building up inside of him. The camp had to contain one hell of a stockpile if the father had gone to this much effort to keep it from being found.

He reached the top of the ladder and pulled himself onto the hut's wooden floor. He stood up quickly, brushing himself down as he looked around at the tree house eagerly. The excitement disappeared almost as quickly as it had arrived.

In one corner lay two dirty mattresses, a thick layer of blankets thrown messily on top of them. To Gabe's right sat a small pile of cooking pots and tools, nothing that his group didn't already have, and to his left were a few shelves mounted firmly to the wall, each weighed down by their own collection of books.

The rest of the hut was completely empty.

He swore under his breath, the numbness that had settled in his stomach being gradually replaced by anger.

It couldn't be. Where were all their supplies? Where were their weapons? And ammunition? And food?

Gabe swore again, this time louder, the sudden noise making Jack jump next to him and shift uncomfortably on his feet. He picked up one of the cooking pots that lay to his right and threw it across the hut. It thudded against the far wall before dropping silently onto one of the mattresses, but before it had reached the bed Gabe had already kicked out viciously at the pile of utensils by his feet, the loud clattering of the metal drowning out his swearing.

"Where are they?" Gabe screamed, throwing another pot in a fit of rage. "Where the hell is everything?"

To his left Jack rubbed his arm nervously and looked quickly down at the floor. Gabe took a deep breath, trying to control his rising fury.

They must have taken what they had into town with them, he thought as he looked around him again at the empty hut. They had to have moved it into the town somehow.

He stormed over to the mattresses in the corner, kicking off the blankets and looking down at the makeshift beds. There was one double mattress and one single. More than enough room for a third person to sleep comfortably.

He scanned the hut for any sign that a mother had been living with them, or anyone else that could have been helping them, but the empty interior stared tauntingly back at him, giving nothing away. His eyes fixed onto Jack, who was standing pathetically in the corner.

Jack shuddered uncomfortably, sensing Gabe's eyes boring into him. He looked up from the floor, but made sure not to make eye contact.

"Where's your lighter?" Gabe said suddenly.

The sharpness to Gabe's voice made Jack flinch, but his hand quickly reached into his pocket and pulled out a small, metal flip lighter.

"Give it to me," Gabe demanded, and snatched the lighter from Jack's outstretched hand.

He flicked back the lid and sparked a small bright flame that curled and spluttered at the end of his thumb.

His eyes glinted menacingly in the light, then the flame suddenly vanished and his cold eyes locked onto Jack once more.

"Get out," he said coldly.

Jack obeyed immediately and hurried over to the opening in the floor. A moment later he had descended down the ladder, leaving Gabe alone in the hut.

Gabe took a deep breath, watching red dots swirl and eddy behind his eyes as his anger intensified. He had expected so much more from the camp in the woods; had expected a vast stash of weapons and ammunition, of food and supplies that he could bring back to the group and keep them going until the spring. But there was nothing. And he would need to return to the group empty-handed despite all their efforts.

He could already feel his hold over them waning.

This wasn't it, he told himself, fixing his eyes on the bookshelves in the corner. The father and son could not have survived for this long with so little. They had taken their supplies with them when they had vacated the camp, assuming that he and his men would find them if they didn't.

He strode over to the bookshelf in the corner of the hut and ran his eyes over the titles on the book's spines. He didn't recognise any of them, but some of them gave him a childish impression and he realised that the little boy must have read some of these books.

He picked up the one closest to him and began tearing out the pages, dropping the shredded paper onto the floor. Then he held up the lighter to what was left of the book and sparked another flame. The dry paper caught instantly and began curling up under the heat. He tossed the burning book on top of the bookshelf and watched as the fire began to spread through the rest of the collection.

Gabe turned his back on the flames and walked slowly to the opening in the floor to climb back down the ladder. As he descended, he saw the other shelves burst into flame before they disappeared from his view. When he reached the ground, he handed the lighter back to Jack and took a few steps away from the tree.

Through the small window in the side of the treehouse he could see the orange glow of flames as they licked the insides of the walls and dark smoke began belching from the roof in a thick black plume.

Gabe watched coldly from the forest floor as the flames burst through the collapsing walls of the hut; engulfing the branches and turning what was once Mark and Jake's home into a giant torch blazing in the trees.

Chapter 25

It took them about half an hour to get back to the library; the oppressive grey concrete of the building's walls dominating the townscape around it. Mark was shocked by how little time it had taken them – he hadn't realised how close they were to the group's camp – and as the building came into sight he felt his stomach start to twist as he searched for any sign that the library had been broken into.

The large door at the front entrance was still intact, the wooden panels no more damaged than when they had left, and as Mark got closer he found himself straining to hear anything from inside the building. His ears were met with a comforting silence and gradually he began to relax.

Ever since they had left the camp he had been fearing the worst. No matter how hard he tried to ignore them, Mark couldn't help but entertain the thoughts that Jake may have been found in the library, or that a Hunter would have somehow got into the building.

Rae must have sensed his anxiety, as she had quickened her pace for the return journey. It meant that as the library had come into view the sun was still hanging precariously in the distance, shining a weak light through the high windows. Mark found the sight was a further comfort; he couldn't bear the thought of Jake being alone when the library's interior was plunged into shadowy darkness.

They entered the small alley that lay at the side of the library and started to climb up the metal staircase that led to the fire exit. The elevation provided the perfect view over the town ahead of them and Mark found himself casting a troubled look over the scene as he ascended.

He saw the usual landmarks which he expected to see; a few monstrous warehouses that loomed in the distance, several blocks of flats that towered above the culs-de-sac around them, and of course the cluster of tired skyscrapers that stood in the town's centre. Beyond the industrial jungle, now far away in the distance and lit palely by the waning sun, the forest stood out as firmly as ever, the trees marching resiliently up the ridge that guarded the town.

Mark frowned. From the top of the ridge, rising gently above the tops of the trees, it looked as if a dark cloud was drifting gently on the wind. He squinted, trying to bring the dark cloud into focus, and watched as the loosely defined edges swirled angrily around each other.

It didn't look like a cloud, he realised suddenly. It was shaped more like a plume and seemed to grow in intensity the longer he stared at it. On the steps above him Rae turned to see what had caught his attention and she too began to squint at the mysterious brume in the distance.

"Is that smoke?" she said, the confusion plain in her voice.

Mark felt his heart sink deep into his stomach and had to fight hard to stop himself from choking. It was smoke. It had to be. And fires didn't start on their own in a winter this cold.

They had found it.

Tears began to brim in Mark's eyes, which he had to blink back firmly, and he felt his lungs deflate as the air rushed quickly out of them. The small hut in the trees had been his home for years and it was the only home that Jake had even known. Now, if they ever saw it again, it would be a pile of ash beneath the burnt out husk of a tree.

Above him he heard Rae curse quietly under her breath, the realisation dawning on her too, and together they stood in silence as they watched the remnants of his home disappear into the sky.

After a few minutes Mark turned and continued to the top of the stairs. When they reached the metal fire exit, Rae turned to him and placed a reassuring hand on his shoulder.

"I'm sorry," she said. Her sympathy appeared genuine.

Mark nodded a reply, turning to give his home one last look before heading through the door.

Inside the library it was dark and quiet, the fading light from the windows casting long, threatening shadows behind every object, and it took a few moments for Mark's eyes to adjust to the gloom. Behind them the metal door slammed shut and they listened as the sound echoed ominously around the building.

"Jake," Mark shouted into the silence. "Jake, it's us!"

The echo reverberated around the room, which now seemed bigger than Mark had remembered it, but neither of them heard Jake reply.

Mark turned to look at Rae, who gave him a shrug before heading towards the banister to look out over the ground floor. He followed her to the edge, resting his hands on the rail as he ran his eyes across the scene below.

The floor was still littered with heaps of books and the endless rows of bookshelves cast ominous shadows that clawed their way over the makeshift carpet. Clouds of dust swam lazily where the shadows ended, basking in the last rays of light before the sun finally set. But apart from the dust the room was still. There was no sign of Jake.

"Jake?" Mark shouted again. This time he was unable to stop his uneasiness from creeping into his voice.

Beside him Rae shifted uncomfortably, her eyes still scanning the room.

"He's probably in the camp," Mark said, turning quickly away from the floor below. "He's probably just fallen asleep."

"Probably," Rae replied quietly.

Mark pushed off from the banister and started walking towards the little maze of bookshelves. He heard Rae begin to follow slowly behind and deliberately focused on moving at a walking pace rather than a run.

He reassured himself that Jake would be in the camp as he approached the entrance to the maze of bookshelves. Around the building he heard his footsteps echoing loudly, but they stopped when he reached the maze's entrance. The echoes were replaced by his short breaths as he stared into the dark path ahead of him.

"Jake!" he called again. He listened as his voice travelled through the maze.

Still there was no reply.

Mark began to navigate his way through the darkness, his pace getting gradually quicker despite his efforts to slow down.

Surely Jake would have heard him shouting by now. Even if he had been asleep the noise should have awoken him.

He shook his head sharply as the dreadful thoughts crept slowly back into his head and this time he found it even harder to drive them away.

They hadn't got Jake, he told himself firmly. They couldn't have got Jake.

He rounded the corner of one of the bookshelves when something made him suddenly stop. He could have sworn he had heard something.

"Jake?" he called tentatively into the darkness.

He turned around to check if Rae had heard the noise as well, but found himself staring into an empty passage. She was nowhere to be seen, and Mark realised that he wasn't even sure if she had followed him into the maze.

Maybe the sound he had heard was her searching somewhere else in the library.

Something wasn't right, Mark thought, as he turned back around and continued on towards the camp.

Something definitely wasn't right.

He tried to focus on keeping his breathing slow and steady and treading more softly on the wooden floorboards, but found that he was powerless to stop his mind from imagining what might have happened to Jake. Each thought was more terrible than the last and the fear they brought with them served only to strengthen his rising panic. It took every ounce of self-control that he had to keep his actions under his control.

He turned another corner in the labyrinth and began to head down the narrow path ahead. He just had to turn right at the end of this passage and the camp would be in front of him – the image of Jake sleeping tightly under his blanket by the fire pit momentarily steadying his nerves.

Mark felt his pace quicken and was about halfway down the passage when suddenly he felt his legs go from under him, and he only just managed to stop himself from falling to the ground.

He looked down at the floor to see what had made him slip, and froze when he saw the dark trail splattered over the floorboards.

Blood. He knew it was blood. There was nothing else it could be other than blood.

Mark's stomach began to somersault inside his body and for a second he thought that he was going to be sick. Cold fear gripped the back of his throat and when he tried to call out Jake's name he could only manage a pathetic wheeze. He forced himself back to his feet and to keep moving down the passage, now absolutely terrified of what he would find at its end.

Maybe Jake had just cut himself on something sharp. Maybe he had fallen over something. He was almost at the end of the passage when his eye caught something else along the trail of blood.

At about waist height, hanging precariously from a small cluster of splinters, was a small scrap of leathery skin. One side was jet black with a thin covering of blood; the other side was coated with a shock of grey fur.

Mark's eyes widened with terror and his heart leapt into his throat. Every last shred of hope had disappeared.

No, he thought. No, no, no!

Panic took over his body and Mark began hurtling towards the end of the passage, his heart beating so fast he thought it would explode. He had barely started moving when the bookshelf to his right exploded, splinters flying in every direction as a flash of grey came crashing out of the darkness.

It hit him before he could react and Mark felt himself being driven through the bookshelves to his left. He slammed into the wood, which snapped easily under the impact, and then landed heavily on the floor, causing dust to be thrown into the air as he screamed at the excruciating pain that lanced through his shoulder.

He tried to roll away, but a heavy weight pinned him to the ground and he found himself staring into the menacing eyes of a Hunter. Its claws dug into his shoulders as it stood on top of him, pressing down hard on his gunshot wound. Black spots began to fill his vision and the Hunter became blurry as his eyes began to water, but somehow he kept himself from passing out.

Mark felt his instincts take over as adrenalin surged into his blood. He tried to move his right hand towards the gun in his pocket, but his arm was pinned to the ground and instead he felt his fingers scrabble uselessly against the floor. The Hunter was still on top of him and Mark looked up at the bloody fur that covered its face, focusing on a gaping hole that sat beneath its right eye.

The Hunter bared its teeth, growling viciously as it lifted back its head to strike at his face. Mark quickly brought his left hand up, gritting his teeth as pain ripped through his shoulder, and jabbed his fingers hard into the Hunter's wound.

The Hunter leaned back and howled in pain, releasing the pressure on Mark's right arm just long enough for him to wriggle it free. He brought that arm up too, stabbing viciously into its eye in a desperate attempt to fight it off.

The Hunter leapt back off him with a yelp, now out of his reach and standing back in the passageway. It shook its head vigorously and sent droplets of blood flying onto the bookshelves before looking back up. Its tail whipped against the floor as it prepared to pounce back onto him, and Mark knew the moment he looked up that it was too late for him to move.

A blur of movement appeared to the Hunter's right and suddenly the beast was on its side, falling heavily to the floor as something smashed into it.

It took Mark a moment to recognise Rae, who had pressed her knee deep into the Hunter's side and had lifted a knife above her head. She brought the knife down hard and the blade disappeared into the fur on the Hunter's face.

The Hunter yelped and began to flail its legs helplessly as Rae stabbed at it again and again. Blood spurted out into the passageway, droplets flicking onto the bookshelves and up onto Rae's face every time that she stabbed with the blade.

Finally, after what seemed to Mark like forever, the Hunter's legs stopped flailing against the floor and its terrible whimpering died away beneath the wet smacks of the stabbing. Only when she was sure that the Hunter was dead did Rae stop her attack, dropping her knife to the floor with a thud as she sat back on the dusty ground, panting with exhaustion.

Mark looked from the Hunter to Rae, somehow feeling worse than he had when it was on top of him.

He leapt up from the floor without a word and ran down the short distance to the end of the passage, charging round the corner at its end to see the empty camp in front of him. The soft, woollen blanket lay flat on the floor by the fire pit.

His eyes darted around the campsite. There was no sign that any struggle or fight had taken place, but there was no sign of Jake either.

"Jake!" he screamed at the ceiling. "It's dead, Jake, you can come out now!"

Maybe Jake was hiding. Maybe he had seen the Hunter and decided to hide until they came back and killed it – but already the deafening silence had filled the library again, its painful message all too clear.

The torrent of thoughts began to flow once more and Mark's mind desperately searched for something that would disprove what was now staring him in the face.

It couldn't have. It can't have. He couldn't go through this again.

He felt his stomach do another somersault and this time he fell to his knees, unable to stop himself from retching bile onto the floor.

Mark stared down at the brown puddle on the floorboards, which swam dangerously in his vision. He had to know.

Quickly he got back to his feet and ran back down the passage to the Hunter's corpse. Rae was still sitting on the floor, breathing heavily and looking nervously up at him, but Mark didn't notice her looking and instead got out his knife as he approached the Hunter's body. He dropped to his knees and plunged the blade into its midriff, slicing open its belly with a horrible tearing sound. Rae scrambled backwards as its insides fell out onto the floor, the organs steaming gently in the cold library air. Mark located the stomach quickly and took a deep breath before cutting it open.

The stench hit him instantly and he nearly threw up again as it caught at the back of his throat. The contents of the stomach were mostly unrecognisable, bits of meat that were either rotted or slowly digesting, but some scraps of fur, that looked as if it had been from a rabbit, stood out to him, as well as a few small bones that were yet to be digested.

He moved around the rest of the contents with the end of his knife, but couldn't see anything to suggest what he had feared.

He sat back with a thud and dropped his knife to the floor, the wave of nausea slowly beginning to subside.

The Hunter hadn't got him. Mark had no idea what had happened in the library, but he knew that the Hunter hadn't killed Jake.

He leaned back his head against the bookshelf behind him and stared up at the vaulted ceiling, allowing the relief to wash over him and the first tears to begin to flow. They would search the rest of the library, just in case Jake was still hiding and was too scared to come out, but Mark knew that he would be gone. Jake was terrified of the Hunters, and the moment he had seen it he would have run as far away as he could.

Mark's relief gave way to panic as the thought of a terrified Jake running blindly through the town filled his mind.

He had promised Jake that he wouldn't leave him on his own, so why had he listened to the advice of a stranger and not taken him with them. He had been certain that what he was doing was for the best, that what he was doing would keep Jake safe.

But he had been wrong. And now Mark could do nothing to protect him.

Chapter 26

Jake had no idea how long he had been crying for, but by the time his sobs finally came to a halt the sun was low in the sky and was doing little to light the room in which he found himself. He was still tucked tightly into a ball beneath the bed, his eyes sore and the back of his throat dry from where he'd been crying. His wrist throbbed angrily from where the gun had kicked it back, making the bruising swell to a dark purple. For a few minutes, he lay still as he listened to the silence that lay undisturbed throughout the house.

Eventually he picked up the gun from the floor beside him and began to edge his way out from under the bed, holding the weapon in front of him shakily as he pointed it at the doorway. Still he could hear only silence in the house. There was nothing to suggest that the Hunter had followed him.

He needed to get outside.

As soon as Mark got back to the library and realised Jake wasn't there, he would be out on the streets looking for him, but there was no way he could search every house he passed to see if that was where Jake was hiding. Jake needed to be on the street, to make it easier to be found. If he headed back towards the library, then he would have a better chance, but in his panic he couldn't remember which way he had come from, and so had no idea how to get back.

He pushed the thought away before it overwhelmed him and caused him to start crying again, and instead began to slowly creep his way out of the little bedroom. His eyes darted around the hallway, lingering in the shadows of every doorway to see if anything was hiding in the darkness, but the hallway was still, and so Jake began to descend the staircase with his gun pointing down at the floor below.

The creaking of wood filled the house with every step he took and he shuddered at the memory of the creaking staircase in the library. When he reached the narrow hallway at the bottom, he crept slowly towards the front door and peeked out through the small window that was at the doorway's side.

The street outside was empty. Some leaves skittered across the floor as an icy wind blew down the road and he could hear the gentle tingle of a wind chime in the distance, but aside from that, it was clear.

Slowly Jake pulled the front door open, his heart jumping into his throat as the rusty hinges squeaked loudly. He poked his head outside to check that the rest of the street was empty before gingerly creeping down the steps and onto the road.

He looked at the houses around him and, to his dismay, found that he didn't recognise any of them. Worse still was that he couldn't see any landmarks he could use to navigate; the gently darkening sky was the only thing visible above the rooftops.

Maybe he should head back home, Jake thought suddenly – the Hunters wouldn't get him there and it was where Dad would look eventually – but his heart sank when he realised that he couldn't see the forest either.

Even if he was able to find his way to the trees, he was on the other side of town and still wouldn't know which way to go.

What if he stumbled into the group's camp instead of his own?

He shuddered involuntarily and accepted that his best option was to try to find his way back to the library. He turned to look down the road that led off to his right before quickly turning to look the other way.

Which way had he come? He couldn't remember. He had been so scared when he was running away that he hadn't paid any attention to where he was going. He only knew that he had wanted to get as far away from the Hunter as possible. He screwed his eyes shut, desperately trying to remember which way he had come. He felt tears build up in his eyes again as his mind drew another blank.

Stop being silly, he scolded himself, while sucking in a deep breath. He would need to just keep moving until he found somewhere he knew, and maybe then he would be able to find his way back.

After a few moments of hesitation he decided to turn right and, with his gun still shaking delicately in his hands, took his first few steps through the abandoned town.

They had started to head back to the camp once the hut had fallen from the branches; the burning wood crashing to the floor in a ball of flame that belched thick, black smoke up through the trees.

Behind them Gabe could still see the spiral of smoke as the wood continued to smoulder and he couldn't help but feel a sense of satisfaction trickle gently over him.

They had been searching for the camp for weeks and now that it had been found it felt like they were making progress. But Gabe had no inhibitions that his task was over and knew that his men would be far from satisfied by his discovery.

They still had a long way to go.

The trees cast dark shadows over the pair as they headed around the outskirts of town. They had been walking for over an hour and throughout their journey the sun had been creeping lower in the sky as night time approached.

Gabe strode boldly ahead, eager to get back and hear what the search party had found in town. Jack followed a few metres behind, his footsteps trudging heavily through the undergrowth. He wrapped his coat tightly around himself to keep out the bitter chill as the sun began to dip below the trees in the distance.

Ahead of them the campsite came vaguely into view, the artificial colours of the tents standing out against the forest. Gabe could see no movement from within the scattering of tents and assumed that the search party must not yet be back.

That was a good sign. It could mean that they had found something.

He looked for the comforting glow of the fire coming from the middle of the tents, but frowned when he saw that the campsite was as dark as the rest of the forest.

What was Mike playing at? It was freezing – and he should have started cooking something by now for when they all returned.

Gabe clenched his fists, feeling annoyed by Mike's incompetence. Everyone in the group had been given a job and they all knew what happened if they weren't completed.

Gabe quickened his pace, hearing Jack follow suit behind him. As they passed the first of the tents at the Camp's perimeter, Gabe noticed that the door flap of the tent to his right was hanging open. He frowned. That had been Dave's tent, and they had already divvied up his possessions between them. He cast his gaze over the rest of the tents scattered around him, but saw the same thing everywhere he looked. All of them had been opened.

"Mike!" Gabe shouted, his earlier annoyance now turning to anger.

The camp remained silent.

"Mike!" he shouted again, storming towards the fire pit and the small congregation of chairs.

Mike was sitting with his back to him in one of the camping chairs, facing the barren fire pit that should have been dancing with flames. His head was tilted forwards to rest on his chest, as if he were asleep. Gabe shook his head in disbelief before making a beeline towards him.

"You lazy bastard!" Gabe shouted, stamping his feet into the frozen ground as he marched towards him. "Where's the fire? Where's the food? What the hell have you been doing all d…"

He grabbed Mike's hair and pulled his head back sharply, stopping short of finishing his sentence when he saw two lifeless eyes staring back at him. For a second, he was completely lost for words.

Mike's face was an absolute mess; completely unrecognisable underneath a mask of blood and cuts. His one good arm was bound tightly to the back of his chair and his feet were bound also, ensuring that he couldn't have escaped. A criss-cross of angry cuts were congealing on his bare chest, the clothes on top having been cut away. A deep, gaping gash ran across his only wrist, allowing litres of blood to gush out and cover his lower body.

Gabe let go of Mike's hair and watched as the lifeless head lolled limply forwards.

For a while, he stood in silence, too stunned to know how to react. Behind him he heard Jack swear quietly under his breath as he, too, saw the brutality with which Mike had been killed. Gradually Gabe's thoughts began to make sense of the scene in front of him and he turned his head to look back at the open door flaps that hung lazily to the floor.

"Check the tents," Gabe whispered breathlessly, and hurried over to check his own. His tent door was hanging open, just like all the others, and he crouched down to look through the opening.

It was gone. His ammunition, his weapons, his food. It was all gone. On the other side of the camp he heard Jack swear loudly as he found the same result.

Gabe stared into his empty tent with disbelief and felt his anger begin to intensify. His face started to twitch and his spine quivered, his rage growing stronger with every second.

They had taken everything.

He lifted his head back and screamed; an angry, wounded scream that cut through the quiet forest and made the birds scarper from the trees. His vision turned a deep red and his lungs began to ache with the intense vibration. When he ran out of breath and the scream came to a strangled halt, he lashed out viciously at the tent, kicking it from its moorings and throwing wild punches at the dirty fabric.

How had this happened? How was he being outsmarted? Why hadn't they killed them already?

When there was nothing left to punch, he stood over the wreck of his tent which now lay uselessly on the floor, panting heavily as he tried to play out the scene around him in his head.

It was a message. The father and his son were sending them a message. Torture one of Gabe's group and leave him in the camp for the rest to see, stealing everything they had left behind in the process. They were trying to make them leave. To make them cut their losses and move on.

Not a chance!

Gabe spat on the floor and stormed back to Mike's body.

If the father wanted to try and scare them, then Gabe would show him it hadn't worked, and if he thought it would make them leave then he couldn't be more wrong. Gabe would not be outsmarted. Not in front of his men.

If the father had thought it would make Gabe and his men leave, then he had done quite the opposite. Gabe was now more determined than ever.

He pulled out his knife and cut the ropes that bound Mike to the chair. His body was heavy, but Gabe hoisted it over his shoulder and started marching towards the edge of the camp. As he walked, he felt cold blood run down his arm and drip silently onto the floor, leaving a bloody trail that led from the chair and out into the forest.

He passed over the edge of the camp and kept walking deeper into the trees, feeling his anger festering dangerously inside of him. Finally, when the camp had disappeared through the trees behind him, he threw Mike's body onto the floor. It landed face down with a heavy thud.

Gabe turned around and started walking back to the camp, barely giving the corpse another glance.

At least, he had found him first, Gabe reflected, tightly clenching his fists to try and keep his rage under control. If the others had come back and found him, then they may have cut and run. The fact that he had been the one to find Mike meant he could make sure that they wouldn't do anything stupid.

As he re-entered the camp, the sun finally disappeared below the trees, casting the forest around him into a murky darkness. Gabe slumped down into his chair and stared into the fire pit, which Jack had just filled with kindling and was beginning to light. The flames licked at each other hungrily as they sparked into life.

It wouldn't be long before the others returned from town, Gabe thought, as he watched the fire slowly take.

With any luck they might have found something.

Chapter 27

They searched the library high and low, but found no sign of Jake, nor any hint as to where he had gone.

The Hunter had come through a window on the ground floor that was at the back of the library, tucked away inconspicuously in a dark corner. Rae had barricaded it with tables and bookshelves while Mark had searched the rest of the building. By the time they were finished, the sun was getting dangerously low in the sky.

"He must have made a run for it," Mark said hurriedly, pacing towards the stairs as he looked around for anywhere they hadn't checked. Rae was standing at the bottom of the staircase with a worried expression on her face.

"He can't have gone far," she said, as they began to climb the creaking stairs. "He's a smart kid. He won't have gone out of sight of the library."

Mark wasn't so sure. Jake was incredibly smart, but Hunters terrified him and at some point the Hunter must have chased him if he had been responsible for the bullet wound below its eye.

A petrified five-year-old being chased by one of his nightmares would struggle to retain much rational thought, even one as smart as Jake, and as soon as he had gotten out of the library he would have tried to get as far away as he could.

Jake may have even tried to find Mark to warn him of the danger before he got back – but that would mean he would be heading towards...

Mark shook his head vigorously, desperately trying to drive away the thought. When he reached the top of the staircase, he began moving towards the fire exit.

Ever since their encounter with the Hunter Mark's mind had been in a frenzy, and there was only one thing that was stopping him from becoming completely insane. Somewhere out in town Jake was alive – of that much he was certain. Mark needed to find him before anything tried to change that.

He reached the fire exit and pushed it quickly open, feeling another jolt of fear run down his spine when he saw how low the sun had got. They rushed down the metal staircase and into the alley below.

Behind them was a dead end marked by a fence that was far too tall to be climbed, so they headed out onto the street at the library's front, scouring the floor for any hint of a trail that they could follow. The tarmacked road gave nothing away and Mark felt his heart sink through the floor as he looked at the houses marching off in endless rows to either side.

"Where now?" he said, panic seizing his voice. "He could have gone anywhere. Where do we go now?"

Tears threatened to drown out his words and he quickly choked back a sob, in an effort to keep his composure. He needed to calm down. He needed to find Jake.

"Over there."

Rae's voice was calm and quiet, a complete contrast to everything Mark was feeling. He followed her outstretched arm and looked across the street to the doorway of one of the adjacent houses.

A cruel surge of hope momentarily blocked out his panic. Between the front door of the house and its frame there was an almost imperceptible crack.

He ran across the street and up to the front door, eyes fixed on the crack in the doorway. He hadn't imagined it. The door was open. He gave it a gentle push and listened to the squeaking of the hinges echo through the empty house.

"Jake!" Mark shouted as he stepped into the hall. He heard his voice echo loudly in the street behind him.

"Shh!" Rae said, appearing at his shoulder like a ghost.

Mark ignored her, instead listening intently for any sign of Jake. Rae moved quickly through the hallway, eyes fixed on the ground as she headed to the back of the house.

Mark went through a door to his right and gave the room behind it a quick once over. The room was empty, so he headed back out into the hallway and made towards the bottom of the stairs. He had just placed his foot on the bottom step when a sharp whistle caught his attention, and he peered down the hallway to see Rae beckoning quickly for him to come over.

He rushed to the back of the house and followed her into the garden. He saw instantly what had caught her attention and found that he was holding his breath as he stared at the overgrown lawn in front of him.

There was a clear trail of flattened grass that led straight down the middle of the lawn, carrying on over the fallen fence and into the next garden. They followed the trail over the fallen fence and saw that on the other side it curved and carried on across further gardens, running parallel to the row of houses to their right.

They were going to find him, Mark began to reassure himself. If they just followed the trail, it would lead them to Jake.

Suddenly the trail took a sharp right and ended abruptly at a patio that led to the back of another house. Mark ran up to the backdoor and tried the handle, but even when he slammed into the door with his shoulder it wouldn't budge.

Locked. There was no way Jake had gone through there.

He turned to his right and saw Rae standing by the side of the house, beckoning him round the corner and down a narrow alley.

Mark followed, hunting desperately for any further sign of the trail. The light was quickly fading and he knew his chances of finding Jake would be far slimmer in the dark. At the end of the alley, he found himself back on another street and what he saw made the hope he had felt moments earlier vanish just as quickly as it had arrived.

They were standing beside a crossroads; four streets all leading off in different directions, each with their own seemingly endless row of houses.

Mark ran into the centre of the junction, turning in circles as he tried to work out which way Jake had gone, but every street looked identical and he could see nothing to suggest that he had gone down any of them.

The trail had gone cold.

Jake couldn't see the sun anymore.

A chill wind blew down the darkening street he was walking in, causing him to shiver with cold and wrap his coat around him more tightly. His legs were aching and it felt like he had been walking for hours.

In that time, he had yet to see anything that he recognised, except for the forest in the distance, which he had decided it was best to avoid. He cast another look over the houses around him, glancing nervously at the black windows that stared emptily down at him. He shuddered involuntarily at the thought of spending the night alone in this place.

Jake trudged on down the street, deciding that he wouldn't give up and find a place to stay the night just yet. He was sticking to the pavement, not wanting to walk so openly in the middle of the road, but too afraid to immerse himself in the dark, ominous shadows that reached out at him from the houses.

He usually didn't mind when it was dark in the forest; he enjoyed listening to the creaking of the branches as they swayed in the wind and trying to identify which nocturnal creature was snuffling and barking in the night – but out here it was different. The whistling of the wind, as it blew through the abandoned streets, was more haunting than reassuring, and Jake found the sounds the animals made weren't as scary when he was in the safety of his home.

At the end of the street, he turned right and started down another road which looked almost identical to the last. At one point, an owl hooted loudly from a rooftop nearby, making him jump with fright and fall quickly to the floor.

He scolded himself for being stupid when he realised what had made the sound. Slowly he stood up from the floor and dusted himself down. He knew the owl wouldn't hurt him and Dad said that if he could hear other animals then that meant there wouldn't be any Hunters around.

Almost as if it had heard his thoughts, the owl hooted again from its perch, and from somewhere in the distance there came another hoot in reply.

Good, Jake thought, as he carried on down the street. Maybe the Hunters have gone to sleep.

He walked for what seemed like another hour before he finally stopped. He still had no idea where he was going and for a second he wondered if he had been walking in circles all day.

He sighed. It was getting really dark now and soon he wouldn't be able to see very far ahead. It was already too dark to see to the end of the street and all he could make out in front of him was the vague outline of yet more houses as they disappeared into the night.

With a defiant nod Jake decided that he should try to rest for the night. He wouldn't be able to find his dad while it was dark and it was too dangerous to be walking around when he couldn't see properly.

He took a look at the houses around him for somewhere to stay and spotted one across the street that looked in slightly better condition than the others. He crossed the road, feeling slightly better now that he knew what he was doing for the night, but when he reached the other side of the street and looked up at the house in front of him, he felt his defiance quickly disappear.

The small steps at the front of the house led up to a thick black door, the wood slowly rotting and covered in cracks. Empty windows stared out from between thick, twisted vines; the shadows within them dark and foreboding, making him think twice about whether he wanted to stay there. The house reminded Jake of how scared he was, and he realised painfully just how much he wanted to see his dad.

Jake took one last look down the darkening street, praying that he would see his dad walking up the road towards him before having to spend the night in the dark.

He was about to look away when something caught his eye and he had to stifle back a yelp of surprise. He squinted into the darkness at the end of the street, his heartbeat starting to quicken.

For a second, he had thought he had seen something move. No, he was certain of it! One of the shadows at the end of the street had definitely moved.

Jake felt a sudden urge to rush down the street towards the moving shadow to see if it was what he hoped, but he stopped himself before he took the first step. It could be a Hunter, he realised with a pang of fear, and he remained rooted to the spot while he tried to work out what he should do.

Dad would want him to hide, to be safe and wait until he could see what it was that had been moving, but there was no way that Jake could do that; not while Dad was out looking for him and he was so lost and alone and scared.

So instead he waited; rooted to the spot as he stared pleadingly into the darkness at the end of the street.

There it was again! One of the shadows was moving. Jake held his breath.

Gradually a shape began to form out of the shadowy darkness. It was moving towards him, at about walking pace, and whatever it was that was moving had to be large.

Jake listened out for the distinctive growling of a Hunter, or the flash of grey that sent fear coursing through every inch of his body, ready to dart into the house the moment he found either sign, but as the shape got closer he realised that it was far too tall to be a Hunter.

The shadow moved too slowly and walked too upright, and looked too much like a…like a…

"Dad!" Jake screamed, his voice echoing around the pitch black street.

Jake started sprinting down the road towards the shadow, which had now stopped and was peering into the darkness to try and see what was running towards it. He dashed over the fractured concrete, his legs no longer aching and his fear from moments before already forgotten. New energy surged through his body and a large smile broke across his face as he got closer to the shadow.

Jake couldn't believe it. He had found him! He had been so afraid, had thought he might never see him again, but now Dad was here! They had found each other again!

Jake opened his arms and ran head on into the man in front of him, hugging his legs tightly as he felt tears filling his eyes.

"I was so scared, Dad!" he started to cry, hugging the legs more tightly. "I was so…"

Jake stopped short when he looked up at the man above him. Then he quickly let go of the legs and stepped backwards. He opened his mouth to speak, but shock stopped him from talking, and his silence was maintained by a cold fear that gripped the back of his throat.

Jake recognised the face looking back at him, but it wasn't the face that he had been so desperate to see.

It was the face of a man. The man he had seen on the other side of the street before he fell through the floor.

Chapter 28

Paul watched Jake trudging slowly in the dark street ahead of him, head bowed low between two slumped shoulders. He was crying, and had been ever since Paul had found him alone in the darkness.

At first, Jake had tried to run back down the street from which he had come, but Paul had quickly grabbed him and forced his hand over Jake's mouth to muffle his screams and shouts. Jake had struggled desperately to escape, flailing his arms helplessly and kicking out at Paul. It hadn't been long before he realised that he couldn't get away and stopped his fighting.

The tears had come not long after that.

Since then they had walked in silence; their only interaction a few grunted commands telling Jake where to go.

Paul still couldn't quite believe what had happened. One moment he had been walking alone in the dark, heading slowly back to camp after a long and useless search in town, when suddenly he'd heard shouting and saw a small boy running out of the shadows towards him.

At first, he had suspected a trap – it was far too fortunate a find for it to be a coincidence – but as he had led the boy through the silent alleys and back streets Paul was yet to see any sign that they were being followed.

He turned his attention back to Jake and found himself struck once more by just how small he was. The effect was exacerbated by the thick, puffy coat that shrouded his frame and Paul realised that he couldn't be much older than six or seven. He couldn't remember the last time he had seen a child that young – or even close to it.

In front of him, Jake let out another sob, his whole body shuddering in fright. Paul opened his mouth to say something, but quickly decided against it.

It would only make it harder, he thought to himself, and so they carried on in silence.

After a while the houses around them began to thin and up ahead the dark, looming shadow of the forest came steadily into view. A small, orange glow could be seen flickering in the darkness and Paul felt a sickening feeling settle in his stomach. He shifted uncomfortably as they approached the fiery glow and suddenly realised how nervous he was.

He looked down at the huddled figure of Jake, who was still crying softly and looking with terror at the glow ahead, and shuddered involuntarily. Paul didn't think he was going to like what was about to happen.

Soon the buildings around them had disappeared and were replaced with the thick trunks of trees that looked down accusingly at them. Paul could now hear voices coming from beside the firelight and a minute later the fire itself came into view, the playful flames partly obscured by the huddled silhouettes sat around it.

In front of him Jake stopped, staring in horror at the group ahead of him. Paul gave him a firm nudge in the back, making him stagger forward and carry on reluctantly towards the fire. He was visibly shaking now and his painful sobs had come to a halt.

Around the fire one of the silhouettes turned to peer at them, the expression on their face unreadable in the darkness.

"Paul?" It was Daniel. "Is that you?"

Paul didn't reply and herded Jake into the small circle of chairs. The light from the fire exposed his red, puffy eyes and tear-streaked face.

Around the fire pit all the men stopped what they were doing, turning to stare in a mix of shock and wonder at their new prisoner.

Paul watched their faces, grimly reading off the expressions one by one. Daniel looked uncomfortable, a deep frown across his face as he stared at the boy; Cal looked more shocked than anything else, probably struggling to come to terms with the fact that he was seeing a child again; Jack sat back in his chair to stare at the new arrival, his face unreadable while his eyes studied Jake coldly; Mike was nowhere to be seen.

Finally, Paul turned to look at Gabe, and shuddered at the cruel expression he found there. Gabe's face was contorted into a bizarre mix of pleasure and rage and his deep blue eyes were staring with suppressed fury at the frightened little boy in front of him.

Slowly he stood up from his chair and began pacing around the fire.

"It's him," Gabe exclaimed slowly, his voice dripping with venom.

Paul nodded in reply.

"Where on earth did you find him?"

"Found him on my way back," Paul replied dryly. "He just ran towards me out of the dark, thinking I was his dad."

"Did he now?" Gabe said, squatting to look into Jake's terrified face. Jake squirmed as his eyes scrutinised him.

"Your dad shouldn't be leaving you on your own," Gabe stated, a cruel smile beginning to play on his lips.

Jake shivered with fright as Gabe's menacing eyes continued to bore into him. Tears were streaking down his face and it was obvious he was trying to keep himself from openly crying. Paul winced involuntarily. He didn't like the look on Gabe's face.

"Where's Mike?" Paul asked, trying to change the subject.

"Mike?" Gabe's eyes flicked up to look at him. "Why don't we ask the little one?" He fixed his gaze back onto Jake and when he spoke next his voice contained a more patronising tone.

"Do you know where Mike is, boy? Do you know where our friend is?"

Jake stood helplessly in front of Gabe, not understanding what he was being asked. The tears continued to flow down his face.

"No?" Gabe went on, his voice getting louder. "Were you not here when daddy cut up Mike? Were you not here when he tied him up and beat him half to death before slitting his wrist!"

Gabe had started shouting, flecks of spit shooting from his mouth and careening into Jake's face. Jake started to cry openly, unable to hold back his sobs for any longer. A large, dark patch quickly grew at the front of his trousers.

"What?" Paul asked, bewildered.

"Mike's dead," Gabe stated. His eyes didn't move. "Daddy tied him up to a chair and tortured him. Then he slit his wrist to finish him off. He left him in that chair over there for us all to see."

Paul looked to where Gabe was pointing and shuddered when he saw the empty chair that was stained with blood. He had thought it was a bad idea to leave only one person to guard the camp, but he hadn't wanted to voice his concerns.

"But I bet Daddy didn't think we would get hold of you," Gabe continued, bringing Paul's attention back to the scene at hand.

The words hung in the air for what seemed like forever and for a while nobody spoke. The only sound to be heard in the campsite was the crackling of the flames and Jake's heavy sobs as he continued to cry uncontrollably.

The rest of the group were frozen to the spot, watching uncomfortably as the cruel smile returned to Gabe's face and a deranged look came into his eyes.

Finally he spoke.

"Give me a knife," he said quietly, holding out an open hand. No one moved.

"GIVE ME A KNIFE!" he shouted. The sudden noise made everyone jump.

Cal was the first to move, pulling a knife from his belt and handing it quickly over. Gabe snatched it and held it up to Jake's chin, using the tip to lift up his head so he could stare into his eyes.

Jake had begun to shake uncontrollably and was staring back wide-eyed. Paul looked on in horror, unable to look away from the scene. He felt sick through to his stomach and realised that he was holding his breath.

He should do something, he thought to himself briefly. He knew that this wasn't right.

"I am going to do to you what he did to Mike," Gabe spat angrily. "I am going to show him what happens when you threaten me!"

Gabe grabbed Jake by the shoulders and tore off his jacket before taking hold of his wrist and holding the knife towards it. Jake tried to pull his arm away from the glinting metal, but Gabe's grip was far too strong.

Jake started to scream at the top of his lungs, an unintelligible sound that was choked with panic. Paul turned quickly away to look at the fire, unable to watch any longer.

"Wait!"

Jake stopped his screaming, his breaths coming in ragged gasps as he screwed his eyes shut. Paul didn't dare to move, afraid of shattering the illusion that time had momentarily stopped. Gabe's knife was still poised on the skin at Jake's wrist and it stayed there as Gabe turned towards where the voice had come from. His cold, blue eyes settled on Jack's beaten face.

"What?" Gabe said quietly, his voice quivering with rage. Jack stared back, with eyes that were dark and serious, refusing to avert his gaze.

"We need him," he stated calmly.

Gabe stared at him, cocking his head to the side as he tried to work out what Jack was trying to do. The rest of the group watched on in suspense, not daring to intervene in the confrontation. They stared at each other for what seemed like an eternity, before Jack finally continued.

"We can use him."

His voice was dull and monotone, completely devoid of emotion. Gabe continued to stare at him coldly, his knife waiting impatiently on Jake's wrist.

"As long as the boy's alive, we have the upper hand. It will draw the dad out and we can make him do whatever we say. Like show us where he's hidden all the stuff he stole."

Gabe's stare lost its edge, and the fury began to fade from his face as he pondered Jack's words.

This pursuit was no longer about gaining supplies. It had become a vendetta; a challenge to his power that threatened to belittle him in front of his men. But the men were angry that their stuff had been stolen, and getting it back would be vital in keeping them on his side. Besides, he also knew that Jack was right.

Jake was far more useful alive, an instrument that allowed Gabe to steer the rest of this campaign in whatever direction he pleased. As long as he had Jake, he realised, he had control over the entire situation.

"Fine," Gabe said eventually. He pulled the knife away from Jake's wrist and tossed it back to Cal.

Jake quickly withdrew his arm, clutching his wrist to his chest as he collapsed into a ball on the floor. Gabe stooped down to pick up Jake's coat, the fabric torn from where he had ripped it off, and threw it towards Jack.

"Tie him up," Gabe ordered, as he walked away from the fire towards his tent. He shouted back over his shoulder before he disappeared inside, "And get him to tell you where his dad is before you go and deliver the message."

Crouched in a ball by the fire Jake was now as white as a sheet and his little body retched heavily as he vomited onto the floor. Sitting uncomfortably in their chairs, the rest of the men were silent, all of them focusing their attention on anything other than the terrified child. All except Jack, who watched Jake huddled up on the floor with an unreadable expression.

His voice made Jake turn, who watched with bloodshot eyes as Jack walked slowly over.

"Don't make this difficult for me, kid," Jack said quietly, crouching down in front of him. "Just tell me where he is."

Chapter 29

The doorframe groaned loudly before splintering with a loud crack. The door it had been holding fell through it and landed in the hallway with a crash.

Rae winced, turning sharply to look at the street around her as the sound echoed around the houses. Beside her she heard Mark enter the now open doorway and call desperately into the house. When there was no reply, he rushed up the stairs to check the bedrooms. Rae waited patiently outside for him to come back down, scanning the abandoned street for any sign of danger.

Ever since they had lost Jake's trail at the crossroads Mark and Rae had been going from house to house in search of anything that would tell them where he had gone. So far they had found nothing, which came as no surprise to Rae. What did surprise her was that they hadn't drawn any Hunters to them with the amount of noise Mark was making.

She heard footsteps on the stairs behind her and turned to see Mark shaking his head hopelessly. It had been the same result every time and she could see he was getting more panicked and desperate with each house they searched. She turned away from him to look down the street, at the houses that marched resiliently into the darkness.

"We need to head back," she said resignedly.

Confusion clouded Mark's face and was quickly replaced with disbelief.

"Go back?" he asked in shock. "What do you mean, go back? We're not leaving until we've found Jake!" As he spoke, he became even more wound up and his frustration was plain in his voice.

"What if Jake's gone back to the library?" Rae tried to level with him. "He's a smart kid. He'll have headed back to the library when he thought it was safe."

"Safe?" Mark exclaimed, his face suddenly turning red with anger. "You mean like how he would have been safe in the library?

It's never safe out here! Jake thinks there's still a Hunter in the library! Why on earth would he go back? He's petrified! Don't you dare tell me what my son would do! It's your fault he ran off in the first place!"

Mark stopped when he realised what he had said and felt his anger suddenly dissipate when he saw the effect of his words. Rae was looking down at the floor in silence, having flinched uncomfortably at every word Mark had said.

He was right, and the worst part was that Rae knew he was right. She did feel to blame for Jake running off and the guilt had been gnawing at her ever since they had returned to find the Hunter in the library and Jake gone.

She had been sure that Jake would have been safe there, that nothing could get in until they returned – but she had been wrong. And now Jake's life was in danger because of her mistake.

She felt indebted to reunite the strange father and son couple before that mistake could get any worse.

"I'm sorry," Mark began to apologise. "I shouldn't hav…"

"No," Rae interrupted him. "You're right. It's my fault."

She raised her head to look him in the eye. Mark was taken aback by the determination he saw on her face.

"And I am going to do everything I can to find him again – I promise you. But we need to go back to the library. If Jake is looking for us, that's the first place he would have gone. And if he is still hiding somewhere else and hasn't gone back, then he will be safe there until we find him. OK?"

Mark stared back at her with a pained expression, turning her words over in his head. He realised there was no right answer, that whatever decision he made was just as likely to lead to a dead end. Eventually he looked towards the ground and nodded in resignation. Rae sighed with relief.

"Let's head back then," she said quietly. "If Jake's not there waiting for us, then we can head straight back out again."

Rae turned and started walking back along the road in the direction of the library. Reluctantly Mark followed, shooting nervous glances into the slowly receding shadows for any sign that Jake might be hiding there. Above them the sky was transforming from a desolate black to a pale and deathly grey as dawn arrived and began softly illuminating the town.

Maybe the light will draw him out from his hiding place, Rae thought, as she passed through a narrow alley.

Ahead of her lay a garden which she quickly scanned for any signs of danger before heading through the tall grass. As she stepped out onto a pathway on the other side of the garden, she felt a sudden wave of relief wash over her and she found herself thinking about the one-armed man she had killed the day before.

Rae had recognised him instantly. The unmistakable leer on his face as he slept peacefully in his chair had sent cold shivers racing down her spine while the blood in her veins had started to boil. He had been one of the men responsible for torturing her husband.

The memory came back to her as if it had only just happened and she began to shudder as she recalled the group taking turns at beating her husband while he sat tied to a chair. She had been watching it happen through a pair of binoculars, knowing that she was too far away to stop them, but not being able to look away.

The one-armed man had been the first to start the beating on that fateful day, though back then he had had two arms, and her husband had managed to grab hold of one of them and bite at it viciously before being overpowered by the rest of the group. She could still see the chunk of flesh in her husband's smiling mouth as the one-armed man writhed in pain. It had been the same arm which he had been missing yesterday and Rae assumed that the wound had gotten infected and eventually needed amputating.

Good, she thought coldly. She hoped it had hurt.

But her husband's smile hadn't lasted long and Rae had watched in horror as they tortured and humiliated him. The helplessness she had felt was like nothing she had ever experienced before, the despair at knowing she was powerless to save him from the pain unbearable.

The anger came when it was finally over. Along with the vow that she would avenge her husband and make every single one of those animals pay.

That was why she didn't regret the brutality of what she'd done. She would do it to every single one of them if she got the chance.

Her only regret was that Mark had been there to see it, that he had witnessed what she was prepared to do to get her revenge. Rae couldn't help wondering if she would have done the same thing if Jake had been with them, if she would have been capable of torturing someone in front of a child.

She couldn't honestly say.

Behind her she heard Mark's heavy footsteps as he scanned every nook and cranny for any sign of Jake. She tried to rouse herself from her thoughts, feeling guilty for not showing the same vigilance, and began looking at the buildings around her. They weren't far away from the library and now that it was getting much lighter their chances of finding Jake would increase.

Suddenly a thought occurred to her that made her stomach turn, and for a moment she thought she was going to be sick. Her pace slowed imperceptibly but she forced herself to keep walking, so as not to give any hint to Mark that something was wrong. She focused on steadying her breathing and gradually the nausea subsided, its place quickly taken by a growing sense of dread.

From the moment they had realised he was missing she had considered the possibility that one of the men might find Jake first, and up to now she had assumed that if they did then they would keep him unharmed while they used him to draw out Mark from hiding.

But she hadn't considered the effect that finding Mike brutally murdered would have on the group, the anger that it would instil within them at the obvious threat, and now she realised the very real possibility that they might take their rage out on Jake in a show of revenge.

A lump of guilt formed in her throat which she quickly swallowed down and she found herself trying to drive the thought away before she lost her focus.

They wouldn't find Jake, she tried to reassure herself as the guilt stubbornly resurfaced. They didn't even know he had run away.

Mark and Rae moved through another garden and found themselves on another narrow street. Over the rooftops the tall building of the library could now be seen, causing them to quicken their pace. Rae took a shortcut through a side alley and emerged on the street directly in front of the library, sensing Mark's anticipation behind her.

The front entrance lay undisturbed and everything looked the same as when they had left. Rae's eyes found the dark metal staircase at the building's side and followed it up to the platform at the top. Her heart sank with disappointment when she saw that Jake wasn't there and behind her Mark let out a harrowing groan.

She realised painfully how sure she had been that they were going to find Jake waiting for them.

Suddenly Mark cried out from behind her, causing her to jump with fright. She turned quickly to look at him, but was met with a rush of air as he sprinted past her and towards the library.

For a moment, Rae was completely bewildered, but when she saw what Mark was running towards her earlier nausea returned and she felt her blood turn icy cold in her veins.

In front of the library's entrance, hanging loosely on a pole sticking out of the ground, something small and dark was flapping gently in the breeze.

It was Jake's coat. She had to stop herself from retching when she recognised it, and a moment later she too was sprinting across the tarmac.

Mark reached the coat ahead of her and ripped it from its stand, staring at the object in his hands as he muttered unintelligibly.

Rae was there a second later and stared down at the coat in horror, still not believing that it could really be Jake's. A whirlwind of thoughts started careening through her mind, desperately trying to make sense of the situation. Beside her Mark fell to his knees and held Jake's coat to his face as he began to scream into the fabric.

They had him. How on earth did they have him?

She tried to fight back her panic as her earlier fears resurfaced; that the group might take out their anger on Jake. Her guilt started to overwhelm her, until suddenly her mind's defence mechanism kicked in and she found herself subconsciously repressing her anxiety.

She let out a low breath as she battled to take control of the situation, to work out a plan that would get Jake back to them safely.

In her confusion, she had almost forgotten that Mark was still on the floor beside her and she only remembered he was there when he stood up abruptly and began walking away from the library with Jake's coat clutched tightly in his hands.

"Where are you going?" she called after him, hurrying down the road to catch him up.

"They have him," Mark muttered helplessly. His eyes were clearly straining to hold back his tears. "I have to get him. I need to get him back!"

"You can't!" Rae said, jogging to keep up with him. "They'll kill you. We need to think of a plan before we resc…"

"WE?" Mark turned and screamed at her. Rae stopped in her tracks and stared at him in shock. He was towering over her.

215

"There is no we! There's just me and Jake! You hear me? There is no we! You told me to leave him, you told me he would be safe! Well you were wrong! And now they have him…now they have my son. And they're going to…"

Mark's voice cracked at the edges before failing altogether and the face that had been so full of anger suddenly melted as Mark fell weeping to the floor.

Rae didn't know how to react and found there were no words of comfort she could offer to him as she watched him desperately clutch Jake's coat on the floor, thick, heavy sobs racking his body. So instead she stood in silence and waited for him to finish weeping, trying to ignore the shame she felt at being a witness to his breakdown.

After a few minutes his sobs seemed to slow and Rae knelt down to place her hand on his shoulder.

Mark looked up at her through eyes blurry with tears, pleading for her to tell him this wasn't really happening, that it was just some nightmare he was yet to wake up from. But the expression on her face told him it was real.

Mark hung his head to the floor and let out a strangled, painful moan. When he looked back up, his eyes were pleading with her again, this time for her to do something to bring Jake back to him alive, for her to help him achieve the seemingly impossible. Rae tightened her grip on his shoulder as she returned his stare, the expression on her face turning hard as stone.

"You're going to get him back," she said to him slowly. "But you are going to have to trust me."

Chapter 30

The edge of the forest was dark and gloomy in the early light, the rising sun doing little to chase away the shadows beneath the trees. In the middle of the campsite, the fire had died down to a few burning embers, which did nothing to stave off the morning's wintry chill.

The group were sat in a circle around what was left of the fire, the damp fabric of the chairs sticking to their trousers and letting the cold leech into their skin. Around the circle Gabe paced impatiently, his head on a swivel as he scanned the trees around him.

They had placed Jake in one of the empty tents after he had told them where his dad was hiding and the group had listened uncomfortably as he had continued to cry softly to himself throughout the night.

None of them had slept.

Ever since Jack had gone to the library to leave Jake's coat they had all been waiting. Gabe knew it wouldn't be long until the dad showed up, and as the morning had drawn nearer the waiting had become more and more tense.

For a while, he had considered getting some of his men to guard the Camp's perimeter, but he had quickly dismissed the idea. Clearly the dad wasn't stupid and would be aware that they would kill his son if they sensed anything was wrong.

Gabe felt a smile creep onto his face despite his impatience. Of course there would be no rescue attempt. It was far too risky.

Instead the dad would have to come crawling out of hiding, begging them for forgiveness and to let his son go. Gabe could already feel his blood rushing at the thought of him begging to spare Jake's life, and he had to bite hard on his lip to stop getting ahead of himself.

Not long now, he thought, as he shot another glance towards the town. Not long now.

It was another half an hour before he finally saw what he had been waiting for.

He stopped pacing around the campsite and fixed his gaze on someone who was slowly emerging from between the houses. It was too far away to make out who it was, but he didn't need confirmation. A cruel smile began to play over his lips.

"Boys," he shouted over his shoulder.

Behind him he heard movement as the men turned as one, slowly rising from their chairs to see what had caught his attention.

The dad was now walking across the barren patch of grass that stood between the town and the forest, hands held above his head as he approached the camp. Gabe felt a shiver of excitement scurry down his spine. He was going to enjoy this.

"Fetch the boy," he demanded, and behind him Paul rushed off. The dad was only halfway across the patch of land, but Gabe could already see the fear that was etched across his face.

That's it, Gabe thought to himself as he heard Jake being hauled from the tent – just a bit closer. He took a deep breath to calm himself before taking out his knife.

Mark passed the first of the tents that marked the edge of the campsite, shuddering involuntarily when he crossed its invisible boundary. He couldn't see Jake anywhere in the camp ahead of him and he found himself fighting off the conclusions that his mind had already drawn.

As he approached the small circle of chairs in the Camp's centre, he felt the men's eyes boring into him. Standing just outside the circle was a tall man with piercing blue eyes, and Mark's throat constricted when he saw the gleeful expression that was plastered across his face. Mark realised this must be the group's leader; he remembered hearing the two men who had killed the stag calling him Gabe.

When Mark was about ten paces away from Gabe, he stopped. His hands were shaking in the air above him to show that he was unarmed. Gabe was still staring at him with a look that said he was enjoying every second of what was happening. Mark instead was still scanning the rest of the campsite for any sign of Jake.

For a while, no one spoke and with each passing second of silence he found himself becoming more and more uncertain.

"Where is he?" Mark blurted suddenly. His voice sounded meek and pathetic in front of the group.

Gabe's expression remained unchanged.

"Search him," came the reply.

One of the younger group members stepped forward from the circle and patted down Mark's arms and legs.

Mark had now locked eyes with Gabe, trying to look as serious as possible as he demanded his question be answered. He ignored the rough pats of the young man who was searching him. The young man turned towards Gabe and shook his head before quickly retreating to his chair.

"Wise decision," Gabe said coldly.

"Where's my son?" Mark repeated, trying to make his voice more firm.

Gabe's smile grew more intense as the sound of someone approaching from the side made Mark turn.

Mark had to stop himself from choking when he saw Jake being marched towards him. He looked terrified, his wide eyes a bloodshot red from where he had been crying and his skin was a shade of deathly white. But other than the obvious signs of shock he looked unharmed.

"Jake," Mark breathed as he was herded towards them.

Jake lifted up his arms and tried to run towards Mark, but Gabe grabbed him before he could get away and pulled him tightly to his side. Mark swallowed back his nausea as he watched Jake struggle and had to stop himself from shouting when Gabe suddenly slapped him across the face.

Jake cried out in pain and instantly stopped struggling. He lowered his head and started whimpering. Mark felt his heart twist painfully in his chest and clenched his fists uselessly as he dropped his arms to his sides.

"I'll make this easy," Gabe said slowly. "You show me where all the stuff you stole is, or I kill your son."

Mark felt his stomach turn and for a moment found that he couldn't speak.

"OK," he said breathlessly. He held out his arms in a pleading gesture. "I'll take you, I swear. Just let him go. He has nothing to do with this. Please!"

Gabe looked at him in confusion, his grip on Jake loosening for just a second. Then he threw his head back and laughed, the deranged sound bouncing around the tree trunks. Only when he was finished did he fix Mark with another menacing stare.

"No," he said plainly, the laughter vanishing from his face as quickly as it had appeared. "That's not how this is going to work. What's going to happen is this. You are going to take me to where

219

you have hidden everything you stole yesterday, and you are going to give it all back. If you don't, or if you try anything – and I mean anything – that I feel isn't right…then I slice his neck open on the spot."

The flash of metal caught Mark by surprise and he watched with horror as Gabe brought a knife up to Jake's throat. Jake whimpered and tried to pull away as the cold metal touched his skin, but Gabe held him firmly in place. Mark fought hard to stop himself from throwing up.

"And if you do exactly what I tell you to," Gabe continued, "then I might not make you watch."

He stopped talking then and left Mark to stare at Jake, who was still shying away from the knife at his throat. He was completely powerless to do anything other than what he was told. He shot glances at the rest of the group, who were watching the encounter with grim expressions. Their faces told him that Gabe meant everything he had said.

He hung his head to the floor, still trying to find some option that would allow Jake to live. He had known that pleading wouldn't work, that they would kill Jake and him the moment they got what they wanted, but a small part of him had still hoped that these men would possess even a hint of sympathy and would let Jake go in return for his own life.

It had been a foolish thing to hope for. Sympathy had died long ago.

"What's it going to be?" Gabe said threateningly, gently rubbing the knife across Jake's skin.

Mark was out of options. He knew he had no choice.

"I'll take you," he said quickly. Gabe smiled and took the knife away from Jake's throat. "Just, please don't hurt him."

Gabe turned and pushed Jake back to someone else in the group, causing him to cry out in surprise at the sudden movement. Mark didn't take his eyes away from Jake as Gabe stepped up to his face, the stale stench of his breath making him flinch with every word.

"If we aren't back in an hour…kill him. If he returns without me…kill him. And if the boy tries to run," Gabe grabbed Mark's face and turned it so he was looking into his eyes.

"Kill him."

Mark pulled his head away and watched as Jake's trembling figure curled up into a tight little ball. The sight awakened a wounded anger deep within him that for a moment cut straight through his despair.

"It'll be OK, Jake," he said, in a voice that was suddenly clear and firm. "Everything's going to be OK."

In front of him, Gabe grunted with amusement and spat onto the ground. Mark ignored him and, with one final effort, turned away and began walking slowly back towards the desolate town.

Chapter 31

They left the forest behind them and began walking amongst the derelict townhouses.

Mark hadn't looked back towards the camp since they had left, knowing that he wouldn't be able to bear the sight of Jake alone with the rest of the group. Instead he had kept his eyes fixed on the road ahead of him, determined to stave off the endless waves of emotion that threatened to engulf him. He needed to keep his focus now more than ever.

Gabe was following closely behind, whistling cheerily to himself as Mark guided them through the abandoned streets. Jack had come with them from the campsite, his face still badly beaten and bruised, and he was now stalking silently behind them as they headed deeper into town. He seemed to not be sharing in Gabe's enthusiasm.

"How does it feel?"

Mark half-turned, just enough to see Gabe's piercing eyes studying him. It was the first thing any of them had said since they left the forest.

"How does it feel to know you've lost? To know that once I get what I want I'm going to kill you."

Mark turned his eyes forward and didn't respond, trying instead to keep his emotions under control. The panic and anger mixing in his chest didn't make it easy.

"Because I am going to kill you. You do know that, don't you? You *and* your boy."

Mark bristled at the mention of Jake and had to clench his fists to stop his hands from shaking. He fought down his urge to lash out and focused instead on pressing his feet hard into the concrete as he walked. They turned a corner and began heading down a narrow alley. The buildings either side began to close in on them and blocked out the weak sunlight.

"When Paul said he had seen a man and a boy when we first arrived, I thought he was making it up. I didn't think there were any children left."

Still Mark didn't look back. Ahead of them he could see the street where the alley ended.

"But then Jack here says he got held at gunpoint by a stranger in the woods."

For a moment, Mark was surprised, and had to stop himself from turning to look at the man who was walking behind them. Of course. Jack was the person he had held at gunpoint only two days ago. So much had happened since then that Mark had nearly forgotten.

Behind him Gabe was still rambling.

"And then four of my men get killed in town. Four! Led into a trap by a mysterious man and boy. Now that could hardly be a coincidence."

The end of the alley was getting closer, like a bright light at the end of the darkest of tunnels. Mark fought to contain himself for just a little bit longer, a task that was becoming increasingly difficult with every passing second.

"And then!" Gabe's voice had started to lose its cheeriness. "I come back from burning down your camp to find Mike – poor, crippled Mike – tortured and beaten to death, left for us to find. Five of my men murdered. By you and your bastard son."

Mark's nostrils flared, his fingers screaming from being clenched so hard. He was almost there. He was so nearly there. Gabe leaned forward and whispered into his ear again.

"I should thank you really," he whispered gently. "They were weak, and you took care of them for me. Five less people to slow me down."

Gabe's breath made Mark flinch as it touched his ear. The tension was unbearable, the pain in his hands screaming at him to let go. He needed to hold on for just a few more steps.

"But you're still going to pay for what you've done," Gabe sneered. "You're still going to watch your son die."

Mark spun round and brought his fist up hard into Gabe's jaw, feeling the bone crack under the force of the punch. Pain shot through his arm, culminating around the bullet hole in his shoulder, as Gabe fell to the floor. Adrenalin quickly kicked in and blocked out his pain as he darted out of the alley and into the street ahead before Jack, who was still behind them, could reach for his gun.

Within seconds, Mark had barrelled through the nearest door and was tearing back through the houses, sprinting as fast as he could in the direction of the forest.

Somewhere behind him he heard Gabe screaming with rage and he knew that it was now a race to see who could get back to the camp first. But he was still unarmed, and there were three men guarding Jake.

Panic began to consume him as he charged through the streets, his intense anger from moments before completely forgotten. He tried to cast off his despair and focus instead on dodging the fallen debris that threatened to trip him up in every house he entered, but all he could think about was the fact that he was now completely helpless in determining the fate of his son.

Instead, Jake's fate rested in the hands of a woman he had known for only two days. A woman he had seen brutally torture a defenceless cripple before executing him. A woman he barely knew.

He would beat Gabe back to the camp, Mark realised, as he saw the treetops appear above the houses. He just had no idea what he would find when he got there.

Jake sat huddled in a ball by the fire pit, still crying softly to himself on the frost-stricken ground. The men left to guard him were sitting some distance away, huddled together as they played a game of cards and did everything they could to avoid looking at him.

He knew that one of them was called Paul, because he was the one that had found him in town and brought him here, and Jake had picked up that the other two were called Daniel and Cal. None of them had said a word to him since Dad and Gabe, the group's scary leader, had left to go into town.

In fact, no one had spoken to Jake since he had told them that his dad was in the library.

He hugged his knees to his chest as he felt another wave of sadness wash over him and wondered what would happen when Gabe returned. Jake didn't want to die, but knew as soon as Gabe got back that the men would kill him and his dad.

Jake couldn't understand it. Why did they want to hurt him? He remembered again how he thought Dad was being stupid when he told him that the people they had seen were dangerous; that he was just being overprotective like he always was. Now Jake knew that he was the one that had been stupid, and that Dad had been right to be afraid.

Jake knew this, but he still couldn't understand why.

He forced himself to stop crying and shook his head vigorously in an effort to keep a hold of himself. It didn't matter why, he thought glumly, it wouldn't make any difference.

In front of him, he sensed movement and he looked up to see Daniel standing up from the card game.

Jake's heart jumped to his throat as he looked for what had disturbed him. He wondered if Dad and Gabe had returned already, but could see nothing moving at the edge of the houses in the distance and around them the treeline was quiet and still.

Daniel began walking slowly to the edge of the camp, his posture relaxed as he entered the forest, and stopped by a tree to unzip his trousers. Jake looked away with a mixture of relief and disappointment.

It was impossible, he thought, as he stared glumly towards the town. He wanted nothing more than his dad to come back and take him away from this nightmare, this nightmare that was worse than anything he had ever dreamt, but deep down he knew what would really happen when his dad eventually returned.

At least, he wasn't scared anymore.

When Paul had found him in town, Jake had been absolutely petrified, and spent the rest of the night crying uncontrollably in fear of what was to come. Now he found he had no more tears to cry, and he was far too tired to be scared.

Instead he found he felt completely numb as the inevitable crept slowly closer, knowing no amount of crying or worrying would change what was going to happen to him. He even wondered if soon he would actually get to meet his mum.

As long as Dad was with him, he reassured himself. He didn't care what happened as long as his dad was with him.

He watched Paul and Cal playing at cards for a few more minutes, his eyes registering their hand movements while his thoughts were focused elsewhere.

Jake thought about his father out in the town, trying desperately to think of a way to escape and free him; about the Hunters, what was once his greatest fear, skulking away and not daring to venture out of their home; he thought of Rae, who had saved his life and wanted him and his father to help her kill these men in return.

Rae, Jake thought suddenly. Had something happened to her?

As his thoughts returned to the camp around him, he realised that only Paul and Cal were sitting around the cards. Jake frowned and turned to look at the tree which Daniel had gone to, but saw to his surprise that the tree was now unoccupied.

He looked around him quickly, confused by the disappearance, but could see no sign of anyone walking around the camp. Paul and Cal hadn't seemed to notice Daniel's absence and they busied themselves with yet another hand as Jake turned back to the forest, scanning the tall conifers for any sign of movement.

He had to stifle a yelp of surprise when he finally saw him.

Daniel was lying on the floor, his head twisted at an unnatural angle from where he had fallen. A deep, red line was sliced across his throat and he lay in a pool of black that was slowly melting the frost on the floor around him.

Jake blinked hard and tried to refocus, the disbelief at what he saw making him doubt his eyes, but when he opened them again Daniel's body was still there, the pool of steaming black steadily growing.

Was it Dad, he thought excitedly, as he searched the camp with his eyes; had Dad managed to escape, and come back to rescue him?

He scanned around the camp again, trying not to look too eager in case Paul or Cal noticed, and froze when he saw a dark figure outlined against one of the tents. The figure was watching the two men playing cards carefully from behind the tent and its hand was poised tensely by a knife at its waist.

At first, Jake thought again that his dad had come back, but quickly realised that he was mistaken; the figure was slighter than that of his dad's, and the thick, knotted mass of hair that twisted down from the figure's head was far too long.

Rae!

He barely stopped himself from calling out her name and stared wide-eyed with disbelief. Rae must have sensed she was being watched, as she turned to meet his gaze and put a finger up to her lips. Jake nodded almost imperceptibly to show that he understood, hardly daring to breathe in case he gave her away.

For a while, nothing happened. Paul and Cal were still engrossed in their game and Rae watched them silently from behind the tent.

She couldn't take them both head-on – if Mark was yet to escape from Gabe then using a gun was far too risky – and a two-on-one knife fight didn't go in her favour. Instead she needed to separate them, so she could take them out one at a time.

Slowly she crept back to the Camp's edge and began to shake the tent closest to her. Jake watched in shock as the loud ruffling filled the camp, causing Paul and Cal to turn sharply towards the noise.

"Very funny, Daniel," Cal shouted, turning back to his hand before placing down another card. Rae shook the tent again, this time more violently, as if the tent itself was possessed. Paul and Cal turned back to the noise.

"Stop playing around, Dan!" Cal shouted in annoyance. "Gabe will be back soon!"

Suddenly the tent stopped moving. The camp fell silent again.

"Dan?" Paul shouted towards the edge of the camp.

"Dan, are you there?"

Still no response. They put down their cards.

"Go check it out, Cal," Paul said, staring uneasily towards the tent that had just been moving. Cal got up from his chair and started moving slowly towards it, his gun held out carefully in front of him. He couldn't see any sign of Daniel, or of anyone else that could have made the noise. He turned to look back at Paul, shrugging his shoulders in a show of confusion. "I can't see him."

"Maybe something got in there?" Paul suggested. "Like a squirrel or something."

Cal shrugged again and carried on towards the tent, his gun still held out in front of him.

From by the fire pit Jake watched on nervously as Cal crept closer and closer. By now he had completely lost sight of Rae and had no idea where she'd gone. He held his breath as Cal got to within a few paces of the tent.

Suddenly something darted out from the trees, a flash of grey that made Cal jump and Jake yelp quietly with surprise. A loud gunshot rang out that echoed around the forest as Cal fell to the floor, his gun flying up into the air and landing out of his reach.

Rae was crouched on top of him, a flash of silver appearing in her hand that was quickly replaced by a spurt of red as she burrowed something deep into the side of his head. Jake watched on with his mouth agape, waiting to hear Cal scream in pain, and shivering when the sound never came.

Paul stood up quickly from his chair and looked at Rae in disbelief. Rae looked up, her face covered with a splatter of blood, and darted towards him.

She moved quickly, but was too far away to reach him in time and Jake watched in horror as Paul moved a hand to his pocket and pulled out a revolver. Rae saw it too and the flash of silver leapt out from her hand and hurtled silently through the air.

The silver disappeared into Paul's shoulder and his gun clattered to the floor as he let out a howl of pain. Rae didn't stop running and before Paul could react she had barrelled into him and driven him onto the floor, causing his head to smack against the hard ground with a sickening thud.

The tussle seemed to last forever and Jake could barely breathe as he watched the desperate struggle. With one hand Paul was trying to reach for a knife which was tucked away in his belt, while with the other he was fending off the constant blows that Rae was throwing at him.

Jake tried to move closer, desperate to help out in any way that he could, but was stopped by the rope that was tied around his legs. It was no use, he realised hopelessly, and gasped as Paul got a firm punch to Rae's face that caused her nose to twist unnaturally.

Rae spat blood out of her mouth and threw another punch. It hit its mark and Paul screamed again as Rae grabbed hold of her knife, that was still in Paul's shoulder, and twisted hard.

For a split second, the pain overwhelmed Paul and he almost blacked out. When he came to, he tried to throw another punch back at Rae, who was now on top of him, but it was too late. Her fingers closed around his throat and he felt the air shut off from his lungs as her grip got slowly tighter.

Panic overtook him and he started flailing helplessly as Rae's cold eyes bored down at him. Red dots began to appear in his vision, which had become blurred as his lungs screamed desperately for air, and the heels of his feet scraped uselessly against the frozen ground.

Gradually, Paul felt the energy ebb from him as Rae maintained her vicelike grip, her eyes boring into his as he continued to struggle. His efforts got weaker and weaker, until eventually the struggling stopped and his eyes clouded over.

Jake sat breathing heavily by the fire pit, his fear beginning to subside as the winner of the fight became clear. Watching the struggle had exhausted him and he felt faint as he watched Rae roll off Paul and onto her back, her breath coming out in heavy steams that drifted up into the sky.

For a while, she lay like that, panting heavily as she tried to catch her breath. Jake waited for her to get up and come over to him, until eventually he couldn't wait any longer.

"Rae?" he said quietly, his voice harsh and dry from all the crying.

Rae stirred and turned on her side to look at him, cursing under her breath when she realised that Jake was tied up. Slowly she got to her feet, grunting in pain with the effort.

Jake was surprised to see that she was covered in blood; a dark red stain on the front of her coat from where one of the men must have bled onto her. She started to shuffle slowly towards him, her face contorting with each step, but fell heavily onto one knee before she had moved more than a few paces. Her hand went to her stomach and when she took it away Jake saw that it was covered in a fresh layer of red. It wasn't blood from one of the men, he realised with horror. It was her own.

"NO!" Jake shouted angrily as she fell to the floor, her face landing heavily on the frozen ground. He began to struggle against the rope that bound his legs, desperately trying to free himself in order to help his friend. Rae lifted her head slowly from the ground, looking up at him with a face that was as white as a ghost's.

Jake stopped struggling and met her stare, her cold eyes freezing him to the spot and stopping him from talking. Her eyes grew slightly warmer as they looked at him and a sad smile tugged gently at the corner of her lips.

She opened her mouth to say something, but thought better of it and closed it again. Then the warmth in her eyes vanished as quickly as it had arrived and her head slumped back onto the cold, hard ground as she finally fell still.

Chapter 32

The sound of the gunshot bounced around the houses, making Mark jump with fright and his blood turn to ice. The echoes made it hard for him to pinpoint the sound, but he didn't need to listen to know where it had come from.

He pushed his legs to move harder, barely noticing the burning pain that travelled up his thighs and throbbed in his shoulder. The cold burned at the back of his throat as he sucked air greedily in, his eyes watering from where the air pummelled into them.

Why was there a gunshot, he thought frantically, as he got closer to the edge of the forest. Rae had said she wouldn't use guns; that she was going to sneak up on the men guarding Jake and take them out quietly. A gunshot meant that something had gone wrong, something potentially catastrophic.

He gritted his teeth together and tried not to think about what that something might be.

Around him the buildings began to thin out again and the green of the forest appeared in the gaps between the houses ahead. His body was screaming at him to rest, but he ignored it and pushed on past the last of the houses and across the gap of no man's land.

The camp lay still and silent ahead of him, the fire pit in the centre obscured by a mismatch of tents and trees.

Mark searched desperately for any signs of life, unsure whether it was good or bad that the camp seemed devoid of it.

He slowed his pace when he passed the first of the tents, his breath now coming in heavy gasps. The centre of the camp came into view and he saw the blackened fire pit with the huddle of chairs placed messily around it. Just outside the circle, lay the dead body of one of the group, the man's eyes staring lifelessly into the sky. By the fire pit lay two other bodies; one large and still, the other smaller and shaking gently.

"Jake!" Mark shouted, and started running again.

Jake looked up, his face streaked with tears, and his mouth fell open when he saw his dad running towards him.

"Dad!" he shouted in reply.

Mark reached him and hugged him tightly, the emotion overwhelming him and sending deep, painful sobs through his chest. Jake was crying too and had buried his face deep into his coat.

Mark couldn't speak, the back of his throat was too thick with tears, and he started stroking the back of Jake's hair softly as he looked up into the sky.

He couldn't believe he had found him. Jake was alive. Alive and unharmed. He had never been so thankful for anything in all his life.

"Where's Rae?" he managed to splutter, remembering suddenly who he had to thank for this moment.

At first, Jake didn't reply and Mark leaned back so he could look into his face. Jake looked suddenly sad again and Mark could see he was on the verge of tears. Weakly he held out a trembling finger and Mark followed it to the other body on the floor.

"Rae!" he gasped, and ran to her side.

When he turned over her body, Rae's head lolled limply to the floor and her cold, dark eyes stared emptily up to the sky. The front of her clothes were dark where they were saturated with blood. Mark held two fingers to the side of her neck and searched desperately for any sign of a pulse, but the cold, unmoving skin beneath his fingers told him what he already knew.

She was dead.

Mark felt a deep sadness wash over him as he looked down at her, caught off guard by the sudden emotion. He had barely known her for more than two days, but she had listened when he had confided in her, and more importantly she had saved Jake's life – twice.

"Thank you," he whispered softly. He leaned forward and used the tips of his fingers to gently shut her eyes.

Behind him he heard Jake struggling and he turned to see what was wrong. Jake's legs and hands were bound tightly by a thick cord of rope and he was struggling desperately to free himself from their grasp.

Mark raced quickly over and began to untie him, the cold in his fingers making him fumble with the tightly bound knots. Eventually Jake was free and he began to scratch his wrists feverishly where the rope had bound them.

"Come on," Mark said, taking Jake by the hand. He scanned the blood-stained ground for any sign of a gun and saw one lying near another body that lay just outside the circle of chairs. He was about to head over and take it when something at the edge of the camp caught his eye.

"Don't. Move."

Gabe's voice was quivering with rage and was as cold as the dead bodies around them.

Mark felt his heart sink. Gabe's face was burning with rage, his cheek a bright red from where Mark had struck him, a trickle of blood running gently from the corner of his mouth.

Mark went to say something, but he knew it would be useless. Out of the corner of his eye he could still see the gun on the floor, just too far away for him to reach without Gabe having time to shoot him. Behind him he felt Jake tightly hugging his leg.

"Who the hell is she?" Gabe shouted, spit flying from his mouth. He was pointing towards Rae's body. Over his right shoulder Jack slowly emerged from behind a tree.

Mark felt his heart sink even further.

"Please," he started to beg.

"Don't!" Gabe cut him off sharply. His outstretched hand was trembling with rage, the gun shaking dangerously at its end. The crazed look in Gabe's eyes made Mark shiver.

"I don…"

The gunshot made him jump and a clump of earth flew up into the air next to him.

"I SAID, DON"T!" Gabe roared, a wisp of smoke drifting up from the end of the barrel.

Behind him Jake had started crying again.

"You've taken everything from me," Gabe continued, his voice shaking. "Everything! Now I'm going to take everything from you."

Mark swallowed hard. He knew what was coming next.

"Come here, boy," Gabe called softly, not taking his eyes off Mark's.

Jake squeezed Mark's leg tighter, refusing to let go.

"Come here!" Gabe shouted again, louder and angrier this time. Mark flinched and began to shake.

"Let him go," he pleaded weakly. His voice was choked with tears. "Please!"

"Come. Here," Gabe repeated, the gun in his hand steadying.

Still Jake didn't move.

"Please let him go," Mark begged again, his voice barely a whisper. The gun on the floor still stared at him from the corner of his eye, the dark metal outlined sharply against the blood-stained ground. He knew he wouldn't reach it before Gabe could shoot him, but he had to try.

His body tensed as he prepared to take the leap.

"Last chance," Gabe said, his finger tightening on the trigger.

It was now or never.

The gunshot caught him off guard, coming much earlier than he had expected and before he had a chance to even move. He gritted his teeth as he braced himself for the impact. Behind him Jake gasped and squeezed his leg tighter, turning his foot numb from the lack of blood.

He waited for the sting of the bullet, the spark of pain to shoot up through his body and switch off his brain, but instead he saw Gabe's head explode from the side, a spray of blood and brain bursting through his temple and splattering onto the trees. His gun fell to the floor as his body collapsed, what remained of his head slamming into the ground and spraying more blood over the frost.

Mark looked on in shock, his brain unable to process what his eyes had seen. He looked at Gabe's body lying on the floor, his head now unrecognisable.

Jack stood to Gabe's right, a gun held out in front of him that was smoking at its end. His face was unreadable behind the angry mask of cuts and bruises, but his eyes were clear and emotionless as they stared down at Gabe. Suddenly he looked up, as if noticing Mark and Jake for the first time, and turned the gun towards them.

Mark shook his head, still too numb from shock to feel his panic. Jack walked closer to them, the expression in his eyes unchanging as he approached.

Behind Mark Jake had stopped crying and was now sniffling gently as he peered cautiously out from between his legs. Jack stepped over Gabe's dead body, the gun still held out in front of him, and stopped.

"Why didn't you kill me?" he asked bluntly, fixing Mark with a cold stare.

Mark looked back in bewilderment, not understanding the question.

"Please, just let my son and I go. We won't hur…"

"Why didn't you kill me?" Jack repeated, more firmly this time.

Mark shook his head in confusion, desperately trying to understand what he needed to say. Then he remembered his encounter two days ago, when he had held Jack at gunpoint on the cliff.

"Wh...why didn't I kill you?" Mark stuttered.

Jack stood still, waiting for what he had to say. Mark began searching for an answer, the most important answer he would ever have to give. His response could mean the difference between Jake living or dying. He could feel Jake now, pressed tightly against the back of his leg, the comforting rise and fall of his chest somehow helping him to concentrate. What was it that Jack wanted to hear?

"Because I didn't need to," he said eventually, wincing at how pathetic the words sounded.

The answer caught Jack off guard and for the first time since he had fired the gun a hint of emotion flashed across his face. He tried to blink back his surprise before searching for any hidden meaning in the words.

For a while, they stood staring at each other, the sound of the wind gently rustling the tents the only thing to be heard. Finally, Jack let out a deep breath, before letting the gun fall to his side.

Mark felt his panic disappear as the gun turned to the floor, like an echo fading into the distance. His whole body flooded with a sudden weariness and he realised how sore his eyes were as he watched Jack turn and head over to one of the tents. Jack reached inside and grabbed a backpack, which he quickly slung over his shoulder before standing up straight and running his eyes over the rest of the camp.

The floor was littered with bodies, the blood that had pooled on the ground gently steaming in the cold. Jack's gaze passed over all of them before finally settling on Mark and Jake, who were still watching him strangely from beside the fire pit. They stood staring at each other for a few seconds, and for a wild moment Mark thought that this might be the last person other than Jake that he would ever see.

"Don't follow me," Jack said suddenly. And with that he turned and began walking towards the road that led away from the town and into the world beyond.

Chapter 33

The sun started its lazy fall back down the sky as the day carried into the afternoon.

Shafts of sunlight drifted down through the trees, thawing out the frozen ground and guiding Mark and Jake as they trudged around the outskirts of town and back towards their home. From the canopy a thrush chirped away merrily, its gentle melody trickling through the forest and searching invitingly for a companion to join in a harmony.

The camp lay far behind them; the abandoned tents now an ugly memorial to the people who'd resided there.

It had taken just over an hour to gather enough wood to build a funeral pyre for Rae. Mark and Jake had watched as her body had gone up in flames, the comforting warmth of the fire reminding them of all she had done for them in the short time they had known her.

They had both said a few words to honour her memory; Jake had said a short goodbye to his friend that he wished he could have got to know better, and Mark had thanked her for saving the only thing he cared about.

"You have your revenge," he had said, as he watched the smoke from her body rising up past the trees and into the endless blue. "Now go and rest peacefully with your husband."

They had left the other bodies where they were.

Mark was tired. He hadn't realised how much until Jack, who had saved them, had gone. It had been nearly forty hours since he had last been asleep and the continual cycle of adrenalin, fear and exertion had left him utterly drained. The pain in his shoulder had also gotten worse since the end of their ordeal and he knew he would need to re-dress the bandage when they got back home.

A thought occurred to him and he turned to look at Jake, who was trudging along by his side. Jake let out a wide yawn, showing Mark that he was equally exhausted.

"Do you know about the house?" Mark asked tentatively, not wanting to break his spirits. Jake turned to look at him and shook his head sleepily. He let out a long sigh.

"It's gone, Jake," he said wearily. "The men found it and burnt it down."

Jake looked down at the floor sadly, his shoulders slumping at the news. The small wooden hut in the trees was the only place he had ever lived – the only place he had ever been able to call home. Mark didn't know what to expect when Jake turned back to look at him.

"Can't we build it again?" he asked curiously, his face scrunched up in thought.

Mark smiled and felt a warmth fill his body which only hours ago he had thought he would never feel again.

"Yes, Jake," Mark replied, laughing softly. "We can build it again."

Jake smiled back, satisfied with the answer, and refocused his attention on the trees in front of him.

He was right, Mark thought reassuringly. They could rebuild the hut. It would take them some time, and a lot of work, but they could do it.

They carried on walking through the forest, sunlight shining brightly down on the town away to their left. It would be spring soon and Mark was looking forward to the longer, brighter days and the warmer temperatures that came with them.

He found himself smiling at the thought of Jake watching the first of the March hares battling amongst the snowdrops, or of the birds hastily building their nests in preparation for the first of their brood. Spring had always been Jake's favourite time of year.

"Dad."

Jake's voice roused him from his thoughts and he turned to meet his expectant gaze.

"Can we have a fire tonight?"

"Of course we can, son," Mark replied, smiling as he put his arm around him. "Of course."

THE END